OBITUARY FOR AN OLEANDER

A HIBISCUS ISLAND MYSTERY

LUCY NORMAN

Obituary for an Oleander
Book 3 in the *Hibiscus Island Mystery* series

Copyright © 2023 by Lucy Norman
ISBN: 978-0-9922664-5-5

All rights reserved. No part of this book may be reproduced in any form or by any electronic or mechanical means, including information storage and retrieval systems, without written permission from the author, except for the use of brief quotations in a book review.

This is a work of fiction. Names, characters, places and incidents are either the products of the author's imagination or are used fictitiously.

Cover by <u>DLR Cover Designs</u>
Editing by <u>Florentia Editing</u>
Map by Illustrated Page Design

Mulberry Ink
BOOKS

For Vairi - the best daughter-in-law anyone could have. My heartfelt thanks for reading unfinished manuscripts, kind critiquing, and plenty of encouragement.

For Trudy - with thanks for always having an open door (home and office), for listening to me (endlessly), and for being an amazing, wonderful friend!

Hibiscus Island

1

January 2nd; Azure Isle

Her lips quivering, Mrs. Anne McGinney re-read the newspaper column.

Dunbar Funeral Home regrets to announce the passing of Mrs. Freda Jane Sinclair née Carleton, 71, wife of the late Harold Sinclair, beloved mother of Sarah and Jonathan (Carol), of 22 Shell Lane, Azure Isle. A private funeral service was held on Saturday, December 31st at St. Peter's Anglican Church.

Drawing in a deep, wobbly breath, she looked at the two other pieces of paper in front of her. Her mouth tightened as she came to a decision. Picking up her phone, Mrs. McGinney scrolled through the contacts until she found the name she was looking for.

~

Later in January; Hibiscus Island

Truffle galloped wildly along the beach, her feathery tail waving in the breeze from the south shore, her little black nose covered in sand, and her mouth hanging open in a doggy smile as she chased the ball Holly Gold had just thrown.

Sunset Cove was completely empty on this Sunday afternoon, except for Holly, her dog, and an exceptionally handsome man just emerging from the sea.

Holly stopped walking to better appreciate the view. Inspector Rob Tucker waved as he removed his mask, then bent over to pull the fins from his feet. Hailing from the south of England, the police inspector's smooth brown skin was a legacy from his paternal Nigerian grandparents; the muscular physique came from working out several times a week at the gym.

Catching Holly's admiring gaze on him, Rob grinned. "The water was fantastic! You should have come in."

Hibiscus Island born and bred, Holly shuddered in dramatic fashion. "No thanks. I'll go swimming again when it's warm. As in July. Maybe. No real islander swims in January, Rob."

"Pitiful. Just pitiful." Rob's eyes gleamed as he drew closer, making Holly back away in alarm.

"You're wet. Keep your distance, Inspector!" She squealed as Rob closed the gap and scooped her up in his arms. "Put me down."

As the inspector headed towards the sea, Holly redoubled her efforts to escape. "Don't you dare do what I think you're thinking! It's freezing! Rob! I'm serious!"

Truffle, hearing the commotion, raced towards the couple, barking furiously. As the curly black cavapoo danced around them, the inspector laughed, swung Holly around in a circle, and put her back on her feet. "Saved by the dog. Good job protecting your mama, Truffle. Even if she is a wimp." He crouched to ruffle Truffle's head.

Holly pulled down her sweatshirt, which had ridden up during the tussle, a smile crossing her face as Rob picked up Truffle's ball and hurled it down the length of sand again. "I'm not a wimp. It's winter, Rob."

The inspector gazed around the white sandy beach that edged turquoise tropical water, then squinted up at the bright sun shining down from a cloudless blue sky. "Mmm. Sure feels like winter to me." He caught Holly's hand in his as they followed Truffle along the shore. "So, what are your plans for the week? Got any new garden projects?"

"Just Thomas's," Holly replied, glancing up at the Big House on the cliff above them where the aforementioned journalist lived. "But there's the big quilt expo this week, remember? I told Becky I'd help with the set-up. The main event's in the library, so even though Myrtle's in charge, Becky's been landed with a lot of the organization."

"Ah, so you'll be busy." Rob grinned. "I, on the other hand, am expecting a lovely quiet week at work. Well, I was going to see if you'd be able to go diving with me on Wednesday, but perhaps we could make it next weekend instead. I haven't seen the wreck yet, you know."

"Diving? Scuba diving?" Holly stopped walking. "But it's cold!"

"Wear your wetsuit." Rob pulled Holly towards him. "Come on, Holls. How does Saturday sound? Is it a date?"

Holly felt herself blushing at the light in his brown eyes. "It's a date," she agreed.

～

"ANYONE SEEN MYRTLE? Where does she want us to set up the tables for nibbles?" Jamie stuck her head into the boardroom of the Bridgeport Library on Tuesday afternoon, then did a double take. "What on earth is that contraption? It looks like some kind of medieval torture device!"

Holly shot her friend an exasperated look from the floor, where she and the head librarian were wrestling with lengths of wood. "You know full well it's a quilting frame, Jamie. And Myrtle's around here somewhere. Have you tried the lecture hall? That's where she was the last time I saw her."

"I just checked there." Jamie inspected the wooden structure with curiosity. "How does this thing work?"

"I have no idea," Becky Dumont responded. "And frankly, I don't really care at this point. All we were asked to do was put the frame together. Someone else, thank heavens, is going to deal with the rollers and put the actual quilt on it. The attendees are supposed to be completing an appliqué quilt while they're here."

Holly sat back on her heels, brushing her red-gold curls off her face. "Yeah, the annual Flower Quilt. Mama did a hibiscus for it."

"Have you seen the quilt already?" Becky asked in surprise. "I thought it was a secret."

"Oh, it is. I only saw Mama's block before she sent it off to whoever was putting the top together. She said they're doing a tropical theme this year—hibiscus, oleander, morning glory, that sort of thing. It sounds very pretty. Last year they did English woodland flowers and Mama made a block with bluebells. She loves quilting."

Becky smiled. "Maggie must be excited about the convention, then."

"She is. And it's good business for the Inn as well. We're

packed solid from Wednesday onwards. In fact, everywhere is."

"It's a big event on the island," Jamie agreed. "Especially since we only host it once every four years. Anyway, getting back to my original question—where should François and I set up the tables?"

"I'll come and show you." Becky got to her feet, casting a glance of dislike towards the pieces of the quilt frame. "Let's find someone else to do this, Holly. I'm sure there's an expert somewhere in the building and I'd like to finish printing the name tags Myrtle asked for. I could use your help if you've got time."

Holly jumped up with alacrity. "I do. I told Gramps I'd be here all day, so he's not expecting me back at the Inn."

A horticulturist like her grandfather, Holly worked in the gardens of the family-owned Hibiscus Inn when she wasn't busy with her own fledgling landscaping business. Her flexible hours and projects meant she'd been able to put work on hold for a couple of days to help set up the Maritime Quilting Expo slated to begin that week in Bridgeport, as she'd told Rob Tucker on the weekend.

Now the three women made their way to the entrance foyer of the library where they stopped to survey the chaos.

The tall glass entrance doors were propped open to allow access for the stream of people carrying tables, boxes, folded quilts, and other supplies into the large lecture hall on the ground floor. Behind the circulation desk, blonde-haired Stephanie, the children's librarian, hummed to herself as she laid out piles of multicolored lanyards, while Mr. Graham, the head of the Historical Society, fussed with lists of paper, cross-checking them with a pile of already laminated name tags.

Becky heaved a huge sigh. "I don't want to complain—"

"But why does every event on the island have to take place in the library?" Holly and Jamie chanted in unison before laughing.

"There's really nowhere else big enough," Jamie said, linking her arm through Becky's. "And it's nice and central. When we did the rebuild a few years ago, the lecture hall and common spaces were designed for just this kind of thing. You don't really mind, do you?"

"The library's always been the heart of Hibiscus Island," Holly added. "And you're keeping the tradition going. Everyone loves coming here. Just like they did when Mrs. Eastham was in charge."

"Aww, look. She's blushing."

Becky's tanned face had flushed slightly but Jamie's comment caused her to swat at her friend, making the other woman duck aside with a laugh.

Holly smiled at their antics. She'd known Jamie since childhood, but Becky was still a relative newcomer to the island, having married a local, François Dumont, just over a year ago. She was also Inspector Tucker's younger sister.

Hailing from the south of England, the petite brown-haired Becky had taken over as head librarian of the Bridge-port Library a few months previously and was already well-loved by both patrons and staff. She had kept the former librarian's programs running smoothly and instituted a few innovations of her own, making the library a vibrant and popular space for all, including the island's teens.

Holly, Jamie, and Becky had become firm friends the summer before when they had helped solve a murder that had occurred at the Hibiscus Inn.

Holly's grin widened as she looked at her oldest and best friend. Jamie White was an extrovert of the highest order, a character trait that served her well in her capacity of owner of the Bean café, one of the most popular places on Hibiscus Island for tea, tasty treats, and a side of gossip. Today, as always, she looked gorgeous, with long dark hair spilling down the back of a purple t-shirt worn over slim black jeans. Gold hoop earrings, a sweep of mascara, and a touch of lip gloss complemented her smooth brown skin, but it was Jamie's effervescent personality and thousand-watt smile that really made her memorable.

Jamie gazed across the foyer to where François, her chef and business partner, waited. "There's your hubby, Becks. Come show us where we can set up. Are we outside in the courtyard or inside somewhere? We just want to get the tables sorted today if we can."

"The food will all be in the courtyard." As they walked towards a smaller open door on the far side of the room, Becky produced a rueful smile. "There's one good thing. The patrons don't seem to mind all this activity at all." She gestured at a number of seniors who watched the hubbub with interest as they sat in companionable groups on benches and chairs in the library lobby, books and maga-zines forgotten.

Jamie grinned. "This convention is the highlight of the month. January's pretty quiet here, so even if people don't quilt, they'll come to this event. It's a good way to catch up with friends from other islands."

"We have one of the nicer venues too," Holly added. "On Coral Island, they have to split it up between three church halls."

"Yeah, it's only Azure Isle that's really fancy with its big resort hotel. The rest of the islands are low-key. You're doing a great job, Becks, so stop stressing." Jamie came to a halt as they reached their destination, a huge smile breaking over her face. "Oh, this is nice! Very nice indeed!"

The paved courtyard between the library and the next-door building held raised beds of plants, scattered trees, and some old-fashioned standing lamp posts. Today, a row of small tents were lined up down the center, their white awnings ringed with lights, while tables and chairs clustered in groups under the trees, creating an outdoor café vibe.

"The tents have sides that can be let down if the weather turns bad," Becky said. "But the forecast is good, and it's fairly cool right now."

François grinned at his wife. "Look at you turning into an islander. Last year you were complaining about how hot it was, but now you think seventy degrees is cool. Which is our tent? This one? Hmmm. Yes, this will work just fine."

"Are you going to be here the whole week?" Holly asked, surveying the food court. "What's happening to the Bean?"

"Oh, we'll be open as usual," Jamie said. "We're providing lunch foods for the convention, but we'll rotate shifts, so someone is here and someone is at the Bean. It'll be a lot quieter in town anyway with the quilt show going on, but I have some high schoolers to help after school around teatime when it could get busy."

"There're going to be a couple of other food vendors here too," François added. "There'll be lots of choices for the quilters."

Becky nodded. "Yes. The Sand Witch from Castlebay, the White Horse, and a few other places will have stalls. We thought a food court would be fun. All the quilting vendors are setting up in the lecture hall, and we're using every other available space for demonstrations, talks, things like that. The communal quilting bee is in the board room of course." A worried expression crossed the librarian's face. "The whole place is going to be packed. I hope the patrons continue to be tolerant."

"They will," Holly assured her. "Seriously, Becky, this is a big deal on the island. Quilting is very popular here. Besides, you'll be doing a book display, won't you? I know Mama always buys books when she goes to this show. That should appease the reading crowd."

Becky nodded. "The Book Worm is bringing a selection —Laura has ordered tons, she said—and we'll put up library displays of course. I have lots of quilt-themed cozy mysteries, for instance. And Frances from A Stitch in Time is also bringing quite a collection. But she'll probably put those on her stall and..."

Her husband put a reassuring arm around her. "Stop worrying so much, honey. It's going to be amazing. What could possibly go wrong? It's a quilt show, for heaven's sake."

Holly and Jamie exchanged amused glances.

"What?" Becky's eyes narrowed. "What are those smirks for?"

Jamie pursed her lips. "Well, you do know there's quite a bit of competition between the clubs, don't you?"

"I'd expect that, yes. But City Hall is hosting the actual quilt contest part in their art gallery, so it's not really my concern." Becky paused as her friends traded glances again. "Stop doing that, you two! What's the problem with the clubs? I know most of the Hibiscus quilters and they're all lovely!"

"There's nothing wrong with any of the clubs when they're by themselves," Holly said, "but—"

"It's kind of an island thing," Jamie interrupted. "We're one big archipelago, but each island has its own... uh... style, I guess you'd say. For instance, Coral Island, although it's a bit bigger than Hibiscus, is less developed, has a smaller population, supports eco-tourism in a big way, and is... hmmm... wilder, if you know what I mean."

"More mountainous. It's a great place for hiking. And diving, for that matter," Holly added.

"But it's harder to get some things. They only have a tiny airport so there are lots of 'back to nature' types over there," Jamie concluded.

Becky looked skeptical. "I didn't notice anything different about the people when we visited for the weekend last year. I thought the island was gorgeous."

"Oh, it is," Holly assured her. "All the islands have their own charm, but they're all different. And it's weird, but the quilt groups kind of reflect the islands they're from, so the quilt show can be... interesting."

Jamie grinned. "Yeah, sparks usually fly when they all get together."

2

———————

François grinned at his wife's dismayed expression. "Don't listen to them, honey. They're just winding you up. Everything's going to be great. I'll go get the tables from the van, okay?"

As he left, Becky frowned at her friends. "You are just joking, right? This club thing can't be that bad."

"Well, personally, I find it highly entertaining." Jamie's grin widened. "The biggest rivalry is between the Tacky Turtles and the Oleander Quilt Society."

Holly giggled. "I just love that name. Tacky Turtles. It's so cute."

"The Turtles got the most points at last year's convention," Jamie explained. "And the one before that as well. They hold the Maritime Thimble Award right now and the Oleanders are determined to take it back. They've won it multiple times in the past. Or so I've been told." Her eyes danced. "The Bean has been buzzing with quilting gossip for the past month. I know all there is to know about the various clubs! Apparently there are six of them coming this year."

Becky nodded. "Besides the two you just mentioned, we have our own Patchworkers, the Quilt Bees from Coral Island, the Sew and Sews, also from Turtle Island, and the Stitch Witches from Juniper Island. This is the first time the Juniper crowd have attended." As her friends laughed, a reluctant smile crossed the librarian's face. "They are cute names, aren't they?"

"Yeah. We only have Oleanders staying at the Inn. They booked out all ten suites months ago. You should see the emails the woman in charge sent Mama last week. Talk about demanding."

"Ahem." An ostentatious throat-clearing behind them caused all three women to turn in surprise.

Silver-haired Myrtle Collier, retired nurse, president of the Garden Club, quilt show organizer, and uncrowned leader of Hibiscus Island society in general, stood in the doorway. Beside her, a stout lady with salt-and-pepper hair gazed at them with interest.

Myrtle's expression was inscrutable. "I've been looking for you three. This is my friend, Anne. She's got something she wants to tell us."

Holly pulled up in front of Becky and François's little cottage and tooted the horn of her car. As she waited for the librarian to join her, she once again wondered what Myrtle's friend wanted to say that was so important.

With all the confusion at the library, plus the amount of work still needed for the convention, it had proved impossible to have any earlier conversation. In the end, Myrtle had invited them all to dinner at her house that evening before sweeping Mrs. McGinney away to finish setting up the quilting frame in the boardroom.

Holly pressed the car horn again, peering through the tiny black wrought-iron gate set into the low wall surrounding the cottage. Becky's garden, miniature like the house, looked like fairyland.

Old China roses intermingled with white plumbago above winter plantings of pink impatiens and pastel-colored candytuft; pale fragrant flowers of *Nicotiana* waved in the evening breeze; and, in the afterglow of the setting sun, the round white berries of a snowberry bush shone almost magically among dark green glossy leaves.

A soft pink *Souvenir de la Malmaison* climbing rose twined around the trellis on the front porch, its full flush of bloom catching Holly's eye. She nodded in approval. She'd helped Becky prune the bridal rose, as it was known locally, in the fall and the plant had responded very nicely. The old roses on Hibiscus Island flowered between October and May, becoming dormant in the summer months. Holly smiled as she remembered Becky taking copious notes about the care of island roses, determined to grow as many varieties as she could.

The front door of the cottage flew open, and Becky hurried down the cobbled path.

"Sorry!" she exclaimed, sliding into the front seat beside Holly. "I had to feed Hibby. François went straight to choir practice after he left the library. Would you be able to drop me back here after dinner, Holly? He said he'll be late tonight."

"Of course." Holly smiled at her friend. "And how is Hibiscus? Too bad she couldn't come with us to Myrtle's. I'd love to see her and Napoleon together."

"Napoleon would eat her alive. Hibby is quite timid

still," Becky replied, referring to the little black kitten she'd recently acquired. "So, what do you suppose this is all about? I sincerely hope there isn't going to be any drama with this quilting convention! Do you know this Mrs. McGinney? Have you met her before?"

"Not that I remember," Holly said, pulling out onto the main road. "But I wasn't here the last time the quilt show was held on Hibiscus. Mama knows her. I asked earlier and she said Mrs. McGinney is a longtime member of the Oleanders. Her specialty is double wedding ring quilts."

"Those interlocking ring ones?" Becky asked, impressed. "They look difficult."

"Mama made one once. A pink and white one for a friend who was getting married. She turned it into a medallion quilt because she got tired of doing the ring blocks, but it was very pretty. And she made a Lone Star quilt for Aunt Laura once. That was really nice. She hand-quilted it with feather patterns. It took forever."

"Have you ever quilted?"

Holly shook her head with a grin. "Mama tried to teach me, but it wasn't my thing at all."

"I like the wall-hangings Maggie did for the Inn. They're like fabric paintings, really, aren't they?"

"Yeah. She likes appliqué more than piecing."

Becky leaned back in her seat. "I've never tried quilting, but I'm interested in learning. Since there'll be a couple of beginner workshops at the convention, I've signed up for one. It's a sampler class, apparently, so they provide all the supplies for nine different blocks. It looks like fun."

"Better you than me." Holly turned onto the narrow drive that led to Myrtle's townhouse. "Look, Jamie's here already."

Being careful to choose a guest spot—the management

at Bluebird Hall, one of the island's few townhouse complexes, was very strict about where visitors could leave their cars—Holly parked her small electric vehicle next to Jamie's car.

There were only six apartments at the complex, all two-story dwellings. Myrtle lived in one of the corner units, enjoying views over the north shore from her upper balcony and a small but charming private garden and patio on the ground floor.

On her way to the front door, Holly paused in the garden. "Wow. Myrtle must have a little microclimate in here. Look how ripe these loquats are! Ours at the Inn aren't this far along."

Becky looked at the clusters of golden fruit nestling among the thick oblong leaves. "Why's the tree so small? The ones I've seen around the island are much bigger than this."

"I prune it. I like to keep it low so I can reach the fruit easily." Myrtle spoke from the doorway. "I grew this one from seed and it always flowers a little earlier than the other trees. Plus, the fruit is sweeter. I make a prize-winning liqueur from these loquats." The septuagenarian smiled at Holly and Becky. "Come on in, you two. Jamie and Anne are in the living room."

Myrtle stood aside to let the younger women enter, then closed the front door behind them.

Although Bluebird Hall retained many of the island's traditional architectural details, such as a stepped white roof, pastel blue exterior walls, and white hurricane shutters on every window, the inside was very modern. Myrtle had opted for pale gray wood-look tiled floors and icy blue walls throughout the three-bedroom apartment. White sofas stood on top of a speckled charcoal area rug, while sleek espresso-colored bookcases, cabinets, and table created a unified look throughout the open-plan living, kitchen, and dining room. Vibrant art hung on every wall, and an eclectic collection of books, arranged by spine color, brightened the shelves.

Jamie was already curled up on one of two enormous white armchairs, a regal-looking Himalayan Persian purring in her lap.

Napoleon's brilliant blue eyes slitted open briefly to inspect the newcomers, then closed again. With his long silky white fur and Siamese color-point markings, he was a beautiful cat. He was also very demanding and bossy, ruling Myrtle with a velvet paw. Himalayans were usually friendly to other animals, but Napoleon proved the exception to the rule. No one ever brought their dogs to Myrtle's house because, despite his stubby legs, Napoleon had a mean right hook and lethal claws.

Across from Jamie and her furry companion, Anne McGinney sat on the sofa, a basket of colorful fabric scraps beside her, silver needle flashing busily through pieces of material.

"Oh, is that a double wedding ring you're making?" Becky asked, sitting down beside the quilter to watch with fascination. "Do you always hand piece them?"

Mrs. McGinney smiled. "I machine sew a lot of my quilts, but I always have a hand-piecing project I can take with me." She spread out the arcs of patched fabric for Becky to see. "What do you think?"

The young librarian peered at the rich batik material. "I love the colors! Do you use a template or something to get the shapes? I read that you can buy acrylic shapes and then just rotary cut piles at one time. Is that what you do?"

"I use these." Mrs. McGinney pulled out some plastic

forms. "I make some of my quilts with the traditional curved edges but this one is a square block pattern. Once the arcs are all made, I'll attach them to the center pieces to make a petal shape, like this." She showed the younger woman fabric that had been stitched together.

"Oh, that's interesting!" Becky exclaimed, fingering the work. "And then you put the four parts together to make the ring? Could I make one of these for my sampler quilt, do you think? I was planning to use a sewing machine to make the blocks."

Mrs. McGinney smiled. "I find it easier to get my points to meet if I hand piece, but if you take your time, and mark the pieces carefully, machine sewing is possible. The double wedding ring's not really a beginner's pattern though. It's probably best to start with the basic sampler blocks if you've never quilted before."

Holly and Jamie exchanged amused glances as their friend continued to cross-examine the experienced quilter.

"Can you imagine how long it must take to make one of those things?" Jamie muttered to Holly, watching Mrs. McGinney make tiny stitches in the fabric.

"It took Mama a year to make hers. And she only did a small one! She said she hated trying to get the points right and that's why she started doing appliqué instead. You can cover up any mistakes, according to her."

Jamie grinned. "I think I'll stick to diving as a hobby. Which reminds me—I'm going out to the wreck of *La Rosa* next week. Do you want to come? I need a dive buddy."

As Holly opened her mouth to tell her friend she already had a dive date, Myrtle called across from the kitchen. "Dinner is ready. Napoleon, I've put your salmon out."

The Himalayan's round blue eyes shot open. Jumping

down from Jamie's lap, he trotted at full speed towards his dish.

"Come and eat, everyone." Myrtle gestured toward the dining table.

Conversation during dinner ranged across several subjects, including the story of *La Rosa de España*, with a fascinated Mrs. McGinney asking a multitude of questions about how the shipwreck had been discovered.

Since the three-hundred-year-old Spanish merchant ship had originally been owned by one of her ancestors, Jamie was always happy to talk about it. She regaled the table with information about the wreck site and what had been found so far, ending with another invitation to Holly— and everyone else—to join her on a dive that weekend.

Mrs. McGinney hastily demurred. "I'm not a diver, but I would love to see the Rose Treasure brooch before I leave. It looked spectacular in the newspaper article about your adventure last year."

Unnoticed, Holly made a small face. Adventure. That was one way of describing it, she supposed, remembering the previous fall when she and the other Hibiscus Island women had helped find out who murdered a pirate and left his remains among the roses. She could do without more 'adventures' like that, thank you!

Jamie beamed at the visitor. "Yes, it's gorgeous. I've lent it to the Maritime Museum, so if you have time to visit, it's on display there." Replete with seafood lasagna, salad, and homemade rolls, she leaned back in her chair with a sigh of pleasure. "That was delicious, Myrtle."

"It was," Becky agreed. "I'd love the recipe, if you're willing to share it."

Myrtle nodded as she pushed her chair back. "Certainly. I'll write it out for you. I think, if you don't mind, we'll take our coffee to the sofa, so we can be comfortable while Anne tells her story."

Mrs. McGinney's smile faded, replaced by a troubled expression.

Noting the anticipatory gleam in Myrtle's eyes, Holly gazed at her with unease. What was Mrs. McGinney about to say? It was always a bad sign when Myrtle looked like that.

Becky, however, directed a kind smile at the Azure Island quilter. "Is something wrong? Can we help in any way?"

"Oh, I do hope so!" Anne McGinney exclaimed. "It's why I came to Hibiscus Island." She hesitated, then in a rush of words blurted out, "I think Oleanders are being murdered!"

3

Becky's expression changed instantly, horrified incredulity crossing her face, but Jamie sat bolt upright.

"What do you mean, 'murdered'? I haven't seen anything about any murders on Azure! When did it happen?"

Myrtle held up a restraining hand as Mrs. McGinney gaped at the younger woman. "Anne will explain over coffee." She shooed them all towards the sofa before placing cups, milk, and sugar on the large coffee table in front of them. "Would anyone like tea instead?"

"I would, please," Holly said immediately. She liked the occasional coffee, but tea was essential if there was even the vaguest possibility they were about to get involved in yet another murder investigation! Holly groaned silently at the thought. How did they manage to attract these things? Remembering Rob's prediction of a quiet week, and their upcoming date, she gave another silent moan. *Please don't let this be a case! Please don't let this be a case*, she chanted to herself.

As she collapsed in one of the armchairs, Napoleon jumped into her lap, turning around a few times. With a loud purr, the cat began rhythmically kneading Holly's jean-clad legs, making her wince as his claws dug in and out.

Jamie flung herself into the opposite armchair, eager expectancy in every line of her face. "So," she began again, as Anne McGinney sat down, "you say Oleanders have been murdered? More than one? How come no one's heard about it?"

Blinking at the rapid-fire questioning, Mrs. McGinney twisted her hands in the skirt of her floral dress. She opened her mouth, then closed it.

"Jamie." Holly's sigh was resigned. "Stop talking. Let her speak."

"Well... I..." The Azure islander tried again, then faltered.

Becky was gazing at the older woman in consternation. "What makes you think members of the Oleander Quilting Society have been... uh... murdered? Because Jamie's quite correct. There's been nothing in the news about it here."

"Well... No one thinks it was murder." Anne McGinney twisted her skirt even more vigorously. "What I mean is... Well..."

"Stop dithering, Anne!" Myrtle handed Holly a steaming cup of tea before crossing to sit beside her friend. "Tell them what you told me. About Daina."

"Who's Daina?" Jamie leaned forward. "She's the person you think was murdered? How? And why?"

"Jamie. Shh." Becky frowned at her friend.

Despite herself, Holly's mouth quirked as she watched Jamie raise her hands in a "What did I do?" gesture at Becky before subsiding beneath the librarian's glare. It was clear to

Holly that her English friend was not as enthralled as Jamie with this latest turn of events.

"Daina Trott. She was a member of the Oleanders. Her daughter, Denise, is several years younger than you. Daina died last year in October." Myrtle's voice was brisk.

Anne McGinney nodded, finding her voice. "Denise will be here for the convention. She's quite a keen quilter herself, you know. Or, she was, before this happened with her mother."

"Really, Anne, is that relevant?"

"Well, Denise is the one who first suggested there might have been more to her mother's condition than we thought."

"Her condition? Was Daina Trott sick?" Jamie asked.

"Breast cancer. She was having chemotherapy." Myrtle poured herself a cup of coffee.

"Chemotherapy? How serious was it?"

"Stage four."

There was a moment of silence, then Holly cleared her throat. "That's tough," she said, sympathy in her voice. "But if Daina had cancer... Well, was there something odd about her death? Was her doctor concerned or something?"

"No," Myrtle replied. "Cause of death was put down to the disease."

"The doctors tried everything they could but eventually nothing worked. Denise was heartbroken when her mother died," Anne McGinney said.

Holly nodded. She understood the 'trying everything.' Several years earlier, completely out of the blue, her dad, Inspector Peter 'Solid' Gold had been diagnosed with acute leukemia. Unable to receive treatment on Hibiscus Island, he and Holly's mother had relocated to Grand Island to do 'everything' that could be done, including a bone marrow transplant. As with Daina, eventually nothing had worked.

Holly missed her father and could sympathize with the unknown Denise.

Napoleon shifted on her lap, nosing her hand. Holly obediently stroked the cat's soft fur, her brow furrowing. It sounded like Daina's death was natural. Why did Mrs. McGinney think otherwise?

Obviously feeling the same, Becky frowned. "I'm afraid I don't really understand. If the doctor felt that Daina's death, sad as it was, was unsuspicious, why do you believe she was murdered?"

"Well, because of Freda, of course!"

All three younger women blinked.

"Who's Freda?" Jamie asked.

"Freda Sinclair. Another Oleander. She died just before Christmas." Myrtle finished her coffee, putting her cup down on the table with a decisive clink.

Jamie's eyebrows shot up. "So, two members of the Oleander Quilting Society have died recently? And you think there's a connection somehow? How did Freda Sinclair die?"

"In a car accident. But—"

Jamie looked confused. "I'm sorry, but how does murder even come into this? It sounds completely natural to me. Tragic, of course, but not murderous."

Myrtle frowned at the younger woman's interruption. "There's a bit more to it. Anne, you'll have to explain in more detail."

Anne McGinney nodded. "Well, it's just that Freda and Daina were both ill as well. Nausea and weakness. The crash was just a... well, an accident."

There was a brief silence, then Jamie's eyes narrowed.

Before she could speak, Holly intervened. "But Daina

was having chemo, you said. That would give her those symptoms. And, as for Freda... Well, it is flu season."

Becky nodded in vigorous agreement. "Yes. A lot of people went down with the flu here over Christmas, I know. Perhaps Freda was just sick from that."

Jamie ignored these hopeful statements, turning her attention to Mrs. McGinney. "What did her doctor say about it? Were Freda's symptoms unusual in any way?"

"According to her doctor, there was nothing wrong with Freda. He said the same as Holly. That it was just flu." Anne McGinney wore a helpless expression as she gazed around at the other women. "That's what everyone keeps saying. No one thinks there was anything wrong. Except me and Denise!"

"Huh." Jamie chewed her lip. "So, why do you think there's something suspicious about their deaths? What's the motive?"

"Well, that's what I was telling Myrtle about earlier," Mrs. McGinney said. "You see, the Oleander Quilting Society is a bit different from the other island quilting clubs."

Myrtle snorted. "Snobbish."

"We are not!" Anne McGinney glared at her friend. "We have a formal structure. There's absolutely nothing wrong with that!"

Myrtle sniffed but stayed quiet.

"An Oleander presidential term is one year," Anne continued. "A president can only serve a maximum of two terms and must have served as vice-president prior to taking over the club. Daina was president last year. And Freda was her vice-president. She had to take over early—halfway through Daina's second term. We had to have an emergency meeting to allow the transition because of Daina's illness."

"So two presidents of the Oleanders have died in a short time. And you think the presidency is the motive?" Becky's expression was politely disbelieving.

"Who's the new president of the Oleanders?" Holly asked.

"Sally Hartley Dill."

"Hartley? That's the name of the woman who's been emailing Mama constantly this week."

"That would be Ellen Hartley," Anne McGinney explained. "Sally's sister-in-law, and the current social director of the Oleanders. She can be a little... uh... bossy at times."

"So you think this Sally person killed the others to become president? Is that it?" Jamie looked dubious. "Why would she want to do that? Do you get paid to be the president of the Oleanders or something?"

Anne McGinney looked horrified. "Good heavens, no! We have a very strict voting procedure. And, although Sally can be extremely annoy—" She stopped, then resumed. "Well, let's just say we've had our differences, but no, she couldn't possibly be a murderer!"

Myrtle sighed in exasperation. "Anne doesn't think Sally's the murderer; she thinks she's the next victim."

LEANING BACK against the car seat, Becky closed her eyes. A soft but heartfelt groan escaped her as she began to massage her forehead. About to get into her own car, Jamie paused to peer into Holly's vehicle.

"How about we meet at the Bean tomorrow for lunch? Becky? You going to be free at your usual time?"

The librarian nodded without opening her eyes.

"Great!" Jamie beamed. "I'll see you then." She waved, hopped into her car, and shot out of the driveway.

Becky groaned again. "Honestly, if I'd had any idea how this evening would turn out, I'd have declined Myrtle's invitation. Quilters being murdered! I can't even!"

Holly suppressed a smile at her friend's indignant expression as she started the car. "I take it you weren't convinced by Mrs. McGinney's arguments then." Holly kept a straight face as she turned onto the road heading towards Bridgeport.

Becky sat up with a jerk, dark eyes flashing in her light brown face. With her short curly hair and long-sleeved pink shirt, she looked like an irate flower fairy as she turned towards Holly. "It's absolutely ridiculous! Who would even *want* to kill the presidents of a tiny quilt club on a tiny island? I've never heard such rubbish in my life! And I'm shocked that Myrtle would support such a silly supposition!"

Holly choked but Becky carried on, barely drawing breath. "I know exactly what's happened. Mrs. McGinney read about that case last September—she even had the newspaper article with her, Holly!—and is now creating drama where there is none! What floors me is that Myrtle and Jamie were egging her on. I mean, really! Words fail me!"

Holly tried not to laugh. Words certainly weren't failing the head librarian.

"Thomas Miller has a lot to answer for," Becky said, in tones that boded ill for the newspaper journalist when she next saw him.

"Oh well, I don't think we can really blame Thomas for —" Holly was overridden.

"If he hadn't written about the pirate in Jamie's garden,

none of this would be happening!" Becky threw up her hands and flung herself back against the car seat, turning an aggrieved look on Holly. "In what universe, Holly, is murder considered exciting? Tell me that! In. What. Universe?!"

Becky's final question was too much for Holly. She gave up the struggle and collapsed in laughter.

4

Having changed the subject and talked her friend into a better mood, Holly dropped Becky at her cottage before driving home to Hibiscus Inn. She parked her little electric car, then went around to the family entrance at the back, pushing open the wooden gate that led into a small courtyard.

Solar-powered fairy lights glowed softly among the branches of the dwarf poinciana tree, now bare of leaves, while more lights illuminated the brick path to the rear entrance.

Pulling out her key, Holly glanced through the ground floor window beside the door. With the blinds still up, she could see her mother curled on an overstuffed sofa, a book in her hand, and a cup of tea on a side table. Beside her, a curly black cavapoo sprawled on its back, four paws twitching in the air as it chased dream rabbits.

When Holly opened the door, the cavapoo leapt up, galloping to greet the young woman with excited moans and wiggles.

"Hello, Truffle," Holly said, laughing as she swept the little dog into her arms. "Missed me, did you?"

Maggie Gold put her book down. "She did. I'm clearly not enough for her anymore." She pulled a sad face, making her daughter laugh.

Crossing the room with Truffle still snuggled in her arms, Holly sat down beside her mother.

Maggie smiled at her. "How was your evening? Had fun?"

Holly rolled her eyes. "Fun? Mama, you won't believe what happened tonight!"

Picking up her teacup, Maggie grinned, leaning back against the sofa cushions. "I'm all ears, honey! Spill the beans."

ALTHOUGH HOLLY WAS UP EARLY the next day, her mother still beat her to the kitchen. Maggie turned from the fridge as her daughter staggered through in blue flannel pajamas, red-gold hair in wild disarray.

"I'm making an omelet for myself this morning. Would you like one?" Maggie hefted a carton of eggs in enquiry.

Holly shuddered. "No thanks. Just tea for me. And toast —if we have any gluten-free bread. Do we? I used the last slice yesterday and forgot to stop at the store."

Her mother grinned. "Luckily for you, I didn't forget. I got cinnamon raisin bread. Want me to pop a couple of slices in the toaster?"

"Yes please." Holly yawned as she slid onto one of the stools at the island, propping her chin in her hand. "I'm all yours this morning if you need help turning the rooms. How many need to be done?"

"Just four," Maggie replied, dropping two pieces of bread into the stainless-steel toaster. "The Martins and Brents are taking the nine o'clock flight to Juniper Island; the other guests check out at noon. Sarah and I cleaned all the rest of the rooms yesterday so if you could tackle the Rose and Lantana suites as soon as you've finished breakfast, that would be great."

"Sure," Holly replied, glancing at the clock. "You know it's seven already, right? The guests will have to leave soon if they're getting the flight to Juniper."

Maggie nodded. "I'll run them to the airport in about half an hour or so. Sarah and I will do the last two rooms after lunch, and then we'll be all set for the onslaught of quilters at three." She made a face. "Although, after what you told me last night, I'm not so sure about having this group. I hope they aren't going to be a problem. Goodness knows, Mrs. Hartley has been somewhat demanding."

Holly accepted a plate of toast with a nod of thanks. Pulling the butter and jam towards her, she grinned. "Oh, I don't think there's going to be any problem with the quilters. My own opinion is that Mrs. McGinney is imagining the whole thing. She has no evidence and both deaths were completely natural, although very sad of course. There was nothing suspicious about them, no matter what Myrtle and Jamie think." Holly eyed her mother. "Did you know Daina Trott? Myrtle said her daughter's coming to the convention. Is she staying here?"

"I met Daina once or twice at past conferences. Nice woman. I was sorry to hear of her illness. And yes, Denise is staying here." Maggie's brow wrinkled in thought as she poured beaten eggs into a pan. "I think she has the Nasturtium Suite. Why?"

Holly swallowed a mouthful of toast. "Mrs. McGinney

said Denise was the one who first suggested her mom might have been killed."

A sympathetic expression crossed Maggie's face. "Perhaps she's struggling to come to terms with her mother's death. Poor girl. It must be difficult for her."

"Well, yeah, but don't you think that's a bit weird? I mean, her mom had cancer. It sucks. We all know that. But most people don't immediately start thinking about murder when someone dies of it. I certainly didn't. And nor did you. When Dad died, I mean."

"No. But you don't know what her circumstances were. Maybe you'll get a chance to talk to her while she's here," Maggie suggested. "Someone nearer her age, who's been through a similar situation, might be able to help a bit."

Holly watched her mother slide the omelet onto a plate. "Mama... Do you still think about Dad?"

Maggie turned around, spatula in hand. "Every day, sweetie. Why? Do you think I'm forgetting him?"

"No, no," Holly said hastily. "It's just... Well, hearing about Daina Trott last night brought back some things, that's all, and I realized I... I don't cry as much anymore. I don't want people to think..." Her voice trailed away.

"Think you've forgotten. No one will." Maggie gazed at her with understanding. "You know, right after your dad died, I read something that's helped me quite a bit. The author compared the grief of losing a loved one to waves in the ocean. At the beginning, the waves are storm driven. They're enormous, relentless, and continually wash over you. But as time passes, the waves spread out. They don't get smaller—the loss never goes away—but the intervals between them get longer. And in between those waves, you're able to remember all the good times, the happy times. But when a wave comes again—and it will—it's okay to grieve in that moment." Maggie paused. "The author had lost her husband as well. Her thoughts helped me quite a bit. Still do, actually."

Holly stared at her mother in silence, then slid off the stool, circled the island, and gave her a fierce hug. "Love you, Mama."

"Love you too, Holly Berry." Maggie smiled at her daughter as she held her away from her. "And that's enough serious talk for now. Didn't you tell me you're meeting Thomas at his garden today? Because if you're going to help me with the rooms, you'd better get moving."

"Oh shoot, yes! I said I'd meet him at ten. I can still do the rooms though. I'll just have to be fast!" Holly gave her mom a hasty kiss before dashing out of the room followed by an excited Truffle.

HAVING HUSTLED at full speed through a shower, Holly dressed quickly, then tackled the two rooms assigned to her as fast as possible.

Located on the second floor of the main house, the Rose Suite had one bedroom, with an adjoining living area. Holly whipped the sheets off the king-sized bed, tossing them into a wheeled basket, before pulling fresh cream sheets, a rose-covered comforter cover, and cream pillowcases from the cupboard in the hallway.

Once the bed was made, she pulled on gloves and tackled the en suite bathroom, leaving it sparkling. Humming to herself, she placed fresh rose-pink towels on the wrought iron *étagère* shelves in the natural stone-tiled bathroom, hung up clean terry robes behind the door, and put out new soaps and shampoos.

In support of local businesses, Maggie ordered a range of natural scented products from a small artisan shop on Juniper Island. Although the Rose Suite featured both rose and rosemary scented soaps and shampoos, guests could select alternate fragrances if they desired, including hypo-allergenic or unscented ones.

Holly swept an assessing gaze around the room one more time, nodded, then pushed the cart out of the room, closing the white painted door behind her. Maggie and Sarah would add fresh flowers later while doing a final check to make sure all was ready for the new guests.

Glancing at her watch, Holly squawked. She would have to pick up the pace if she was going to meet Thomas Miller at the Big House on time. Remembering that the Lantana Suite had two bedrooms to tidy, she scampered along the hallway at full speed, pushing the linen cart ahead of her.

HOLLY WAS ONLY two minutes late for her appointment at the Big House, also known as Rosedon House, home to Thomas Miller, journalist and owner of the local newspaper, *The Island Gazette*.

The Miller family had owned the Big House since the early eighteenth century, but since Thomas's grandfather had relocated to the East Coast of the United States, his son and grandson had lived in Boston, visiting the island only occasionally. Thomas had fallen in love with the ancestral home, eventually moving to Hibiscus Island the previous fall.

The Big House had undergone significant renovations as Thomas reversed the thirty-year neglect of the colonial house, and now, four months later, it was once again considered an architectural jewel.

Occupying the cliff opposite Jamie's tiny Rose Cottage, the Big House sat at the top of a steep hill. As she drove up the road, Holly eyed the shrub borders on either side with satisfaction. When he'd heard she was launching a landscaping business, Thomas Miller had immediately commissioned her to draw up designs for the borders along the main drive, as well as a small garden area outside his library, becoming her first paying client.

Holly had carefully chosen wind-and-salt tolerant plants for the driveway, including shrubs like the sea ox-eye with its silver leaves and small daisy-like flowers, the similar-looking tassel plant, and the tall, spiky Spanish bayonet yuccas, which produced huge clusters of cream flowers from spring to fall.

With more creative license in the sheltered library garden, she had taken great delight in filling it with roses, lantana, daylilies, plumbago, and other ornamentals. The library garden was designed for summer use, but Holly had mixed in other plants to create interest in the winter months, including the variegated lily grass that edged a small, red-bricked patio partially shaded by a pretty little silver buttonwood tree.

Today, Holly was meeting with Thomas to look at the flower beds around his pool, as well as a small courtyard outside the room he used as an office. Both areas faced south, overlooking Sunset Cove, with the island known as Wreck Rock visible on the horizon, and both were quite exposed to the elements.

Since Thomas had said he wanted to discuss the possibility of enclosing the areas—to provide more shelter without losing the stunning views over the south shore water—Holly hoped to persuade him to consider traditional island dry stone walls. She had the name of a contractor who specialized in this somewhat dying art, as well as a portfolio of his work. If Thomas agreed, she would set up another meeting with the three of them later.

Parking her electric car in the circular driveway outside the main entrance, Holly grinned at the excited little dog on the front seat beside her. "Just hold on a second, Truff. Let me get all my stuff first."

Holly gathered her binders and laptop, then grabbed Truffle's leash before she hopped out of the car. With the cavapoo leaping and prancing beside her, Holly approached the wide-open front door and poked her head inside.

"Hello? Thomas? You in here?"

A volley of barks broke out before a pretty fawn-colored whippet careened into the front hall. A fat pug waddled after the whippet, barking loudly when he saw Truffle.

"Hi, Kimi. Hey, watch my laptop!" Holly squeaked as the ecstatic whippet leaped up to lick her face. "Down, girl. Down."

Overjoyed to see her friends, Truffle raced in circles around Holly's legs, wrapping her leash tightly around her owner, while, adding to the chaos, the pug plopped down at Holly's feet staring at her bug-eyed as he continued to bark.

The man who entered the hall laughed at the sight of the tangled Holly. "Beau! Stop that noise! Kimi, get down. Holly doesn't want your wet nose in her face. Beau! Quiet, I said."

The pug paused, eyed Thomas with scorn, then gave one last defiant woof before waddling away.

"Disobedient dog." The journalist bent down to unclip Truffle from her leash. As the whippet and cavapoo took off through the house, Thomas grinned, taking the laptop and binders from Holly. "Come on through to the office. Do you want a drink or anything? Something cold?"

"No, I'm good, thanks."

As Holly followed the fair-haired man through the house, Thomas glanced over his shoulder. "Did you know I'm in disgrace?"

"What? Here, let me get that door." Holly pushed ahead of him to hold open the office door. "What do you mean you're in disgrace?"

The journalist placed Holly's binders and laptop on the large desk in front of tall windows overlooking the south shore. He grinned, gesturing to her to take a seat before commandeering the second of two armchairs in front of the desk.

"I popped into the library this morning," he said.

"Ohhhh." Holly grinned. "I guess you saw Becky."

Thomas nodded. "Oh yes. And I got an earful. Apparently, it's entirely my fault there's a hysterical quilter dreaming up fictional murders!"

5

—————

Grinning, Holly surveyed the smirking journalist. "She told you about our evening at Myrtle's, huh?"

"Oh yes. I heard all about it. You may be interested to know that if I hadn't written that article last fall, this McGinney woman wouldn't have formed an entirely erroneous impression of certain people's detecting abilities and those same certain people wouldn't now be getting ready to gleefully poke and pry into things that didn't concern them. Things which, by the way, were obviously completely invented and are without any credence whatsoever, and, even if there was some slight possibility that these ludicrous accusations were true, should be left to the police, who are trained, competent, and fully capable of solving crimes."

"Oh, come on. She didn't really say all that! Did she?" Holly gurgled with laughter at his imitation of an on-fire Becky.

"Oh yes, she did. Our head librarian was not happy with me." Thomas assumed a mock-injured expression at odds with the mirth in his grey eyes. "I tried to tell her all I did was report the news, and got blasted again. So I crawled away to lick my wounds over a cup of coffee."

Holly rolled her eyes. "Sure you did. You went to the Bean, didn't you? So, what did Jamie say?"

"Well, I'm afraid I struck out there as well. Miss White was swamped with customers all clamoring for coffee and edibles, so was unable to chat." Thomas paused. "Not that I think she was in the mood to talk to me anyway. I received quite a glare from those gorgeous brown eyes, by which I suspect she may still be peeved I caught two more lionfish than her on the weekend."

Holly tried not to laugh. Lionfish were an invasive species in the sea around Hibiscus Island and many islanders had licenses to spear them. Until Thomas's arrival, Jamie had been the acknowledged champion in lionfish hunting, with more catches than anyone. In the annual tournament the previous November, Thomas had almost beaten her, causing Jamie to become even more competitive in the weekly hunts than she normally was.

Holly gave a brief shiver at the thought of going lion-fishing in winter. Jamie and Thomas had thicker blood than her.

The Millers and Whites had a shared history going back three hundred years and relations between the families had been acrimonious to say the least. Recent events had caused Jamie to rethink her stance on the Miller family, but she and Thomas continued to butt heads frequently.

Holly and Becky were secretly convinced the two antag-onists not only enjoyed their never-ending sniping but were also quite attracted to one another. Getting either of them to admit to that, though... Well, it wasn't going to happen soon, that's for sure.

Thomas grinned at her. "So, you're my last hope, Holly.

Before we go check out the gardens, I beg you, fill me in on the murder gossip. Please?"

HOLLY GLANCED in her rearview mirror as she left the Big House driveway, in time to see Thomas vanishing at full speed into the house. A wry smile crossed her face. The journalist had asked a myriad of questions about Anne McGinney's story, paying very little attention to his gardens until Holly had recalled him, with some annoyance, to the project in front of him.

His grin had been unrepentant, but he had stopped asking questions and she had been pleased to get his agreement to create a design that incorporated dry stone walls.

Now, as she drove towards Bridgeport, Holly sighed in resignation. Thomas, ecstatic at the thought of another investigation, was undoubtedly already researching recent deaths on Azure Isle, while Myrtle and Jamie... Well, who knew what they were doing!

"Rob's going to have a fit if they start causing trouble, Truffle. You know that, right?" Taking one hand off the wheel, she rubbed Truffle's head. "I think maybe we won't say anything just yet. Perhaps it will all blow over. After all, he did say he was planning to enjoy a quiet week."

Truffle tilted her head, giving an interested woof.

Holly laughed. "Yeah, I'd like a quiet week too. And I know Becky doesn't want to get involved in any crime solving! Not now, anyway."

Remembering the news Becky had shared with her best friends the previous weekend, a wide smile spread across Holly's face.

"I'm only just three months along," Becky had said,

beaming at their exclamations of delight. "Due in July, but just keep it to yourselves for now, okay? We want to wait till four months to tell everyone. Rob knows, though, and both sets of parents, of course. But you're the only other people we've told."

Truffle tilted her head to the other side as Holly continued. "And she has enough to do with the quilting convention anyway, right, Truff?" She grinned when the little dog woofed in reply. "Good answer. Oh look, there's a parking spot."

Holly parked the car, then clipped Truffle's leash onto her collar. Cutting through Waterfront Park, they emerged on Windward Street right beside the Bean café.

Truffle's tail whipped back and forth furiously. Although well-behaved dogs were welcome in the café, Truffle, as a privileged friend, was allowed upstairs in the staffroom, where she could spend some time with Jamie's standard poodle, Teddy, who accompanied his mistress to work most days.

Holly took Truffle up the back stairs, dealt out biscuits to the two dogs, then descended to the ground-floor café.

"Over here!" Becky hailed her from a corner table.

"Are you okay?" Holly eyed the librarian with concern as she pulled out a chair. "You look a little pale."

"Green, you mean. Morning sickness has stretched into lunchtime today." Becky looked at her ginger ale with distaste. "I'm sticking to toast."

"Aww." Holly patted her friend's hand in sympathy. "Aren't the symptoms supposed to go away soon?"

"Yeah. But my mom was sick for her entire pregnancy—and so was my grandma. I'm really hoping I don't take after them!"

"Here you go." Jamie came up behind them, putting a

plate of toast in front of Becky before sliding into an empty seat. "François said you're to eat all of it. And there's a pot of your favorite jam as well." She glanced at Holly. "Do you know what you want? How about pasta? We have a gluten-free one with pesto sauce and chicken." At Holly's nod, she jumped up. "Be right back."

Holly grinned across the table at Becky. "Jamie's taken you under her wing, I see."

"Uh-huh. She and François are in cahoots. I have to have lunch here every day now so they can check up on me."

"How's the quilt convention going?"

"Fine. A couple more vendors still have to set up this afternoon, but everything should be ready for tomorrow's opening. All the name tags are done, the quilting bee thing is set up, we've got every possible book about quilting arranged in displays all over the place, and, at the last minute, we've turned the Children's Library into a babysitting area."

"Oh, that's a very good idea! Who's manning it?"

"Stephanie and some volunteers on the weekdays—it'll only be preschoolers probably—but I have teenagers for the weekend. They'll tell stories, and we have a jigsaw table and Legos. It should be enough to keep any kids occupied while their parents enjoy the convention."

"Here's your tea, Holly." The young barista who worked at the café placed a cup and small teapot on the table.

"You read my mind." Holly smiled at Angie. "Thanks."

"And lunch." Jamie barreled over with two plates. "You okay if I take a break, Angie? Give me a shout if you need me."

Her employee grinned as she headed back to the counter. "Will do."

"So!" Jamie beamed at her friends as she grated

Parmesan cheese with vigor over her own plate of pasta. "The Hibiscus Island Detective Club has a new case! What are your thoughts? How are we going to tackle it?"

Becky groaned. "I knew it. I just knew it." She leaned across the table, looking Jamie in the eye. "Listen to me carefully. There. Is. No. Case. Two people died of natural causes. Tragic, yes, but not murder. And really, this detective club thing needs to stop!"

Jamie tutted. "We can't disband the HIDC, Becks. Look how much help we've been to Rob. And Mrs. McGinney seems certain there was foul play." She twirled pasta onto her fork. "Now, I think we need to keep an eye on this Sally Hartley Dill person. Just in case she develops mysterious symptoms, you know. She's staying at the Inn, so that can be Holly's job. And Myrtle says she'll guard Mrs. McGinney."

"Guard her? Guard her from what? Her own imagination?" Becky's voice was laced with exasperation as she replaced her empty glass on the table. "Jamie, no one is murdering quilters, and there is no case to solve." Ignoring her toast, she got to her feet. "There is, however, a quilt convention to get through. In my library. Which I need to get back to. I'll see you both later, okay?"

Jamie's eyebrows shot up as the librarian left the café. "Gosh, she's in a bit of a mood, isn't she?"

"She's not feeling well. Morning sickness."

"Ohhhh. Hmmm. That's a point. Maybe she shouldn't be involved in this case."

"Maybe you should wait till you have actual proof that something happened." Holly held up a hand in the face of Jamie's immediate protest. "Personally, I'm with Becky. I think this is a case of an overactive imagination."

"*Et tu*, Holly?" Jamie exclaimed, placing a dramatic hand

on her forehead. "Where's your sense of adventure? Your social conscience? Hibiscus Island needs us."

"Uh-huh. You go on telling yourself that." Holly couldn't suppress a grin at her friend's theatrics as she took a sip of her tea. "Let's just put murder on hold for a while, okay? Didn't you say you needed a dive buddy? When are you going out to the wreck? Because Rob would like to go as well —we were thinking of Saturday."

Jamie paused in the middle of another theatrical sigh. "Saturday? I can't. I'll be doing lunch at the quilt expo. Sunday's free, though. Could Rob go then instead?"

"I don't see why not. I'll ask him." Holly grinned at her best friend, then dug into her pasta with relish.

Having spent a profitable afternoon pricking out winter seedlings with Gramps in the Hibiscus Inn slat houses, Holly trailed into the Inn foyer in time to see Sarah Flynn pushing a loaded trolley into the small breakfast and tearoom.

"Oh, are those Mama's raspberry scones?" Holly asked, stopping to eye a plate piled high with delectable treats.

Her mother's business partner laughed. "They are indeed. And these aren't gluten-free, so hands off. There's a plate for you in the kitchen."

Holly pulled her hand back with a grin. "Have all the quilters arrived, then?"

"Oh yes." Sarah's dark brown face crinkled with amusement. "That Mrs. Hartley can rival Myrtle for organization, I'm telling you. She had them all checked in and sorted into their rooms in no time. And since they'll be here for tea in moments, Holly, if you could go grab the other trolley, that would be a huge help."

"Will do."

Maggie was topping up the hot water tea urns when Holly entered the large Inn kitchen.

"Oh good, you're back! Can you take—"

"—the trolley through. Yep. Aunt Sarah already issued orders. I'm on it."

"Thanks, honey. I'll boil the kettle for our own tea, then. I made—"

"Raspberry scones! I saw. I'll be right back." Holly whisked the tea trolley out of the room to the accompaniment of her mother's laughter.

As Holly entered the tearoom, a young man turned from contemplating the baked goods Sarah had just put out. "This all looks delicious! Can I help with that trolley?"

"I've got it, thanks." Holly eyed him with interest.

He was decidedly handsome, with lightly tanned skin, close cut brown hair, and unusual amber eyes rimmed in long, dark eyelashes. The Azure islander looked her over with equal curiosity, hands in the pockets of well-cut slacks. His polo shirt was lemon yellow and should have been casual but somehow looked elegant and expensive.

His gaze was appreciative as he held out his hand. "Derek Hartley. I'm here for the convention."

"Holly Gold. Nice to meet you. Are you a quilter?"

"Do I look like one?"

Holly smiled. "Well, lots of men quilt. You could be."

"True, but I'm not one of them. I'm actually a jeweler."

"A jeweler? Do you sell quilt-themed things or something?"

"Yeah." Derek fished out his phone. "Here, have a look. These are some of my designs for this year's conference." He rocked back on his heels, shoving his hands into his pockets again as he watched Holly flick through the photos he'd pulled up.

"Wow! These are fabulous!" she exclaimed, scrolling through pictures of gold-and silver-enameled quilt block charms set in pendants, bracelets, and necklaces. "I have to get my mother some of these. She'd love them."

"I'll have a booth at the convention," Derek said, smiling at her enthusiasm.

"Derek." An impatient voice came from the doorway.

Holly turned to see a very elegant woman in a dressy black suit, with white hair pulled back in a chic chignon, and pursed lips. "I thought you said you took all my luggage to my suite."

"I did, Grandmama," Derek replied. "Why?"

"My small case is missing."

"I found it, Sybil!" Another woman appeared in the doorway, peering in with interest. She beamed at the sight of the pastry-laden trolley. "Oh my! Those look delicious. And I could certainly do with a cup of tea! You should have one too, Sybil. Oh, and take one of your joint pills. You're limping again."

"I don't remember asking for medical advice from you, Wilhelmina." Derek Hartley's grandmother stared down her nose at the newcomer before raising an eyebrow at her grandson. "Perhaps you could take this remaining case to my suite, Derek?"

"Sure thing, Grandmama."

Holly hastily handed Derek his phone as he started to follow the older woman from the room. He gave her a brief wink. "I'll see you later, Holly. Make sure you visit my booth at the show, okay?"

"I will." Holly grinned before turning to tell an eager

Wilhelmina about the various tea offerings.

6

The Maritime Quilting Expo formally opened at noon the following day. Becky was standing just inside the lobby area when Holly finally arrived late in the afternoon.

"Hi. How's it going?" she asked her friend. "Looks busy in here."

"So far, so good," Becky replied. "The opening ceremony went off well and there's been a steady stream of people coming and going all day. We're using the Teen Library for the quilt classes, and they've been very popular."

Holly smiled. "Have you been to yours yet?"

"No, it starts tomorrow. One of the quilters from Juniper Island is doing the sampler class." Becky's voice was abstracted, making Holly look at her more closely.

"You okay? You're not feeling sick, are you?"

"What? No, no, I'm fine. It's just..." Exasperation entered her voice as the head librarian gestured across the room. "Look at that. There they go!"

"There who go?" Holly peered in the direction Becky was pointing. "Oh. Never mind. I see."

"Well, don't just stand there grinning. Stop them!"

"From talking to people?"

Becky rounded on her. "They're not just talking, and you know it!" she hissed. "They're investigating! Interrogating people! Making a nuisance of themselves at my quilt convention. It has to stop. Do something, Holly!"

Holly tried to wipe the grin off her face as she watched Jamie and Myrtle disappear into the lecture hall.

"Did I hear something about investigating? Who's investigating what?" A man's amused voice caused both Holly and Becky to turn around.

Inspector Rob Tucker, chief of police on Hibiscus Island, smiled down at his diminutive sister before grinning at Holly.

Holly smiled back. "You heading to the golf course? Nice shirt. It's very... islandy."

"That's what I thought." Rob glanced down at his bright pink shirt with complacency before turning an enquiring look on his sister, eyes twinkling. "What's got you all riled up, Becky?"

"It's not funny!" Becky glared at him, then at Holly. "Never mind. I'll go sort it out myself."

As she stomped off, Rob's eyebrows shot up. "What did I say?" A worried expression crossed his face. "Is she feeling okay? Should I go find François?"

"Why on earth would you get François?" Holly asked.

"Well, because she's—"

Holly rolled her eyes. "She's pregnant, Rob, not incapacitated. She's just annoyed at Jamie and Myrtle, that's all."

"Annoyed at..." Rob's voice trailed away. "Wait a minute. Investigating? Oh no! They're not!" He studied Holly's face before emitting a heart-felt groan. "What could they possibly be investigating at a quilt show?"

Holly grinned. "Possible murder?"

"Murder?" Rob's eyes narrowed. "You're kidding me, right?"

"Well, we heard something the other night when we went to Myrtle's for dinner, and now—"

Rob held up a hand. "Say no more. I'll go put a stop to this right now."

Holly's grin widened as she watched Rob hurry into the lecture hall after his sister.

"I just don't understand why you feel the need to tell Rob everything now," Jamie complained that evening, slouching back on the small sofa in Holly's private apartment at the Inn. "This was our case, not his. And you told Miller too!"

Holly helped herself to another handful of popcorn. "First of all, you don't even know there's a 'case'; secondly, it was Becky who told Thomas, not me; and third, Rob's a policeman. Don't you think he should be told if you think someone's going to be murdered?"

Jamie waved a hand in irritation. "That's not the point. It's *our* case. Myrtle and I were discreetly asking questions" —Holly snorted, receiving a glare as her best friend continued—"when Rob comes barreling over, drags us across the room, and launches into a lecture about leaving police work to the police."

Holly grinned at this exaggerated account. "I was there, you know. I didn't see any barreling or dragging. I saw a quiet conversation at the side of the hall."

"Whatever." Jamie looked indignant. "And then he told us we weren't to upset Becky at this delicate time in her life!"

Holly choked. "He did not."

"Yes, he did! I mean, who talks like that, Holls? 'Delicate

time'? Does he think we live in the Regency era or something?"

"He's just concerned about his sister." A muffled giggle escaped Holly. "Did he really say 'delicate'? What an old-fashioned sweetie."

"Sweetie?" Jamie looked at her friend in disgust. "The man's a dinosaur."

Holly grinned again. "So what did he think of your 'case'? Does he agree? Does he think someone's murdering Azure Isle quilters?"

"He refused to even listen to us! He just stalked off!"

"Oh." Holly's lips quirked as her friend's scowl returned in force. "So, of course, you're going to—"

"—keep investigating. Naturally!" Jamie took a handful of popcorn while leveling a stern look on Holly. "And you're going to help!"

～

"Weak. That's what I am, Truffle. Spineless even. I should have said no. Why didn't I say no? What exactly am I supposed to say to this girl? 'Hi, I'm Holly. I hear you think your mom was murdered.' I mean, really, Truff. How's that going to sound?"

The little dog tilted her head as she trotted beside Holly the morning after the discussion with Jamie. "Woof."

"Exactly." Holly sighed, then squared her shoulders as they approached the entrance to the Nasturtium Suite.

Located on one of the lower terraces on the Inn's grounds, the outdoor entrance to the Nasturtium Suite was accessed via a tiny sunken paved patio edged with raised stone planters. At this time of year, they were bursting with candytuft, a favorite of Holly's grandfather, but by March these pastel annuals would be replaced with the signature flower of the suite, the bright yellow and orange nasturtiums that grew wild around the island.

Yellow-flowered hibiscus shrubs clustered beneath the windows, which were wide open to allow the breeze in. Holly could hear voices inside.

As she raised her hand to knock, the door opened. Derek Hartley stared at her, then smiled. "Holly, right?" He looked down at Truffle. "And who's this little cutie? Hey girl, how are you?"

As Derek crouched to offer a hand to the tail-wagging Truffle, a girl in her early twenties appeared in the doorway behind him. She wore no make-up, her long, dark hair was piled carelessly on top of her head as if it took too much effort to brush it properly, and there were dark shadows under her eyes.

The girl gave a wan smile. "Hi. Are we late for breakfast? Sorry. Derek just came to get me."

"No, not at all." Holly hesitated. "Are you Denise? Denise Trott?"

"Yes. Who are you?"

Derek glanced up from where he was rubbing an ecstatic Truffle's ears. "This is Holly Gold, Denise. She's Maggie's daughter and she's responsible for the gardens here." He grinned as he stood up. "I met your grandfather yesterday. Mr. Mackintosh, right? We had a nice chat."

"Then you should know it's Gramps who's in charge of the gardens." Holly smiled. "I just help him out."

"You're Holly? You're one of the people who solved that murder in September last year?"

Holly blinked in surprise at Denise's abrupt question. "Well, uh, actually, the police—"

She was cut off.

"Mrs. McGinney said you and your friends found out who did it. She said you might be able to help me. Have you spoken to her yet?"

Holly's mouth dropped open. "Uh..."

"Denise," Derek began, his smile fading. "I don't think—"

"You said you agreed with me, Derek! And Mrs. McGinney said they could help!" Denise rounded on Holly again. "Well? Will you? Will you help me find out who killed my mom?"

As the girl's eyes filled with tears, Holly gazed at her in dismay. Why, oh why, had she allowed Jamie to bully her into this?

JAMIE'S EYES lit up as Holly finished telling her about Denise's request. Her coffee forgotten, she leaned across the café table. "She actually said she thinks her mom was poisoned?"

Holly nodded with reluctance. She took a sip of her tea and prepared for battle.

"And this Derek person agreed with her?"

"I think he's ambivalent. I get the feeling he's just trying to be a good friend." Holly put her cup down on the table. "Look, Jamie, the girl is obviously very upset about her mom's death, but she has no real reason—that I could see anyway—to believe she was murdered. I really think they've all worked themselves up into a frenzy because of two tragic circumstances."

"Mmmm." Jamie fingered her lip, obviously not listening to a word. "This Derek Hartley has a jewelry stall at the convention, right?"

"Yes, but like I said—"

"I've been thinking the Rose Treasure should be looked over by a jeweler again. It's kind of tarnished, you know, and should maybe be cleaned. But I'd want an expert opinion on that."

"You've been thinking no such thing," Holly retorted, half-amused, half-exasperated.

"Maybe Mr. Hartley would be willing to do a consultation. And then I could just ask a few questions about the case as well. What do you think?" Jamie beamed at her friend.

"I think it's ridiculous."

Jamie glanced at her watch. "I'm heading up to the library in twenty minutes for my lunchtime shift at the convention. François has made the cutest little quiches today, packed in bento boxes with crudités, dips, and fresh baked rolls. If you're not doing anything, you could help me load the van, hand out the lunches, and then we can check out the jeweler together. You can introduce me. Sound good?"

"Well, since you ask, I'm forced to say, 'Not really.'"

Jamie pursed her lips as she surveyed her friend. "Stop faking, Holls. You know you want to find out what's going on as much as I do."

"Uh, no." But Holly wilted under Jamie's glare. "Fine. I'll introduce you!"

"Great." Jamie bounced up, beaming. Collecting Holly's now-empty teacup, she headed towards the kitchen, calling out to her co-worker as she passed the counter. "I'm going to take the food up to the library, Angie, okay? I'll be back in time for the teatime rush."

Angie gazed around the nearly empty café. "Take your time. Looks like there'll be more business up at the convention than here." She grinned as Holly approached the counter. "I take it you've been drafted to help. Go on back. I think François has everything ready to load up."

Holly nodded, then passed through the swinging door into the kitchen of the Bean. François looked up from the stainless-steel working space where he was counting brightly colored plastic bento boxes.

"Hang on a minute... Fifty-eight, fifty-nine, sixty... Yep, all present and accounted for. The van's out back, Holly. If you can just help me load these into the cartons, you two can get going."

Within fifteen minutes, Holly and her friends had packed the insulated cartons with the smaller bento boxes and loaded the cartons into the van.

Jamie hopped into the driver's seat with a grin. "Let's go."

The Bridgeport Library was only a block away. Jamie turned down Spinnaker Road and into the smaller parking lot on the side of the building. She and Holly unloaded the van, placing the cartons onto a small trolley before wheeling them up the accessibility ramp into the far end of the foyer.

"We'll take them straight to the courtyard," Jamie said. "Get that door for me, Holls."

Other vendors were setting up their lunch offerings under the small tents, and a happy buzz of chatter filled the air.

"What on earth is that?" Holly stared at the table beneath the Bean's tent. What appeared to be a rectangular paddling pool reclined on top of it.

"An inflatable buffet." Jamie grinned. "Pretty nifty, huh? I'll just go grab the ice from the van. You can start unloading the boxes, then we'll pop them into their ice bath to keep them cool for the customers."

She was back in moments with two large plastic bags of ice cubes, which she dumped into the buffet.

"How does this work?" Holly asked, inserting boxes into the ice. "Do you get the boxes back?"

"Yep. We were told we had to be eco-friendly, so people are either using compostable or reusable containers. The attendees return our boxes when they finish eating, we take them back and sterilize them, then refill them for tomorrow. And we don't take any money in. It's all on a ticket system. All lunches are charged at the same rate—attendees buy tickets, we collect them as they choose their lunch, and then we get reimbursed for the number of tickets. It's been working great so far."

Jamie shoved one more box into the ice. "There. That's all that will fit right now. We can leave the rest in the cartons and replace as necessary."

As the first hungry quilters appeared in the doorway of the courtyard, Jamie grinned. "It's a bit like feeding time at the zoo at the beginning, Holls. You take the tickets; I'll refill the buffet as the boxes go. Oh! I forgot the menu sign." She dove under the table, re-emerging with a whiteboard easel. Hastily scrawling the menu on it, she propped it up beside the table. "Okay. Ready, set, go!"

The next half hour was hectic. Holly collected tickets, repeated the menu a million times to those quilters who, for whatever reason, couldn't read the sign, answered allergy-related questions, explained the box return system to newbies, and in between times helped to refill the buffet.

The bento boxes were popular and, to the great disappointment of latecomers, all gone within thirty minutes.

"What's on the menu tomorrow?"

Smiling as she recognized Wilhelmina—the elderly quilter did love her food—Holly hesitated. "Um…"

"Sliced baked chicken, zucchini caprese, and fresh berries," Jamie interjected. She glanced at the woman's name tag. "Make sure you get here early, Ms. Carson."

"It was our turn at the Quilt Bee this morning," Wilhelmina explained. "We all lost track of time."

Jamie grinned. "Well, the Sand Witch has some fabulous chicken salad just a few tables down which you might enjoy. And I believe there's soup and rolls at the White Horse table."

"Come on, Wilhelmina." The woman beside the hungry quilter tugged at her arm. "Stop chatting or we won't get anything to eat."

Holly and Jamie exchanged amused glances as Wilhelmina was dragged away by her friend.

"Right! Let's pack up quickly, hand in our tickets, and then," Jamie rubbed her hands together in anticipation, "let's go check out the jewelry stall!"

7

Holly hadn't been into the lecture hall since the convention had started and was surprised at the number and variety of stalls in the room. Booths lined the walls and marched in rows down the center of the room, all of them overflowing with a remarkable assortment of goods.

"I didn't realize there'd be so many different things for sale!" Holly's head whipped from side to side, taking in the variety of offerings. "Wait, Jamie. Look at these!" She paused at a table covered in individually wrapped sugar cookies frosted to look like quilt blocks. "How cute are these? I wonder if there are gluten-free ones."

The woman behind the table smiled, gesturing towards a basket. "These are gluten-free. We also have vegan and dairy-free versions."

Holly eyed the basket with delight before glancing at the sign on the table. "Cookie Encounter. I've never heard of you before. Where's your bakery located?"

"Coral Island. It's just a small home bakery but we do ship orders to the other islands. We supply a couple of bed and breakfasts with treats. They're quite popular."

"I'll bet they are!" Holly exclaimed. "Our guests would love these! I wonder if Mama's seen them. Do you create custom designs?"

The woman nodded. "I'll give you our information."

Jamie inspected a cookie closely as Holly took the brochure. "How'd you get all these here? On the ferry?"

"No. My husband's a pilot. He has a small plane, and this gives him an opportunity to fly back and forth. My daughter's my business partner, and she makes a fresh batch every other day, then John zips them across. It's only a twenty-minute flight." The woman smiled. "I take the ferry myself. I'm not fond of small planes at all."

"Well, these are fabulous," Holly said. "I'll take half a dozen gluten-free ones for me—and I'll be telling my mom about them for sure."

Having paid for and accepted the bag of cookies, Holly eyed the nearby tables with interest. Jamie nudged her impatiently.

"You can browse another time, Holls. Where's this jeweler guy?"

Holly scanned the room. "Over there."

The two women made slow progress through the room. Holly couldn't resist stopping at several stalls, despite Jamie's repeated admonitions.

"He's not going anywhere, Jamie! And I may not get a chance to come here again. Oh look! Look at these!" Holly paused in front of a table display of antique teacups and packaged teas.

Jamie's groan made the woman behind the table laugh out loud.

"Not a tea fan?" Her brown eyes twinkled at Jamie, who had the grace to look somewhat abashed. "Oh, don't worry about it. Tea's not everybody's... Well, cup of tea." She laughed again.

Holly grinned at the woman, liking the look of her. She was about their age, maybe a little older, with tawny skin and shoulder length brown hair. Gold hoop earrings dangled from her ears above an off-the-shoulder red peasant-style dress.

"This is the first time we've been to the quilt conference," the woman continued, smiling at Holly. "My sister chairs our quilt club, and she thought people might like some tea-related items since they all drink it by the gallon when they meet up. I manage our shop with my other sister, so we thought we'd try it out and see whether there's any interest."

"Oh, are you from Juniper Island?" Jamie asked. "We heard there was a club from there attending. The Stitch Witches? Is that right?"

"That's us. It's been... okay... so far."

Holly looked up from inspecting the label on a packet of tea. "You know, I think we order soaps and lotions from you. My mother owns the Hibiscus Inn."

The woman's eyes lit up. "Oh, you're Maggie's daughter! Yes, you're one of our best customers actually." She smiled. "We first met your mom when she and your dad came to Juniper for a week for an anniversary trip, I think it was. They found our shop on the first day, and by the end of the week, I think Maggie had sampled every single item. Solid used to sit outside with a cup of tea and talk to my dad. We were so sorry to hear of his passing. He was a good man."

"I remember when they went on that trip. He called you..." Holly's voice trailed off in confusion.

"The three witches plus dad. Yeah, he and my dad

thought it was hysterical." The woman rolled her eyes, then laughed, holding out her hand. "I'm Tansy Craft. It's a pleasure to meet you, Holly."

Jamie grinned. "Are you witches?" She held up one of the packaged teas and tapped the label, raising an enquiring eyebrow. "The Black Cat?"

"Well, some people think our soaps and teas are magical." Tansy's answering grin faded to be replaced by a more enigmatic expression. "So you're the detectives I've heard about. There's been a lot of chatter among the quilters about those murders you solved last year."

Holly sighed. "We're not—"

"We've solved some cases, yes," Jamie interrupted.

The tea seller's smile blossomed again. "There seems to be a difference of opinion here."

"Ignore her." Jamie eyed Tansy thoughtfully, then leaned across the table, lowering her voice. "You haven't by any chance heard any talk about more recent murders? Say, among the Oleanders?"

"Oleanders?" The Juniper islander's amused expression disappeared completely. "Is this about Daina Trott? What's Denise been saying to you?"

HOLLY GLANCED sideways at Jamie as the two women threaded their way through the tables heading towards the far end of the room. "You're just unbelievable sometimes, you know that?"

"If you don't ask questions, you don't get answers." Jamie's smirk was complacent. "And we certainly couldn't talk here with all these listening ears! I can't wait to hear what Tansy's going to tell us!" She performed another little shimmy of excitement.

"She's probably going to say Denise is a distraught and upset young woman and we shouldn't listen to anything she says," Holly hissed.

"Oh, just relax, Holls. You know, you're really being a bit of a wet blanket about this case. Where's the old Holly gone? Rob is turning you into a stuffed shirt!"

"He is not! And I'm not a wet blanket!" Holly scowled at her friend. "I just don't think—"

"Yeah, yeah. I know. You just don't think there's a case. Blah, blah, blah. Well, come with me to Highwood House tonight then. Maybe what Tansy has to say will make you more interested in being a real member of the Hibis—"

Jamie came to an abrupt halt. "Whoa! What is that I see ahead of me? Is that him? The jeweler? My, my, my!" She fanned her face rapidly before turning an accusing look on Holly. "You didn't tell me he looked like that!"

Ignoring Holly's attempt to speak, Jamie sashayed up to Derek Hartley's table. He glanced up, then paused, eyes widening in admiration.

Holly had to admit his reaction was justified. Her best friend's single-minded focus on solving nonexistent crimes could be annoying, but she did look amazing today. With her long hair pulled back in a braided ponytail, amber drop earrings, and a burnt orange silk shirt worn loose over black leggings, Jamie could have graced the cover of any fashion magazine. Looking down at her slightly scruffy jeans and plain black t-shirt, Holly sighed, then cleared her throat as she approached. "Allow me to do the honors. Derek Hartley, Jamie White; Jamie, Derek."

"Enchanted, Miss White." Derek's smile was somewhat wolfish as he looked Jamie up and down.

Repeating his actions, she grinned, unfazed. "Ditto."

Trying not to roll her eyes at the mutual admiration society in front of her, Holly turned her attention instead to the pendants, earrings, and bracelets reclining on velvet trays on the table. The display surprised an exclamation out of her. "Wow!" She turned to the jeweler. "This looks great, Derek! You must be getting tons of sales!"

Derek Hartley tore his gaze away from Jamie. "Yeah, they've been decent so far. Maggie's been by a couple of times, by the way." He grinned at Holly as he handed a bracelet to her. "This piece seemed to catch her eye." He shot a wink at Jamie, who laughed.

"Really?" Ignoring the flirtatious byplay, Holly turned the bracelet this way and that, admiring the diamond-shaped enamel charms. "It's lovely. What do you think, Jamie? Mama's birthday's coming up soon."

"It's very pretty," Jamie agreed, taking the bracelet from Holly to examine it more closely. "Not quite my style, but I can see why quilters would like it. And yes, I think Maggie would love it."

"Why, thank you." Derek's amber eyes gleamed at the compliment. "I do actually create more contemporary pieces in my shop on Azure." He eyed Jamie in appraisal. "You ever considered modeling? I have some things that would look fantastic on you. Of course, they're nothing like the Rose Treasure. Now that's a work of art. And may I say it looked stunning on you, although I'm not sure the newspaper photos did it—and you—full justice."

"They didn't," Jamie agreed with a grin and complete lack of modesty. She cast a quick sidelong glance at Holly before continuing, "Funny you should mention that. That's why we're here." She leaned against the table, directing a wide smile at the jeweler. "Would you be willing to take a look at the Rose Treasure? In a professional capacity, I mean."

Holly gave an inward resigned sigh as Derek's eyebrows rose.

"Is there something wrong with it?" The question was wary.

"No, no. It's a bit tarnished though and I wondered if there was a way to make it, I don't know, brighter or something."

"Possibly. I'd have to inspect it. You need to be careful with antique gold, especially if there are gemstones set in it. I could take a look on Sunday, if that suits you. The booths are closed so we can all have a break, restock, that kind of thing."

"Oh. No, Sunday won't work. We're planning to go out to the wreck then." Jamie pursed her lips. "Maybe an evening?"

"Sure." Derek seemed to vacillate, then asked. "Is that the wreck of *La Rosa de España* you're going to?"

"Yes. Why? Do you dive?" Jamie eyed him with interest. "You do? Would you like to come with us? Holly's bringing her boyfriend and I need a dive buddy."

Holly opened her mouth, closing it as Derek accepted the invitation without hesitation.

"You have an open water qualification, right?" Jamie asked. At his nod, she leaned more comfortably against the table and began to tell him all about the wreck and what to expect on the dive.

"I'm sorry, Holly, I can't. I thought we'd settled on Saturday, so I told Sir James I'd play golf with him on Sunday afternoon."

Holly sighed as Rob gazed at her in apology over the top of his cup. "That's okay. I should have told you sooner. I'm sure I can find someone else to be my partner." She gazed around the nearly empty Bean café. "Maybe. Seems to me everyone I know is involved with the expo. And although the stalls are closed on Sunday, they'll all be up at the City Hall art gallery checking out the competition, I'm sure."

She took a sip of tea before popping a piece of scone into her mouth. Jamie, engaged in animated conversation with Derek Hartley, hadn't protested when Holly left for her standing Friday afternoon date with the inspector.

Rob frowned in thought. "Well, Becky can't go now. What about Miller? Have you asked him yet?"

"No. And I'm not sure that would be a good idea. Jamie seems kind of... Um, how shall I put this? ... enamored of this Azure Isle guy."

Rob grinned. "Enamored?"

"That's probably not the right word but... Well, I wouldn't want Thomas to get upset."

The inspector shook his head in amusement. "You and Becky. You're like high school matchmakers."

"We are not," Holly protested. "We just think they'd make a cute couple. All that arguing and bickering has to mean they like each other."

Rob laughed. "Like I said. High school. I don't think Miller will mind in the slightest, but you know what? Ask him yourself. He's just coming down the street and looks in dire need of a coffee."

He leaned over and tapped on the glass window, drawing the attention of the passing journalist, who grinned at them, then breezed into the Bean.

"Hey there, Inspector. Holly." Thomas pulled out a chair and collapsed into it. "What's up?"

"Holly here needs a diving partner on Sunday. You free?" Rob got straight to the point. "I'm golfing."

"Sure. *La Rosa*, I presume. I'm at your service." He leaned back in his chair. "So, Holls, you ready for the murder meeting tonight?"

8

_____

"The what?" Rob exclaimed, turning an incredulous eye on Holly before glaring at Thomas. "What are you talking about, Miller? I thought I nipped Jamie and Myrtle's investigation in the bud!" He groaned. "What is this obsession you all have with being armchair detectives?"

"I'm not obsessed!" Holly protested. "I've told Jamie repeatedly I want no part of any of this!"

Thomas Miller sniggered. "Which is why you were talking to Denise Trott this morning, right?"

Holly flushed. "Actually, she talked to me. And I was only there because Jamie wanted..." Her voice trailed away as Thomas guffawed. "How do you know what's happening tonight anyway?"

Thomas lowered his voice to a mysterious whisper. "My sources tell me everything." He laughed. "Actually, I popped into the library to check out the expo, get some photos, see if there was anything newsworthy, and Myrtle nabbed me the second I walked through the door. I hear we're going to Highwood House tonight to talk to the Juniper Island witches."

"Stop!" The exclamation burst from the sorely tried inspector. He massaged his forehead. "I knew I should have cross-examined Jamie and Myrtle more closely!" His look at Holly was rueful. "And I probably shouldn't have cut you off when you were about to tell me about it."

"This is true," Holly agreed. "Although, to be fair, at that point I didn't know anything about the Juniper witches."

Rob took a deep breath. "Right. The witches. Okay, you two, tell me what's going on."

Holly beat Thomas to the punch. "Well, in a nutshell, Denise Trott, an Oleander quilter from Azure Isle, is convinced her mother was murdered. She and Anne McGinney, another Oleander, also think Freda Sinclair, the former president, was murdered and that the current president will be the next victim. One of the Juniper Island quilters, who sells tea, told us she needs to talk to us tonight about Daina Trott. I don't know what she's going to say."

The inspector's face held utter disbelief. "They think someone is murdering the presidents of a quilt club?"

Holly's lips twitched as she nodded.

"And this is what Jamie and Myrtle were doing yesterday? They actually believe this?"

Holly nodded again.

Rob looked at Thomas. "And what's your part in all this, Miller?"

The journalist grinned. "There might be a story in it."

"A story. Right." Rob wore a pained expression. He took a deep breath. "So, did these Oleander quilters—you said Oleander, right?"

"Yep."

"Did they say why they thought quilt club presidents were being murdered?"

"Mrs. McGinney was a bit shaky on that," Holly admitted. "And we haven't spoken to Denise yet."

Rob stared at her. "Shaky?"

"Well, actually, she went into hysterics."

Thomas snorted in amusement. "She thinks she might be next on the killer's list," he told the incredulous police inspector.

"After the current president, Sally Dill," Holly added.

Rob closed his eyes briefly, then opened them again. "Dare I ask if they have any evidence for these allegations?"

"Both women who died had nausea and weakness, but Daina Trott had cancer and was having chemo, and Freda Sinclair's doctor said she had the flu when she had her car accident." Holly eyed Rob. "Is there any way you can confirm that, do you think? Maybe contact the police on Azure—you know them, don't you?—and ask if there was anything suspicious. Because otherwise, Jamie and Myrtle are going to run wild with this. I certainly can't stop them!" She cast a sideways glance at Thomas. "And some people aren't interested in even *trying* to rein them in!"

"Nope," the journalist agreed with a wide grin. "Watching Myrtle in full-on detective mode is one of the highlights of my life. Besides, there's always the possibility they're right, and if so, I want to be in on all the action."

Rob ran a hand over his face. "In on the action," he muttered to himself. "Oh, that's lovely. Just lovely. Once again, citizens are running amok, interfering in police business, aided and abetted by the free press."

Holly tried desperately to keep a straight face as he glared at her. "I'm not running amok." Her lips quivered.

"And it's not police business yet, because, so far, we don't even know if there's been a crime. It's all still supposition,

Inspector." Thomas smirked. "But the free press is pretty interested, yes."

"Are *you* going to talk to these people?" Rob asked Holly.

"Well, if I don't go, I won't know what's happening," she pointed out.

"And besides, she's curious too. She just pretends she's not," Thomas added, ignoring Holly's indignant look. "But you don't need to worry about Becky, Inspector. Everyone agrees she should sit this one out."

Rob stared at them both in silence, then gave a resigned sigh. "Well, that's something, I suppose." He pondered a moment, before heaving yet another sigh. "I can't believe I'm saying this but I'll contact the police on Azure and see if there's anything in this at all. And you'll keep me informed about... Well, about anything you hear that might cause problems. And that includes any shenanigans Myrtle and Jamie might be planning! Okay?" He frowned at Holly. "And don't do anything daft!"

"'Daft' is not in my vocabulary, Inspector Tucker," Holly said in dignified tones, before smiling at him. "Rob, I really don't think there's anything in this at all, but yes, I—we— will let you know what's going on. Right, Mr. Miller?"

Thomas grinned. "Totally, Inspector. Totally."

"YOU NEED TO CALM DOWN," Holly advised her excited passenger as she drove into the parking lot of Highwood House.

"I'm completely calm." Jamie bounced out of the little electric car as soon as it stopped moving. "Come on, Holls. Myrtle's already here. And— Wait a minute! Is that Miller's car I see? What's he doing here? Who invited him?"

She turned an accusing look on Holly, who held up her hands. "Don't blame me. Myrtle told him."

Jamie huffed. "Honestly. That woman!"

"He was pretty useful in our last case."

"Our last case? Ooh, then you do think there's something going on! I knew you'd come around, Holls. This is more like it! The HIDC is back in action!" Jamie beamed at Holly, who had regretted her words the minute they'd left her mouth.

"I just meant... Oh, whatever. Have it your way." Holly eyed her friend in amusement. "I don't think you'll ever grow up."

"Who wants to?" Jamie replied in cheerful tones, linking her arm through Holly's as they approached the front door of the guesthouse. "'The secret of genius is to carry the spirit of the child into old age.'"

"What?"

Jamie gave a shout of laughter at Holly's stupefied look. "I've been dying to use that quote! It's a good one, isn't it? Aldous Huxley wrote it."

"Aldous Huxley? I'm impressed, White! *A Brave New World* fan, are you?" Thomas Miller grinned at the two women as they entered the front hall.

"Huh? What are you talking about, Miller?"

"Aldous Huxley. He wrote *Brave New World*. Or were you talking about a different novel?"

"It's a quote, Miller. A quote. That's all."

Holly giggled at the confusion on the journalist's face. "She just likes them, Thomas. Quotes, that is. She used to collect them when we were at school and drop them into conversations." She looked at her best friend in amusement. "I didn't know you still did it. You don't even know who Aldous Huxley is, do you?"

"Nope. And I don't care. It's a great quote though." Jamie dismissed the conversation, peering around the well-lit foyer. "Where is everyone?"

"In here." Looking somewhat impatient, Myrtle, attired in one of her signature suits, this one a muted teal green, stood in the doorway of an adjoining room. "Come along!"

Grinning, Thomas motioned to Holly and Jamie to precede him.

Holly hadn't been to Highwood House for several years, but she'd always liked the old-fashioned guest house. Gazing around what the proprietor, Miss Greta Golding, referred to as the 'morning room,' Holly smiled as she realized that, although it had been freshly painted, the room still held the same bright floral sofas and antique wooden coffee tables with their glass-shaded Tiffany lamps.

A fire burned in the brick fireplace at one end, but Miss Golding had set out her rose-patterned china tea set on a small table near the window, where Tansy Craft and one other woman were already seated.

Beaming, Jamie hustled towards them. "Here we are!" She held out a hand to the unknown woman. "Hi. I'm Jamie White."

Tansy grinned. "This is my sister, Sage. She's the quilter in our family. Sage, this is Jamie, her friend Holly, and Thomas, the owner of the newspaper here on Hibiscus."

Sage Craft smiled. Like her sister, she had light brown skin, but her eyes were hazel green instead of brown, and her dark hair was worn in a multitude of long braids. Jamie eyed her with interest.

"Tansy and Sage. Your mom likes herbs, huh?"

"And flowers," Sage agreed, with another smile. "Our youngest sister is called Marigold."

"Sage is the tea blender in our family; Marigold and I

run the shop," Tansy explained. "And we all make the soaps and lotions and other things. We have a sort of partnership with the perfumery on Turtle Island."

"Is that the one that still uses the old techniques?" Thomas asked. "I've forgotten what they call it. En... En something."

"Yes. They use the *enfleurage* method. It's a way of extracting scents and oils from plants, even fragile ones. Like frangipani, for instance." Sage glanced at the fair-haired, grey-eyed journalist with approval. "We use many of the aromatic oils from Plumeria in our products."

Pulling out a chair next to the Azure islander, Thomas grinned at her. "I've been thinking of visiting them. It sounds like it would make a good feature piece in the paper. I want to have a Maritime Island section—highlight events on other islands as well, not just Hibiscus."

"You should hold off on that until spring then," Tansy advised. "They're having a group of perfumiers descend on them sometime around May, I think. To learn the art of *enfleurage* apparently. It might make a better story for you. I was talking to a Tacky Turtle today, and she told me it's a pretty big deal for the perfumery."

"Thanks. I'll look into that." Thomas made a quick note on his phone. "It's a nice alliterative name, isn't it? Plumeria Perfumery. I wonder if it means anything."

"Plumeria is the botanical name for frangipani," Holly told him as she sat down next to him. "You know the tree, don't you? We have them growing here. They flower in the summer. Yellow and white flowers mostly, but we have some pink and peach ones as well."

"And there's an interesting story that connects the frangipani flower and perfume. Have you heard it?" Sage asked.

Holly grinned. "I have."

"Mr. Miller?"

"No, and he's not going to now!" Jamie frowned at first Thomas, then Holly. "We're here for a reason. Not to chat about flowers and perfumes! No offense, Sage."

"None taken. Perhaps another time, Mr. Miller."

"I'd be delighted," Thomas assured the tea blender.

Glancing sideways at Jamie, Holly saw her friend's scowl deepen as the journalist smiled at Sage.

Myrtle cleared her throat, and all eyes swung her way. "Jamie's correct. Perhaps we could start with you, Sage. I understand you provided Daina Trott with some special teas of your own making. Is that correct? And that they were in her possession when she died."

9

S age pursed her lips as she gazed at the older woman. Her voice was cool. "I'm not quite sure I like the implication you seem to be making, Myrtle."

The septuagenarian raised an eyebrow. "There's no implication. Anne McGinney told me Daina regularly ordered products from The Black Cat, including several herbal teas. Is that true?"

"She liked our rose soap," Tansy agreed, a trace of a frown on her face. "The same one that Maggie buys for the Hibiscus Inn, I'd like to point out. And some essential oils—lavender, rose, jasmine—all of which we get from Plumeria."

"Anne mentioned teas," Myrtle repeated. "Did you supply Daina with those as well?"

"Yes. We grow some of our own flowers for teas, like chamomile, honeysuckle, jasmine, and hibiscus," Tansy said, "but we outsource a lot as well. Not everything grows on Juniper."

"What about a tea called..." Myrtle consulted a piece of paper in her hand, "... *pau d'arco*? Do you make that?"

"It's made from the bark of a tree that grows in the rainforests of South America," Tansy said.

"*Tabebuia*. Pink Trumpet Tree. There's one in the Botanic Gardens here," Holly murmured, then blushed when everyone looked at her. "Sorry."

"We source our supply from Paraguay." Sage paused. "And it's not poisonous. It's used to reduce inflammation."

There was a moment of awkward silence, then Tansy gave an impatient sigh. "Look, we wanted to talk about Daina because we know Denise has been telling everyone that she thinks her mother was poisoned. Well, it has nothing to do with us!"

"Are people saying it does?" Thomas asked.

Sage shrugged. "They're not saying it to our faces, but business has dropped off. Daina sent a lot of online customers from Azure our way."

"In person ones too," Tansy added. "You need to remember we're about the same distance from Turtle and Azure as you are from Coral Island. The ferries run regularly, and so do the planes. We get a lot of weekend visitors."

"Including Daina Trott and Freda Sinclair, I understand," Myrtle said.

Holly blinked in surprise. *What?*

"Yes." Tansy made a sour face. "They were great customers—something which appears to have backfired on us. They both loved the sorrel tea that Sage makes. And they just liked Juniper Island. They'd visit four or five times a year, if not more. Heck, half the Oleander quilters come to Juniper. Sybil Worthington's a great customer. So's her daughter, Ellen."

"What's sorrel?" Thomas asked, looking up from his notes.

"It's a type of hibiscus," Holly offered.

"The ones that grow all over the island?"

"No. Different species. Those are *Hibiscus sinensis*—ornamental, mostly. Sorrel is another name for *Hibiscus sabdariffa*. You can make tea from the flowers. It's really popular in Jamaica."

"And in our islands too." Sage's face was impassive as she added, "Sorrel, mixed with ginger and orange, was a favorite tea of both Daina and Freda."

"But there's absolutely nothing wrong with it!" Tansy exclaimed. "Unless you're allergic to hibiscus—and neither woman was—then it's perfectly safe to drink. Historically it was used to treat sore throats, but a lot of people drink it now for high blood pressure or just because they like the taste. Regardless, it has no real side effects. Certainly not the nausea and weakness that Denise is telling everyone about!" Tansy looked exasperated. "And Daina had cancer. She was on chemo, for goodness' sake! Of course she was nauseous."

"Freda Sinclair didn't have cancer though. And we've heard she was feeling ill when she crashed the car. You say sorrel tea is used for high blood pressure. Could it lower blood pressure so much that it would cause symptoms of nausea or dizziness?" Jamie's face wore a shrewd expression as she looked at the Juniper Island women.

"Well, technically, I suppose yes, it could," Tansy replied. "But you'd have to have low blood pressure to start with, and it would only be temporary. And Freda ordered tea from us for at least two years! She would know how it affected her."

"Were there any other things they both ordered?" Jamie asked.

Sage hesitated but Tansy snorted. "Of course there were! You know they were friends, right? They both liked having weekends at Serenity—a spa on the island—and they would come by the shop before they left to check out anything new that we had. I know they both liked that apple seed oil stuff you make, Sage, right?"

The older sister nodded with some reluctance, opened her mouth, then closed it again. Holly eyed her with curiosity, wondering what the Juniper islander had been about to say.

Tansy leaned back in her seat. "You all have to understand. We liked Daina and Freda! And we even met Denise a couple of times when she came with her mom. Why would she think we had anything to do with her mom's death?"

"Denise hasn't specifically accused you," Myrtle said, eyeing the two Azure Island women with speculation. "However, I find it interesting that you both think poison was the means by which Daina and Freda died."

"Well, what else could it be, Myrtle?" Jamie's voice was impatient. "They weren't strangled or shot or pushed off a cliff, were they? If they didn't die naturally, they had to have been poisoned!"

There was a small choking sound from Thomas as Myrtle stiffened. Pressing her own lips tightly together in an effort not to laugh, Holly spoke hurriedly. "Do you know of anything that would produce the symptoms they had? Nausea, vomiting, weakness?"

She instantly regretted her question when Jamie shot her a beam of approval, before frowning at Myrtle.

Sage's tone was cool as she answered. "You mean something herbal? I'd have thought, as a horticulturist, you'd know your plant poisons pretty well, Holly."

Holly blinked, then flushed. "Oh, well, I prefer the landscaping side of horticulture. And herbal teas aren't really my thing. I like plain old English breakfast the best."

"Me too." Tansy's companionable grin made Holly feel better. "Actually, Sage and I have been thinking about this, ever since we heard the rumors about Daina. It's one of the reasons we wanted to come to the quilt expo, actually. We didn't want all the islands thinking we might be involved."

Jamie and Myrtle stopped glaring at each other and turned as one to look at the Juniper Islanders.

"And?" Jamie asked. "What are your thoughts?"

Sage shrugged. "All herbal supplements can have side effects if misused. And they can interact with prescription medicines as well. But those specific symptoms? Hard to tell. They're common side effects of St. John's Wort, for one."

"But we don't sell that," Tansy interjected.

"Sage tea, if you drink too much, can cause vomiting and dizziness." Sage's smile was wry. "Even too much black or green tea can cause nausea at times." She shrugged. "And don't forget the flu was going around when Freda had her accident. I had it myself. It was a pretty nasty strain last year."

Tansy raised her hands in appeal. "The thing is, we don't know what, if anything, happened to Daina and Freda. We just wanted you to hear our side of the story. Especially since Denise has asked you for help. Besides," she continued with indignation, "I'm tired of seeing Oleanders look at me like I'm Lucrezia Borgia or something. And we know you've solved mysteries in the past."

Thomas grinned as both Jamie and Myrtle immediately preened themselves. "They have. But Holly and I also spoke to Rob earlier—that's our Inspector Tucker—and he agreed he'd reach out to the Azure Island police and see if there was anything unusual at all about the two women's deaths. Medically speaking, that is."

"You spoke to Rob?" Jamie frowned at the journalist, then at Holly. "But Mrs. McGinney already told us the doctors said there wasn't anything unusual."

Tansy threw up her hands. "See? So why're they spreading rumors?"

"I don't know. But it won't hurt for Inspector Tucker to double-check, will it?" Thomas smiled at the Juniper islanders.

"And in the meantime," Myrtle intervened, "we'll see what we can find out from the quilters themselves. The Oleanders are a snobbish bunch, but they're definitely disturbed by these two deaths. It's not just Anne McGinney and Denise who are suspicious, so there has to be some reason for everyone to be worked up about it."

"Who else is suspicious?" Jamie demanded, turning another frown on the older woman. "What do you know that we don't? We're supposed to share information, Myrtle!"

The smug expression Myrtle usually wore when she knew something the others didn't was missing from her face. "Well, for one thing, Rosalie Becknell is very worried about Sally."

Everyone looked blank.

"Who's Rosalie Becknell?" Holly asked. "And why's she worried?"

"Sally? You mean Sally Hartley Dill, current president of the Oleanders, right?" Thomas was instantly alert. "What's wrong with her?"

Jamie spoke at the same time. "Is she sick? Does she have the symptoms Daina and Freda had?"

Myrtle looked impatient. "I don't know, Jamie. I've been very busy organizing the expo, so I've only had a brief word with Rosalie. I'm having tea with her tomorrow and will get more details. But I can assure you that Rosalie Becknell is a very level-headed woman. If she says she's worried, then there's something to worry about!"

~

"Well, that was pretty useless. All hearsay and rumor. Nothing concrete at all." Jamie slumped back in the passenger side of the car. "I can't believe I'm actually saying this, but I'm beginning to think you're right, Holls. This case might not be a case after all." She heaved a huge sigh.

Holly's lips quirked involuntarily at the gloomy look on her friend's face. "Oh, I don't know," she demurred. "Something's got the Oleanders all worked up—and if nothing else, the rumors are hurting Tansy and Sage's business. Even if all we do is find out there's nothing going on, it'll be a help to them, right?"

"I suppose." Her friend huffed again, staring moodily out the window.

"Maybe Myrtle will learn something more from her friend Rosalie tomorrow."

"Mmm."

"And you never know, Rob might hear something exciting from the coroner on Azure."

"Maybe."

Holly sighed, wondering how the tables had turned and she was now the cheerleader for murder. Eyeing her friend sidelong, she changed the subject. "So. About the dive on Sunday. Did you tell Derek Hartley a time? I'm assuming you want me to bring him to the boat."

A tiny grin appeared on Jamie's face as she turned towards Holly. "That would be great actually. I've got Captain Rick booked. We'll leave from the Mousehole, if that's okay."

"Not a problem."

"You said Rob hasn't been out to the wreck yet, didn't you?" Jamie's voice was considerably more cheerful. "He'll love it. And you haven't seen it for a few weeks either. The Historical Society has had a team of divers down there regularly. They've found another cannon, so that makes two now. And a couple of other things."

Holly nodded, clicking her turn signal as they approached the road that led to Jamie's little cottage. "Yeah, I saw photos of those carpenter's tools Mr. Graham found. I knew a ship would carry someone to help repair it but seeing the actual tools makes it more real, doesn't it?"

"Yep. But I'd still like to find something more interesting. Like china or gold!" Jamie grinned then sighed. "Unfortunately, it's beginning to look like *La Rosa* didn't have much of a cargo—or it was all divvied up onto other ships when that pirate captured her."

"The cannons are great though," Holly said, trying to appease her. "And it's a fabulous dive site. Everybody wants to go out there. Some of our guests have been quite annoyed that it's not open to the public yet." She paused. "And by the way, it's not Rob who's coming with me. He's playing golf with Sir James and can't cancel. I've asked Thomas to be my dive buddy." She raised an eyebrow when her friend's head whipped towards her. "Unless that's a problem?"

Jamie took a deep breath. "Why would it be a problem?" she asked, nonchalance oozing out of her. "He's been poking around out there practically every weekend."

Holly grinned. "Oh good. So, what time do we need to be at the boat again?"

10

The following day Holly was up bright and early, getting Truffle ready for her weekly visit to Castlebay House, one of the island's nursing homes. The little cavapoo, who had done some therapy dog training, was a favorite visitor at the home.

Holly was brushing the small dog's fur when Maggie stuck her head into the room.

"I'm going to go drop off my entry to the show—the deadline's noon today—and then I'm helping your Aunt Laura at the expo today, Holly. Sarah and her niece are handling the rooms, but would you be able to set out afternoon tea? I'm not actually sure how many guests will be here, but I'd hate for them not to be able to have tea if they want it."

"Wait! Is that your entry there?" Holly paused, one hand on Truffle to prevent escape, and pointed to the bag Maggie was holding. "Let me see it first!"

"You've seen it before," Maggie protested.

"Not finished, I haven't! Let me see it, Mama." As her

mom sighed but pulled out a tissue wrapped bundle, Holly craned her head forward to watch Maggie unwrap a small quilt. "Oooh, that's so pretty! What did you decide for a name?"

"*Through the Garden Gate*. Do you recognize it?"

Holly gazed in delight at the appliquéd wall hanging. Maggie had created a pieced background out of what looked like hundreds of shades of green, giving an impressionist feel. Over this she had appliquéd larger roses in shades of pale pink, white, and very pale yellow, then sewn a wrought iron gate in black fabric over the top.

"It's Becky's garden! Mama, it's lovely! You're sure to win something!"

Maggie laughed, carefully folding the quilt and wrapping it up again in its tissue paper. "Oh, I don't think so. There are some very talented quilters in this competition. But it was very satisfying to complete this one. I think I'll give it to Becky as a gift. Do you think she'd like it?"

"She'll love it!" Holly was definite. "And I still think you'll win!"

"We'll see. Now, are you okay to set up tea this afternoon? I thought you might have a date with Rob."

"No. We were going to go diving, and then when that fell through, we arranged to go to Spanish Cliffs for a walk instead, but then Sergeant Hollis called in sick, so Rob has to take his shift. We're going to watch a movie tonight instead." Holly smiled at her mother. "So I'm totally free this afternoon. Is everything in the kitchen?"

Maggie nodded. "Shortbread, lemon blueberry loaf, and some tea sandwiches. I kept it simple. And you'll remember to do the urns in advance, right?"

"Yes, Mama." Holly grinned. "I can handle it. Once Truff

and I get back, we're helping Gramps, so I'll be on site. He wants to replant one of the rock outcrops on the trail."

Her mom frowned. "See if he'll let you do that, Holly. It's time that man accepted the fact that he's nearly eighty."

"Ha! Good luck with that!" Holly snorted, knowing full well that her grandfather would have a fit if she suggested he stay on the ground and hold the ladder. "But at least I'll be there if he falls like he did last time."

Maggie sighed. "Tell him to be careful. And to wear his shoes."

She waved and disappeared, leaving Holly to her dog grooming.

"There's no way I'm telling Gramps to wear his shoes," Holly muttered, brushing Truffle's feathery tail. "I value my life too much. There, Truff. Don't you look smart! Come on. Your fans await."

Truffle gave a happy woof as she trotted beside Holly to the car.

"Pass those Chinese violets up, Holly."

"Coming. Please don't lean over like that, Gramps." Holly scampered up the tall ladder leaning against the rock face, carrying a tray of small plants. "Mama will be upset if you fall."

"Pfftt." Stuart Mackintosh snorted in disgust. "I'm not going to fall. Your Mama worries too much."

Holly rolled her eyes and balanced on the ladder to watch her grandfather, barefoot and wearing shorts and a sweater fit only for the trash, upending tiny pots and deftly planting the seedlings into the pockets of earth in the huge stone outcrop.

"That'll look really nice when it starts to trail over the edge," she noted in approval. "What else are you putting up here? It's a bit shady with the spice trees overhead."

"Mmph. Snowberry, I think. Maybe some philodendrons. I want stuff that will grow wild. Minimum maintenance."

Holly gazed around from her vantage point on the ladder. Below her, the small trail meandered through the spice tree woods that grew down the terraced hillside in this part of the Inn property. Gramps had deliberately kept a few acres of land as natural woodland, only removing invasive trees and plants to replace them with natives or perennials enjoyed by the resident and migratory birds and insects. Hibiscus Island had no larger wild animals, unless you counted the feral chickens, lizards, and the odd turtle in the ponds.

A splash of red and yellow caught her eye in a small clearing. "Is that milkweed down there?" she called to her grandfather.

He glanced down, then nodded. "That's where that tree came down in the last storm. Made a natural clearing. Milkweed flowers all year, so I threw some seeds in there when the last lot podded."

"We could make it a proper butterfly garden," Holly suggested. "Add some pentas, passion flowers maybe—and a bench or two. Then people can sit and watch the butterflies. There'll be tons in the summer."

Gramps grunted. "I'll leave that to you. You know more about that kind of thing than I do. Good idea though." He stood up and stretched. "Right. That'll do for today. I'm going to Elma and Stanley's tonight. What are you doing?"

"Watching a movie with Rob." Holly backed slowly down the ladder, trying not to make it appear she was keeping an eye on her grandfather as he started down. "Is Roxie going with you? If not, she could come hang out with Truffle and us. Truff had a busy day in Castlebay but she loves seeing Roxie."

A dark brindle Boxer, Roxie was getting up in age and now spent most of her day napping in the sunshine.

Gramps dismissed the suggestion. "Roxie loves coming to the Fosters. Besides, Elma said she's made cassava pie, and Roxie enjoys a small piece of that."

"Cassava pie? Now? Whatever for?"

Holly was surprised. Cassava pie was a traditional Christmas dish on the island, and while it could be eaten at any time, it was unusual to hear of it being included in meals outside the holiday season.

"Elma's got some quilter woman coming to dinner as well. Apparently she's well-known for her cassava pie. Gives it to everyone and not just at Christmas. Elma's got her knickers in a twist and wants to show off her own recipe, Stanley says." Gramps snorted as he finally, laboriously, reached the ground. "As long as it doesn't have chicken, I don't care. Can't stand my cassava pie with chicken."

"I don't like any cassava pie," Holly said, making a face. "Who's the quilter? Do you know?"

"Why on earth would I know that? Stop asking silly questions, Holly girl, and help me with this ladder. Can't leave it on the trail. Where are my shoes?"

Holly grinned and held out the ancient footwear before picking up her end of the ladder.

THE WEATHER the following day was gorgeous, but Holly mentally groaned as she packed her wetsuit, mask, fins, towel, and sunscreen. The water was going to be so cold! She pulled out a couple of thermoses and turned on the kettle, then trotted to her room for a fleece, knowing she'd need it when she surfaced.

A short while later, she met Derek Hartley in the foyer, and directed him to put his gear in her small electric car.

"You have a sweater, right? Or a jacket?" When he nodded, she smiled. "We'll get you a wetsuit and dive gear from Captain Rick. He rents to visitors all the time." She put her bag of thermoses and snacks into the car.

"Where do we get the boat?" Derek asked, swinging into the passenger side.

"There's a tiny little cove on the south shore we call the Mousehole. Captain Rick keeps his boat there. It's a perfectly protected little harbor and it's the fastest way to get to Wreck Rock from there."

"Where's the actual shipwreck? Is it close to the island?"

Holly laughed. "Oh, that's a deep dark secret. When Jamie's ancestor took his compass bearings from the wreck, he focused on some part of Wreck Rock. Jamie's only shared the bearings with a small group. We don't want tons of people out there, you know."

"Oh, so I'm one of the privileged few, am I?" Derek looked pleased at the thought.

"You are."

Despite the low speed limit and narrow winding roads, Holly made good time and zipped into tiny Mousehole in under twenty minutes. A pristine white sandy beach curved around the edge of a small bay, which was guarded by rocky headlands. Only a small gap showed between the rocks, making Derek whistle.

"I can see why you call it the Mousehole. You sure this guy can get his boat through that?"

"He's an expert," Holly assured the jeweler. "Oh, hi, Thomas. Hey, have you met Derek yet?"

The journalist grinned. "No. Nice to meet you, Derek. You joining us on our dive? Does Jamie know?"

"She invited me. Is she here yet?" Derek looked around the beach. "Oh, there she is. I'll just head over. Nice to meet you, too, Tom."

The journalist's eyebrows shot up as he watched Jamie greet the Azure islander. "So, who's this guy again?" he asked Holly.

She handed him her bag of supplies, before hauling out the dive gear. "He's from Azure and is staying at the Inn with the rest of the Oleanders. He's a jeweler. And he knows Denise Trott. Jamie wants to pick his brains about Daina Trott."

"Huh." Thomas frowned, watching Derek laugh at something Jamie said. "He's a jeweler, you said? What's he doing at a quilt show?"

Holly stifled a smile. "He makes jewelry that's shaped like quilt blocks. It's pretty. I bought Mama a bracelet yesterday. He's the son of one of the Oleanders—Ellen Hartley, the social secretary or some such thing."

"Huh," Thomas repeated before turning back to Holly. "Well, come on, dive buddy. *La Rosa* awaits!"

THE WRECK of *La Rosa de España*, an eighteenth-century Spanish merchant ship, lay about a mile off the south side of Wreck Rock, the smallest island in the archipelago.

Uninhabited, Wreck Rock was visible from the south shore of Hibiscus Island. It was a mountainous island, a former volcano which had collapsed so that the crater formed an almost completely circular natural swimming pool. Now a nature reserve, it was a popular place for hikers, divers, and those who just wanted to swim and sunbathe in a place of natural beauty.

Two tall rock stacks stood sentinel against the winds that came from the south, and the island was ringed in shallow reefs.

As Captain Rick's boat chugged out to sea, Holly looked at the island, wondering exactly what feature Jamie was taking her bearings from. She suspected it might be one of the stacks, but couldn't be sure.

"Look, Mr. Graham's out here too!" Jamie called over the wind, gesturing at a boat in the near distance. "I wonder if he's uncovered anything new."

As they drew closer, Holly recognized her Uncle Phil, who ran a fishing charter business out of Castlebay. She waved to him, noticing he was dangling a handheld fishing line over the side. A dive flag flew on his fishing boat.

"Hello, you lot," Phil Connolly called. "Jeff Graham's down there already with someone from the Ocean Science place."

Jamie nodded in acknowledgement. "We won't bother him." She turned to Derek Hartley. "So, the wreck lies in about seventy-five feet of water, and there isn't really all that much to see since the wood has disintegrated. We're hoping there might be some remains buried in the sand pocket, but the Ocean Science people aren't starting the big excavation until the spring when the weather's more settled."

"But there're a couple of cannons up against the reef that are cool," Thomas interjected.

"And it's a pretty dive no matter what. Plus, there's always the possibility you'll spot something." Holly made a wry face as she pulled on her wetsuit. "Mind you, I haven't found anything yet."

"Don't touch anything, though," cautioned Jamie. "None of us are qualified underwater archaeologists so we'll let the proper people know and they'll tell us how to handle any retrievals. Mr. Graham found some old tools on one dive and was allowed to bring them up, but we do have to wait to be given permission."

"Got it." Derek nodded, sitting on the edge of the boat to pull on his fins. "Hands off but eyes open." He winked at Jamie.

Thomas shot an incredulous look at Holly. *Seriously?* he mouthed, before holding up an underwater camera. "I can take photos if you do spot something."

Jamie's eyes lit up. "Oh, good idea, Miller. Okay, we only have thirty minutes bottom time everyone. This is a non-decompression dive, so watch your time. Everybody ready? Remember to stay with your buddy. Let's go."

"FANTASTIC!" Derek Hartley pulled off his mask with a flourish, unslung his scuba tank, then unzipped his wetsuit. "Absolutely awesome! And that grouper was huge!"

"Yeah, I saw that one too. A black grouper. And I also saw the moray eel poking its head out right above it!" Holly shivered as she stripped off her wetsuit at full speed, grabbing her fleece and sweatpants. They stuck to her barely dry body as she wriggled into them. "I can't stand morays." Teeth chattering, she rummaged through her bag for her thermos.

Jamie, who had already stripped off her wetsuit and

didn't appear to feel the cold at all, wrapped a towel around herself. Ignoring the talk about fish, she shot an eager look at Thomas. "What's that photo like, Miller? Is it any good? Did you make sure you got some identifying features on the reef? That's super important!"

The journalist grinned. "It looks pretty decent to me. Have a look." He held out the camera to her.

Holly, warming her hands on her thermos cup, peered over Jamie's shoulder.

"It looks old, doesn't it?" Jamie appealed to her. "What do you think it could be?"

"Hard to tell with all that stuff on it, but it looks like glass to me. Maybe a wine bottle? I guess we'll have to wait for someone to retrieve it." Holly beamed at her friend. "This is so exciting. Call Natasha, Jamie. Maybe she can come out next week."

Natasha was a marine scientist at the Ocean Science Research Center on nearby Turtle Island, and one of the organizers of the wreck project. She and Jamie had clicked and become good friends when Natasha first came to Hibiscus Island to help locate *La Rosa*.

"I didn't bring my phone, but I'll call her as soon as we get back to shore." Jamie's grin was wide. "Did you see the photo, Derek? Come and look!"

The Azure islander smiled as he looked at the camera. "Nice!"

Catching sight of Thomas's pronounced eyeroll behind Derek's back, Holly smothered a smile of her own.

She and Jamie were still speculating about the possible find from the wreck as their boat approached Hibiscus Island and little Mousehole Harbor when there was a loud exclamation.

Thomas had pulled out his cell phone and was staring at the screen in shock.

"What's the problem, Miller?" Jamie asked with a grin. "Is there a crisis in the newsroom?"

"You could say that." He held the phone out to her. "Sally Dill's just been found dead!"

11

Jamie glared at Thomas. "Honestly, Miller, could you have been more tactless? The poor guy. Imagine hearing that his aunt had died like that!"

"I've said I'm sorry! I forgot the connection between them in the shock of the moment."

"And if you were shocked, how do you think Derek felt?"

Thomas threw up his hands. "Oh, let it go, White, why don't you? I spoke without thinking, okay? I'm sorry. You can console the man later!"

As Jamie drew in an outraged breath, Myrtle interrupted, disapproval written all over her face. "I think this subject has had more than enough time devoted to it. Let's move on, shall we?"

As soon as they'd disembarked from Captain Rick's boat, Holly had driven a silent Derek Hartley to the island's hospital, where he had been met by his mother, Ellen, as well as Myrtle and Inspector Tucker.

Drawing Holly aside, Rob had told her he would make sure the Oleanders got back, before dismissing her with a nod of thanks. Unable to ask any questions—Rob was in full

Inspector mode—she'd returned to the Hibiscus Inn to find Jamie pacing up and down in the family quarters, ready to verbally rend Thomas into shreds. When the journalist, accompanied by Myrtle, arrived thirty minutes later, Jamie had erupted.

Now she directed her scowl at Myrtle.

"I thought you had a source at the hospital. How come you haven't found anything out yet?"

Myrtle frowned in reproof. "I quite understand you're upset, Jamie, but there's no need to be rude. And although I was on the scene at the time of Sally's collapse, I didn't think it was the time to cross-examine anyone, engaged as they were in trying to save a life!"

"Oh." Jamie blinked, then suddenly looked embarrassed. "Sorry."

An expression of sadness crossed Myrtle's face. "I've known Sally for many years. You may not be aware, but when I first relocated to the islands, Azure Isle was where I lived. I had a nursing position there and Sally and I became good friends, even though she's quite a few years younger than me. When I moved to Hibiscus some years later, we kept in touch. And of course, we've always enjoyed quilting as a common interest."

"I'm sorry, Myrtle." Holly's voice was gentle. "This must be very difficult for you. Are you sure you want—"

"To find out who prematurely ended her life? Absolutely!" Myrtle straightened in her chair. "Sally Dill was a good woman! And so were Freda and Daina. We must find out who murdered them!"

"When you say you were on the scene," Jamie began after another moment of silence, "what exactly do you mean by that? Where were you?"

"Why, right here, of course. We were having tea in the

garden. Ellen, Sybil, Wilhelmina, Rosalie, Anne, Sally, Elma, and myself. We get together every year at the convention on the Sunday for tea. It's tradition. Freda and Daina used to be part of our group as well." She paused, then shook herself briefly. "It was lovely weather today, so Maggie kindly set up for us under one of the little pergolas."

Holly gaped at her. "Sally died at the Inn?"

"She collapsed here, certainly. I called an ambulance immediately but..." Myrtle's voice trailed away as her eyes teared up. She cleared her throat. "Could I have another cup of tea, Holly?"

"Sure." Holly hopped up from the sofa she was perched on, her mind racing as she headed to the kitchen to turn on the kettle. "Anyone else want anything?"

Sally Dill had collapsed and maybe died at the Hibiscus Inn! Holly's ambivalent feelings about being part of another investigation underwent an abrupt change.

"Does Mama know what's happened?" she asked suddenly, turning around with a teabag in her hand. "Where is she, anyway?"

"She's probably still with Denise Trott," Myrtle replied. "The poor girl heard the ambulance arrive and went into hysterics when she found out what happened. Doc Eastham is with them. And Rosalie stayed with her. She was a good friend of Daina's and is Denise's godmother. The Oleanders have taken Denise under their collective wing since Daina was a single parent, you know. Denise had only just graduated from college when her mother died. She's very young still."

"Is that Rosalie Becknell you're talking about?" Jamie's voice was subdued. "She's an Oleander too, right?"

Myrtle nodded. She slipped off her canary-yellow jacket, leaning back on her chair to accept her cup of tea with a sigh. "Our little group consists of all Oleanders other than myself."

"And Auntie Elma," Holly reminded her, returning to her spot on the sofa. She balanced her own cup of tea on a jean-clad leg as she helped herself to a cookie from the plate on the coffee table.

"Oh yes, of course. Elma joined us the last time the convention was held on Hibiscus. She doesn't often travel to the other islands, but she is an expert quilter. I fully expect her to win the pieced traditional category again this year. You've seen her quilts, haven't you, Holly?"

Myrtle obviously needed a little more time to collect herself.

"I have one. She gave it to me for my sixteenth birthday. A tumbling block pattern. It's gorgeous." Holly smiled at the older woman, happy to talk about quilts if that would help her.

Thomas, who up until now had been silently listening, leaned forward, clearing his throat. His voice was gentle as well. "Are you able to tell us exactly what happened at the tea party, Myrtle?"

The septuagenarian sighed, then took another sip of tea before answering. "I'm fine. And I appreciate your consideration." She straightened up, her voice becoming brisk. "Unfortunately, I was a little late arriving. I got there just in time to see Sally collapse. Naturally, I rushed over but she was already unconscious, and, from what I understand, was pronounced dead on arrival at the hospital."

There was another brief silence. Jamie shot Holly an appealing look, and made subtle shooing motions with her hands, mutely asking Holly to lead the questioning. Before Holly could comply, Myrtle spoke again.

"All I've found out so far is that Sally apparently

suddenly became breathless, then appeared to have a seizure before collapsing completely. She was still breathing when I got to her, but, as I said, unconscious."

"Did she have any health concerns?" Holly asked.

Myrtle's head shake was definite. "None. Sally was as healthy as a horse. Walked several miles a day, did yoga, ate properly. She had a tinge of joint pain at times, but who doesn't as they age? No history of any heart disease in her family or anything like that. She was absolutely fine. Someone killed her."

"This Rosalie Becknell you mentioned..." Thomas's gaze was thoughtful. "You said she was worried about Sally. Has she told you why yet?"

"No. We had to cancel our tea on Saturday—there was a crisis at the art gallery I had to deal with—and obviously I haven't had a chance to ask her today. But you can be sure I will. As soon as possible."

HOLLY HAD JUST TIDIED AWAY the last plate and cup when her mother came in.

"Mama, you look exhausted. Come sit down." She dragged Maggie over to the sofa. "Would you like something to eat? Some tea? A glass of wine?"

Maggie's smile was weary. "Tea would be lovely." She leaned back against the sofa with a sigh.

"How's Denise?" Holly took her mother's favorite teacup from the cupboard. "Is someone with her?"

"Rosalie's sleeping in there. We set up the sofa bed for her and she'll keep an eye on Denise tonight. I don't expect she'll wake though. Doc Eastham gave her a fairly strong sedative." Maggie closed her own eyes briefly, then opened them with a nod of thanks as Holly set a steaming cup of tea on the coffee table in front of her.

"How's everyone else?" Holly perched on the armchair beside the sofa, directing an anxious look at her mother. "The other quilters, I mean."

"Shocked, but coping. Ellen and Sybil went to the hospital, of course." At Holly's enquiring look, she added, "Ellen is Sally's sister-in-law and Sybil is Ellen's mother. They came back with Derek a short while ago and have all gone to Ellen's suite. Ellen told me they've contacted Jonas, her husband—Sally's brother—and he'll be arriving tomorrow." She massaged her temples. "He'll go into the Lantana suite with Ellen and Sybil. It's lucky they chose a two-bedroom because we have no more rooms available."

"We'd have figured something out," Holly said. "I can pick Mr. Hartley up from the airport if that'll help."

Maggie gave her a grateful look. "It would. Rob will be here in the morning to ask some questions, so it's probably best if I'm on site for that. Jonas said his flight will land at nine thirty."

"I'll be there." Holly nodded, then gave her mother's hand a gentle tug. "You'd better get some sleep. I'll close up."

JONAS HARTLEY LOOKED HARRIED as he walked towards Holly at the airport. A slim, dark-haired man, he carried a small case in one hand and held a phone to his ear with the other. Holly caught the end of his conversation as he approached.

"Fine, fine... Yes, reschedule my appointments today... No, I'll be back on the island tomorrow... Yes, yes. Good." He pocketed the phone in an irritated move as he read the sign Holly held. "I'm Jonas Hartley."

"Holly Gold." Holly gave him a smile. "Do you have any luggage to collect?"

He made an impatient gesture. "Just this. I'm not planning on staying. I need to be back in my office tomorrow."

"Oh. Okay. Well, the van is this way." Holly tried not to show her surprise as she led the Azure islander to where the Inn van was parked.

The man's sister had just died. Surely he would want to be here to find out what happened. And what about his family? Holly held the door open for Mr. Hartley, raising her eyebrows when he climbed into the back without a word of thanks, immediately taking out his phone again.

It was a silent ride back to the Hibiscus Inn. Holly pulled into the circular front drive before turning to her passenger.

"I can show you the way to the Lantana suite if you'd like, Mr. Hartley. Mrs. Hartley and Mrs. Worthington are staying there."

Receiving a grunt of acceptance, Holly led the way along the narrow path to the two-bedroom Lantana Suite, situated on a lower level.

As Holly approached the pretty little patio outside the Lantana rooms, Sybil Worthington, snowy white hair arranged in her usual chignon, looked up from the table at which she was sitting.

"Well, Jonas, this is a surprise."

"Sybil." Jonas Hartley greeted his mother-in-law with a curt nod. "I fail to understand how my presence here is a surprise. I informed Ellen I was coming."

Sybil produced a saccharine smile. "It's surprising to me that you could bear to leave your office for any amount of time, let alone travel to Hibiscus Island." She waved an elegant ringed hand. "But no matter. I'm sure Ellen will be glad of your support. And certainly, having a lawyer present may be helpful."

Jonas Hartley narrowed his eyes. "I trust Ellen hasn't made any statements. I specifically said she and Derek were to wait for my arrival."

"Derek, I'm afraid, is manning his booth at the quilt expo." Sybil ignored the man's huff of irritation, continuing in a bland voice, "But the delightful police inspector will be here shortly to take Ellen's statement. And mine, of course, but that isn't your concern, is it, Jonas? Perhaps you'd like to see your wife? She's in the sitting room."

With another huff of annoyance, the lawyer stalked inside. Sybil Worthington smoothed down her pale blue suit jacket before turning a sweet smile on Holly.

"Holly, dear child, would it be possible to have some tea and scones delivered to our suite? I'm sure the inspector will appreciate a little sustenance while he interrogates us."

Holly blinked. "Uh, sure. I'll see what I can do."

Her eyebrows shot to the top of her head as she watched Sybil Worthington, after another smile, saunter inside the Lantana Suite. Mind working busily, Holly returned to the Inn.

12

H olly's phone rang as she reached the foyer of the Inn. "We're all at the Bean. Can you join us?" Jamie asked.

"Let me just check that Mama doesn't need any help and I'll be right there." Holly paused. "Who's 'we'?"

There was a laugh at the end of the phone. "The HIDC, of course. Oh, and François has made gluten-free apple cake, so I'll have a piece for you when you get here. See you."

BECKY WAS the first person Holly saw as she pushed open the doors to the Bean café. Beside her, Myrtle, attired today in salmon orange, carefully poured tea from a china pot.

"Oh good, you're here!" Jamie hailed Holly from behind the counter, where she was making a coffee-to-go for the only other customer in the café. "I'll be right over!" As Holly made her way to the table in the corner, Jamie turned to call into the kitchen. "François, can I get a piece of that cake?"

Pulling out a chair, Holly met Becky's resigned gaze over the slice of toast the librarian was nibbling. Holly produced a wry smile in return. So much for their theory Mrs. McGinney had imagined things.

"Still feeling queasy?" she asked, sympathy in her voice.

Becky nodded. "It's getting better though."

"Mint tea." Myrtle's voice was brisk. "And small meals throughout the day. Keep those blood sugar levels up. Pregnancy is a completely natural event. There's no need to coddle yourself."

Holly smothered a grin as Becky rolled her eyes. Obviously the retired nurse had discovered her friend's secret. The good thing about Myrtle was she knew how to keep personal information confidential; the not-so-good thing was Becky was now going to be the recipient of non-stop unasked-for advice for the duration of her pregnancy.

A slice of apple cake was slid under Holly's nose. "Thanks," she told her friend before gazing around the empty café. "Not very busy here, is it?"

"What do you expect? Everyone's buzzing around the expo because of what happened yesterday. Even people who don't know what a quilt is are up there today, being nosy looky-loos! Now!" Jamie rubbed her hands together as she took her seat at the table. "Let's get started!"

"Has it ever occurred to you," Becky interjected, "that it's not normal for one small place to have this many murders in such a short space of time?"

Jamie paused. "It's only been three."

"In about half a year!" Becky retorted. "I feel like I'm on the set of some television murder mystery series!" She caught sight of Myrtle's expression and winced. "That sounded awful. I'm sorry, Myrtle. I know Mrs. Dill was your friend."

"She was, but your comment is not unfounded. We do seem to have had more crime than usual on our small island. I'm sure, however, this is an anomaly and life will soon revert to its usual idyllic state."

As Myrtle gave Becky's hand a reassuring pat, a tiny involuntary smile crossed Holly's face. Sadness still lurked in the older woman's eyes, but her use of pompous language was a sure sign Myrtle was feeling more like herself.

The septuagenarian straightened, determination written all over her. "In the meantime, it is incumbent upon us to discover who is responsible for the deaths of Daina Trott, Freda Sinclair, and now Sally Dill. I have some information."

"Of course you do." Jamie grinned, then sobered as Holly directed a quelling frown at her. In more subdued tones, she asked, "Is this from your friend Rosalie?"

"Yes. I popped up to the Inn and had a quick word with Rosalie this morning. Denise, poor child, was still asleep, so Rosalie and I sat outside and had a coffee." Myrtle paused.

Jamie waited a beat. "And?"

"According to Rosalie, Sally had been having small, irregular bouts of queasiness, nausea, headaches, and dizziness since just after Christmas."

"Like Daina Trott and Freda Sinclair!" Jamie exclaimed.

"They appear to have had similar symptoms, yes. Rosalie told me Sally had been to the doctor, but they were unable to ascertain a cause."

Jamie fingered her lip in thought. "Did Rosalie have any ideas what it might be?"

"If you mean, did Rosalie tell me she believed Sally was being poisoned, then no, she didn't." Myrtle took a sip of tea. "However, she did confirm there are rumors circulating among the Oleanders—about the Craft sisters and the products they supply."

Becky sat upright in surprise. "Tansy Craft? That pretty girl from Juniper Island who has the tea stall at the convention? But... but she's lovely! And Sage is so sweet. She's teaching my sampler class, you know. What rumors are people spreading?"

"Oh, that's right, you weren't with us the other day. Tansy basically told us people think their teas and stuff might be poisoned." Jamie toyed with a sugar packet.

"You're not serious!" Becky was indignant. "That's absolutely ridiculous. Why, we don't even have proof that poison is involved!"

Jamie wiggled her hand from side to side. "Well, it does seem quite likely. All three women have had similar symptoms, and Sally Dill collapsed suddenly. If they were killed, then I think we have to consider poison."

"Aha!" Becky pounced. "You said 'if'! That means you're not actually sure there's anything nefarious going on at all!"

Holly's lips twitched. Nefarious? Myrtle's language seemed to be rubbing off on Becky.

Myrtle intervened. "I think there's no real doubt that murder has occurred, Becky, but certainly some research is required. First, we need to know what poisons could cause the symptoms all three women experienced, and second, we need to know which ones might cause a sudden collapse such as the one Sally had. I think this is your provenance. Let us know what you discover."

Ignoring Becky's dropped jaw, Myrtle continued, "I'll contact my sources at the hospital to see if an official cause of death has been noted and will then get eyewitness statements from the women who were at the tea yesterday. Holly, you said Inspector Tucker agreed to contact the police and coroner on Azure Island. Perhaps you can follow up with him on that and report back to us. Jamie—"

"I want to talk to Sage Craft again," Jamie interrupted. "She had a funny look in her eye when Tansy was talking about those rumors, and I want to find out why."

Holly blinked in surprise. "You know," she said slowly, "I saw that too. She did seem a little reluctant, didn't she?"

"Exactly." Jamie leaned across the table as another sound of protest escaped Becky. "I'm not saying I think she killed anyone, Becks. I think that as a person who mixes teas and lotions and whatnots, she knows about the properties of the plants she uses. And I think she knows more than she told us!"

"Aren't you manning the Bean today?" At Jamie's reluctant nod, Holly spoke diffidently. "Well, I could have a chat with her before I head back to the Inn. Unless, of course, Thomas already has." She paused as a thought struck her. "Hey, where is Thomas? Why's he not here?"

Jamie gave a dismissive snort. "Miller's not part of the HIDC."

"Oh, come on," Holly protested. "Of course he is. Besides, the man's like a ferret. He can nose out information like nobody's business." She eyed her friend with disapproval. "You have to stop this ridiculous squabbling. I thought you'd settled your differences with him. What's going on? Is this because of Derek?"

Becky straightened in her chair. "Derek? That good-looking jeweler?"

"Derek Hartley," Myrtle supplied. "He's Sally Dill's nephew."

"Oh." A dismayed look crossed Becky's face. "Oh, that's awful. Poor man. How's his family doing, Myrtle? Have you seen them today?"

"I picked Derek's dad up from the airport this morning." Holly frowned, remembering. "He says he's going back to Azure tomorrow though."

Myrtle snorted. "That's Jonas Hartley for you. Work has always taken precedence over family."

"Oh, so he wasn't close to his sister?" Holly asked.

"I don't believe Jonas Hartley is close to anyone, but no, he and Sally had virtually no relationship at all."

"Why'd he even come here then?" Jamie's voice was curious.

"Mrs. Worthington told him they hadn't made any statements yet," Holly offered. "He's a lawyer, right? Maybe it's so the family has legal representation."

"Jonas Hartley doesn't represent Sybil Worthington. There's no love lost between those two, I can assure you." Myrtle was definite. "They've been at each other's throats ever since Ellen and Jonas's wedding."

Becky's eyes were round. "But why?"

"It's one of those generational things. Worthingtons and Hartleys are the Azure Isle equivalent of Whites and Millers. Sybil disinherited Ellen when she married Jonas."

"What? But she's staying in the same suite as her!" Holly protested.

"Oh, Sybil still loves her daughter. But she's not taking any chances of Jonas Hartley getting his hands on the Worthington property. Ellen can't inherit the land or the resort but she's Sybil's heir to the Worthington money. No, there's no animosity between Ellen and Sybil about money."

There was a moment of silence as all three younger women exchanged disbelieving looks.

"Wow," Jamie breathed. "Well, that's something alright."

"You mentioned a resort." Becky leaned forward in curiosity. "Which resort is that?"

"The Daylily."

Jamie bolted upright. "Are you telling me Sybil Worthington owns the Daylily Resort? That enormous place on the mountain? But... but it's worth millions!"

"Yes." Myrtle nodded, then drained her tea. "However, it wasn't Sybil Worthington who was murdered. And since she and Sally have always had an amicable relationship, I don't think—"

"But Sally is—was—a Hartley too," Jamie interrupted. "How come Sybil's friends with her but not her brother?"

"For the same reason, I imagine, that you and Mr. Miller manage to be civil to each other from time to time. The feud was a long time ago, and Sybil picks her friends for their character, not their family connections."

"I..." Jamie paused, narrowing her eyes at the septuage-narian, then gave a shame-faced grin. "Point taken, Myrtle. I'll fill Miller in on what we're doing."

"THAT'S GOT to be the strangest set of relationships I've ever heard of." Becky glanced sideways at Holly as they walked back towards the library. "Don't you think?"

"It's definitely weird," Holly agreed. "Although I suppose it's good that Ellen and Sybil haven't let money or land come between them. I wonder what happens at times like Christmas though. Do you suppose Jonas doesn't go? Or they don't get together? Or what?"

Becky shrugged. "I've no idea. I'm glad François's family is the way they are." She grinned at Holly. "And you'll be glad to know the Tuckers will welcome you with open arms and hearts when you join us."

"What? Wait— What?" Holly stopped dead in her tracks. "What are you talking about?"

Her friend laughed. "I'm just teasing, Holls." She tugged on Holly's arm to get her moving again.

"We've only been dating a couple of months." Holly was flustered. "And I don't think—"

The laughter left Becky's face. "Oh Holly, I'm sorry. I didn't mean to upset you. I was just joking. It was a silly thing to say."

The dismayed expression on her friend's face made Holly pause. She took a deep breath and forced a smile. "No, no, it's okay. I'm sorry. I just kind of panicked there for a minute. Rob's never said anything to me about... well, about anything like that. And I haven't thought about it either."

Becky was contrite. "I shouldn't have said anything. It was really stupid of me. It's just... Rob's never been this happy and I... I guess I'm just hoping that things will work out for you two. I won't mention it again, I promise."

"It's okay." Holly took another breath, then smiled, linking her arm through her friend's. "Come on. You have some research to get started unless you actually want Myrtle breathing down your neck." She sighed, glancing at her friend. "Looks like we were wrong, Becks. And Mrs. McGinney's suspicions were right."

Becky heaved a sigh of her own. "Yes. I still find it hard to believe though. And we don't know for a fact that Mrs. Dill was murdered." Her voice was hopeful. "Maybe she had a stroke or... or something."

"Maybe. It would be kind of coincidental though, don't you think?"

"Yeah." The word came out as a sigh. "But what's the point of researching possible poisons? It's like hunting for a needle in a haystack!"

As her friend's voice rose in exasperation, Holly interrupted. "I have some time to help. I'd like to talk to Sage, but I can do that later."

"Come to my sampler class. She'll be there." Becky frowned. "Although I still don't think she or her sister have anything to do with... well, anything."

"Let's hope not," Holly agreed.

13

"Good grief! Jamie was right. Everyone and their grandmother is here today!" Holly stared in disbelief at the crowd of islanders in the library foyer. An excited buzz of conversation surged around them, making her raise her voice more than she'd intended.

Becky made a sour face. "It'll be good for business, but really, it's a bit morbid, isn't it? All these people here because of a death."

"Mmm. It's slightly embarrassing, I must say." Holly frowned. "But this number of looky-loos, as Jamie calls them, means gossip is spreading 'round the island. I wonder what everyone's saying?"

Becky nudged her, jerking her head towards the other side of the lobby area. "Look, there's Thomas! I'm sure he'll know what's going on. Let me just check with Stephanie and Mr. Graham that I'm not needed, and then we can go to the archives. They're not being used for this event, so it will be quiet down there." She glanced at her watch, then pursed her lips. "I only have another forty minutes or so before my sampler class, though, and I really don't want to miss it. Are you sure you can help me with some research? You don't have any jobs to do?"

Holly shook her head. "Gramps and I were supposed to finish some work on the north trail today, but he bailed on me. Said he's taking the day off to go fishing with Uncle Stanley. I need to go home and work on the butterfly garden we've decided to make, but I'm free for a little while." She eyed the now-laughing Thomas Miller with suspicion. "I'll go pin down our journalist friend and see what he's found out so far."

As Becky nodded in acknowledgement before hurrying off to check on her employees, Holly pushed her way through the crowd, keeping an eye on Thomas's fair head. The journalist was deep in conversation with an elderly lady whose dark skin crinkled into a wide smile as Holly approached.

"Well, Holly child. It's been a while since I've seen you. Why haven't you been by to visit?"

Holly kissed the proffered cheek. "Hi, Auntie Elma. Yeah, sorry about that. It's just been super busy up at the Inn lately. And I've had a couple of landscaping projects as well." She grinned. "I hear Uncle Stanley's out fishing today."

"Humph. He's promised me some whitewater snappers, so he'd better not come back empty-handed."

"Hope Gramps gets some too. I love those!" Holly smiled, thinking about the pretty, yellow-striped pink and white fish. "Dad and I used to catch tons off the old oil docks on the south shore."

Thomas raised an eyebrow. "I haven't heard of them before. Good eating, huh?"

"Delicious," Holly assured him. "Dad used to fillet them, then panfry them."

Auntie Elma nodded. "That's what I do too. Nice local dish, Thomas. If Stanley comes home with any, I'll send some over to you." She looked across the lobby. "Now, if you'll excuse me, I need to get to my station. I'm on duty at the Patchworker stall today. Violet Greenley will be all atwitter if I fail to relieve her on time." Elma Foster adjusted the enormous handbag on her arm. "Now, Holly child, you make sure you find the time to visit me, you hear?"

"Yes, but wait a minute, Auntie Elma. About what happened yesterday... Uh..." Holly hesitated, unsure how to word her query.

Sadness filled Elma's eyes as she paused. "Such a dreadful thing, Holly. Sally Hartley Dill was a lovely woman. Just lovely."

"You were present when Mrs. Dill collapsed?" Thomas asked, interest coloring his voice. "Could you tell us what happened?"

"Is this for the newspaper?" Elma Foster frowned when Thomas and Holly exchanged looks. "Oh, I see. You're interfering in police business again." She tutted in disapproval.

"Police business?" Thomas pounced. "Is this a case for the police, then? Was there something suspicious about Mrs. Dill's collapse?"

A severe look appeared on Auntie Elma's face, making Holly wince. The older generation of Hibiscus Islanders had no problem putting youngsters in their place if they felt they'd been disrespectful.

Thomas blinked, then flushed. "Sorry. I didn't mean to—"

Auntie Elma held up a hand, cutting him off. "No need for apologies, Thomas. Your profession is an honorable one. Just make sure you keep it that way. We don't need ghouls on Hibiscus Island."

Holly pressed her lips tightly together as Thomas looked even more discomfited, then cringed when Auntie Elma turned an equally disapproving look on her. "Are you and Jamie getting involved in this? May I remind you of what happened the last time you decided you were detectives?"

"Uh, well..."

Auntie Elma swept on. "You found yourselves in a very dangerous situation, that's what. I would suggest, Holly, that you restrain your curiosity and allow our very capable police inspector to do the job for which he is eminently qualified." She eyed the young woman sternly. "I'm quite sure Inspector Tucker will not be happy if you put yourself at risk again. And I sincerely hope Mrs. Dumont is not involved in any of this. This is a delicate time for her, and she should be taking care of herself, not prancing around the island trying to solve a murder."

"Murder? So you do think—?" Thomas quailed again at the look he received.

"I shall have a word with Myrtle," Auntie Elma said with reproval.

Thomas and Holly watched her sail away then looked at each other.

"Boy, she sure knows how to put a person in their place!" Thomas grinned. "Did we overstep or what?"

"I swear she thinks I'm still ten years old." Holly sighed. "She won't share what she considers to be private information with me. Or you."

Thomas's grin broadened as he watched Auntie Elma bustle into the lecture hall. "Oh well, as long as she tells Myrtle everything she knows, I'm okay with that. Now, what are you up to, Holly? What's Myrtle told you to do?"

"I like that you assume Myrtle's in charge of me," Holly

complained, "but, if you must know, I'm going to help Becky do a little research on potential poisons."

"Hmm. Good idea. I looked into Sage Craft's suggestions by the way. She's right that St. John's Wort and sage can cause symptoms like dizziness, nausea, and such, but I saw nothing to indicate they could cause a total collapse like the one Sally Dill purportedly had."

"And you haven't heard anything about the cause of death from any of your 'sources'?" Holly made air quotes around the final word.

Thomas smirked. "You're dying to know who they are, aren't you? No, there's been nothing determined yet, as far as I know, but don't worry, I'll fill you in as soon as I find out anything." He nodded across the room to where Becky was waving. "Our head librarian wants you. I'm going to amble around and see what gossip I can pick up. I've never known a place where people find out things so fast. It's a journalist's dream."

"Just don't be a ghoul," Holly admonished with a grin, ducking away with a laugh when he lunged at her.

BECKY GLANCED AT HER WATCH. "I'm going to have to stop now, Holls. My sampler class starts in a few minutes. What about you?"

"Research really isn't my thing." Holly looked at the computer screen in front of her with distaste, and then at the paper in front of Becky. "Look how much you've found out compared to me. It's like you have magic or something!"

"Practice, that's all." Becky laughed as she shut down her own computer. "If you'd helped as many high school students as I have with research, you'd be an expert too."

She frowned at her list. "I still think we're going about this the wrong way. The symptoms the three women experienced are just too vague. There could be so many reasons for them. I really think we have to wait to find out what the cause of death was for Mrs. Dill—if there was one, beyond a stroke or aneurysm or something like that. We could be looking for something that doesn't exist."

"I'll let you explain that to Myrtle and Jamie." Holly stretched her back out with a groan. "But I agree. Let's wait till we have a diagnosis before we do any more of this. I'll come check out your sampler class before I head home. Maybe I can have a quick word with Sage."

"Oh sure. People drop in and out all the time. Did I show you what I've already done?" Becky rummaged around in the large canvas bag at her feet. "Look. I finished my nine-patch block!"

Holly took the twelve-inch square of fabric from her friend, admiring the alternating patches of green and yellow material. "Very pretty."

"Oh, well, that's the easiest one." Becky's shrug was self-deprecating. "This one is a... a... Hang on." She consulted a piece of paper in her bag. "Oh yes, this is the log cabin, and this one is a pinwheel. It was a bit harder."

Holly smiled as Becky shoved more squares into her hand. "I like your color scheme. How big's this going to be?"

"I thought I'd make it crib sized."

"Aww, you're making a baby quilt. Becky, that's a great idea. And these are perfect colors for a baby." Holly eyed the blocks. "I guess you don't know what you're having yet, huh?"

Becky beamed. "Nope. We want to be surprised. But I love green and yellow, and those are the colors we're going to have in the nursery." She glanced at her watch again, then squeaked. "I've got to dash or I'll be late. Will you shut down your computer and turn out the lights?"

Holly nodded. "I'll be right behind you."

AFTER THE QUIET of the archives, the noise in the library foyer broke over Holly like a wave. Threading her way through the crowd, she stopped to admire one of Becky's library book displays.

"See any you like?" Stephanie, the children's librarian, smiled at Holly as she added another book, filling an empty stand. "Patrons have been gobbling these up."

"I like the quilt theme you've got going," Holly replied, looking at the covers. "Lots of cozy mysteries, I see."

"Yeah, and some romance, women's fiction... There are quilt-themed books in lots of genres. Laura's got more technical books at the Book Worm booth, if you're interested."

"I'll leave the quilt books to Mama." Holly grinned. "I prefer mystery or fantasy myself."

"Yeah? What fantasy authors?" Stephanie paused, interest flickering over her face.

"Anne McCaffrey, David Eddings, Tamora Pierce..."

"Great choices. I'm a fan of McCaffrey myself. I like her Pegasus series the best. You?"

"Oh, Pern for sure." Holly laughed. "I'd love to ride a dragon!"

"Wouldn't we all?" Stephanie grinned, then lowered her voice. "So, Holly, what do you think about this rumor going round about quilters being poisoned?"

Holly sobered instantly. "Is that really being said out loud? Who'd you hear it from?"

"People are muttering. I've had no less than four people

today tell me Mrs. Dill was poisoned. One person said with arsenic, one said strychnine, and two are convinced it's some rare undetectable substance." Stephanie paused. "We've had a lot of murder mysteries checked out. Agatha Christie in particular. Seems there was a Christie film festival recently on Azure and the quilters from there have all been chatting about her mysteries. They've got people a bit stirred up."

"Good grief." Holly shook her head. "Mind you, I don't know why I'm surprised. This island thrives on gossip."

"Sure does." Stephanie popped a final book into the display. "You guys helping the inspector again?"

"Uh... You know what, Stephanie, I need to get to the teen section. I told Becky I'd drop in on the sampler class."

"Ah, gotcha. You can't tell me. Well, good luck anyway." The librarian frowned. "Weird how we've had all these murders lately, isn't it? Usually nothing happens on Hibiscus."

"Not exactly the reputation we want, that's for sure," Holly agreed. "But perhaps the rumors are just that. Rumors."

Stephanie looked skeptical. "There's no smoke without fire, Holly. No smoke without fire."

14

The teen section of the Bridgeport Library had been added as part of the renovations some years earlier and was an immensely popular place. Located on the ground floor of the west wing, it featured diner-style seating and study spaces, as well as a media lounge that could be booked for movie nights. Today, it was a sewing center.

"Wow." Holly stopped in the doorway, gaping at the sewing machines that lined the walls where computers used to sit. Chatting women, and a few men, sat in front of them, running strips of fabric beneath the busily moving needles. "Where'd all these come from?"

A young volunteer at the door laughed. "From A Stitch in Time. The owner's lent them for the expo. She runs classes at her shop, you know."

"I didn't know," Holly replied, scanning the room for Becky. "But this is very cool. I guess they've been popular. Your classes, I mean."

"Very. This is the first year anything like this has been done at the Maritime Quilting Expo," the volunteer said proudly. "Everyone is loving it!"

Holly smiled. "It looks like it. Is it okay if I go watch? I came to see Becky."

"Oh yes, Mrs. Dumont's over there. She's making a baby quilt, you know." The volunteer beamed. "She's due in July. But I guess you already know that."

"I do." Holly tried not to smile. So much for Becky's attempts to keep her pregnancy a secret. It looked like the whole island already knew. "I'll go see what she's doing."

Becky had her bottom lip gripped between her teeth as she carefully fed material through her sewing machine. Sage Craft stood behind her.

"Relax, Becky," the Juniper islander laughed. "It won't eat it."

Becky grinned, pausing the needle. "I know. I just want it to be perfect. Oh, hi, Holly. Look, I'm starting a flying goose block."

"Flying geese," Sage corrected.

"I've graduated to triangles."

The pride in Becky's voice made Holly smile. "Very impressive."

"She's doing a great job. By the time the expo's over, she'll have all nine blocks pieced and will be able to put them together and start quilting them." Sage glanced at Holly. "And speaking of quilting, Maggie's block for the Flower Quilt is lovely. I put some stitches in it today when we had our turn at the Bee. If I don't see her, will you let her know?"

"Sure. Did you make a block for the quilt as well?"

Sage nodded. "I did a yellow allamanda flower. We have them growing outside our shop on Juniper Island. I've always loved the vine, and the Flower Quilt has a tropical theme this year, so it worked out nicely. It's the first time I've contributed a block, but I must say I really enjoyed making it."

"Oh bother!" Becky's exclamation had Sage immediately redirecting her attention.

Holly watched the Juniper Island woman straighten out the patch Becky was sewing before gesturing to her to continue. Although Sage smiled, her eyes were somber and there were dark shadows under them, as if she hadn't slept well. She was also very busy with her class, so Holly shelved the idea of questioning her, waved a cheery goodbye to Becky, then headed back to the Hibiscus Inn, determined to get at least a little work done on the butterfly garden.

AFTER A QUICK BITE TO eat in the empty Inn kitchen, Holly raided Gramps's slat house, loading a wheelbarrow with starry-flowered pentas, a few passionflower vines, a couple of Michaelmas daisy bushes, not yet in flower, blue and white plumbago, and an assortment of annual and herb seedlings.

Hibiscus Island was home to several species of butterfly, including monarchs, fritillaries, buckeyes, cloudless sulfurs, and cabbage whites, with occasional visits from red admirals. A variety of sphinx moths also inhabited the island, and since Holly loved their fat green caterpillars, she intended to include some of their food plants in her new garden.

Walking through the spice tree woods, Holly pushed all thoughts of murder from her head as she trundled the wheelbarrow along the narrow path. White-eyed vireos chirped from the branches of the surrounding trees, while the melodious song pouring from the highest point of a

Norfolk pine tree made Holly stop to search for the bright red singer. It was a little early to hear cardinals, but this one was clearly on the hunt for his mate already.

Reaching the spot where the milkweed grew, she contemplated the space. Apart from the red and yellow butterfly plants, there were a few weeds, which were easily dealt with. A couple of wheelbarrow loads of soil would be needed, but there were plenty of loose limestone rocks lying around which could edge the borders. It wouldn't be a large garden, just big enough for a chair or two and a lot of butterflies.

Holly rubbed her hands on her trousers and got to work.

As SHE LEFT the slat house with a final load of soil, Holly heard her name called. Blowing a red-gold curl off her face, she looked around, finally spotting Denise Trott waving to her from the level above.

As Holly paused, Denise hurried down the winding stone steps towards her.

"Holly, do... do you have a minute? I... I really need to talk to someone."

Denise's eyes were red and puffy, her hair was piled up haphazardly on top of her head, and her t-shirt looked like it had been slept in.

Holly eyed her with concern. "Of course." She hesitated a second. "I'm just taking this along to the butterfly garden I'm working on. Why don't you come with me? It's a nice stroll, and then we'll go back up to the Inn for a cup of tea and a chat."

Denise nodded. "O...okay." She gave a wan smile. "I only got up a little while ago. Aunt Rosalie was here but she had to go to the expo. She just left." The girl yawned. "I still feel a little groggy. Your doctor gave me some stuff to help me sleep and boy did it work. I don't take things like that normally. Well, except when... when my mom..."

"I got prescribed something when my dad died." Holly's glance was sympathetic. "It helped me too. I don't need it anymore now."

"How long ago was that?"

"Over two years now. But time's not really that important, is it? I mean, they'll always be part of our lives."

"Maybe. I hope so." Denise was quiet for a while as they walked along the trail. "This is nice. Peaceful."

"I like it. There's a small pond at the very end of the trail that my dad loved." Holly smiled, remembering. "There are some diamondback turtles that live there. Pretty little things. I fell in once trying to catch one and dad had to jump in after me. We were filthy! But he caught the turtle for me to look at. We laughed the whole way back to the house. Boy, did we smell."

A small smile crossed Denise's face. "My mom and I used to go for walks along the beach. She loved collecting shells. There's one beach on Azure that has hundreds and hundreds of keyhole limpets. She would make me necklaces of them when I was little."

"That's a lovely memory."

Both women were quiet until they reached Holly's destination.

"This is a butterfly garden, you said?" Denise's voice was curious.

"Yes—or it's going to be. Gramps tossed some milkweed seeds in here last year, and they're doing pretty well so I thought we may as well try and lure some more butterflies.

Want to help? I've only a few more things to plant and then we'll go get that tea I promised you."

Holly upended the wheelbarrow of soil into the curved bed she'd made, then picked up a pot to hand to Denise.

The younger woman stared at the clusters of star-shaped pink flowers. "What's this?"

"Pentas. It's the food plant for a sphinx moth caterpillar, as well as being a nectar plant for butterflies. Go ahead. Plant it somewhere. Here's a trowel."

"Anywhere?"

Holly pursed her lips as she looked around. "Put it over there. It'll spread about two or three feet, so we'll give it some room to grow." She started to level the soil she'd just dumped, watching Denise out of the corner of her eye.

After a moment's hesitation, the Azure islander made her way to the spot Holly had indicated and began to dig a hole. When she'd finished, Holly handed her a passionflower, and pointed out a spot for it at the bottom of a dead tree.

"This is the food for the fritillary larvae. It's a tiny bit shady for it here, but I'm hoping it might still take."

"What's that you're planting?" Denise asked, taking the potted vine.

"Dill, cilantro, and some borage." Holly glanced down at the tiny seedlings, then up at the trees. "Cardinals love borage and there was one singing his little heart out earlier. Maybe he'll come visit the garden."

Denise smiled suddenly. "My mom loved cardinals." She drew in a deep breath, looking around. "This is lovely. Th... thank you, Holly."

"I've always found gardening to be soothing." Holly cast a glance over her shoulder at Denise. "Hurry up and plant that passionflower and we'll go get some tea."

~

As the kettle boiled, Holly placed milk and sugar on the table before opening the fridge to see what goodies lurked inside. "There's shortbread, lemon blueberry loaf, a couple of carrot muffins, and a few sugar cookies. What do you fancy? You know what, never mind. I'll just bring a selection."

Denise giggled as Holly slid a full plate in front of her. "I'll never eat all that."

"Well, try the shortbread at least. It's delicious." Holly poured boiling water into a fat teapot covered in roses and carried it to the table. "I'm being fancy today. Usually when it's just me, I stick a teabag in a mug, but it's fun to use the pretty china sometimes." She smiled at Denise. "You look a lot better."

"I feel it." The younger woman's answering smile was grateful. "Thanks for taking me out there. It... helped."

"The woods are a great place to go when you need a little peace and quiet." Holly grinned. "Even if I put you to work out there." She hesitated as Denise laughed, then gently touched her hand. "I know it's hard right now, but I promise you, it does get easier as time goes by, Denise." She took a sip of tea, eyeing the Azure islander over her cup. "Do you feel like talking about it?"

"You mean about why I think my mom was killed, don't you?" Denise's eyes teared up suddenly. She took a quick gulp of tea. Holly waited as the young woman drew in a deep breath. "Sorry. I'm not going to be hysterical again, I promise."

"I'd imagine Mrs. Dill's death was a shock." Holly was sympathetic.

"Yeah. I wasn't at the tea party, but I was just on my way

up to the Inn when I saw her collapse." Denise's voice was wobbly, but she seemed to be regaining control. "You must think I'm nuts, Holly. Thinking my mom was poisoned. Right?"

"Not nuts, no, but I do wonder why you think it." Holly sipped her own tea. "Mrs. McGinney told us your mom had cancer."

"She did." Denise drew another deep breath. "And yes, she was on chemo. And yes, I know that causes the symptoms she had. And actually, I didn't think anything was wrong until Aunt Freda had her accident. But then..."

"Then?" Holly prompted as Denise's voice trailed away.

"Well, Aunt Freda had the same symptoms! And then she had the car accident. And people are saying it's because she collapsed while she was driving."

"And you don't think she just had the flu?"

"She'd had the flu earlier in the year—in September—and I know that because she wouldn't come visit mom—because she was immune-compromised, you know."

Holly looked dubious. "Well, maybe she caught a different strain in December."

A mutinous expression crossed Denise's face. "I don't think so. Derek was suspicious too. He thought she might have been poisoned as well. He told me so."

"Derek told you?" Holly leaned back in her chair, staring at the younger woman. "Did he say why he thought this?"

Denise squirmed. "Well, he hasn't exactly said she was poisoned, but he was suspicious, I know. He kept asking me about my mom's symptoms, and one time he asked me if I'd noticed anything about Aunt Freda."

Holly raised a dubious eyebrow. "How did he know Mrs. Sinclair? Were they friends?"

"She was a customer of his," Denise explained. "She'd

commissioned a piece of jewelry for her daughter for Christmas, and she was actually in his shop when she had one of her episodes."

"Episodes?"

"Yes. Nausea, dizziness, weakness. Derek said she had to sit down and catch her breath. He wanted to call her daughter, but she refused to let him. Then a couple of days later, she had the car accident. You see?"

Holly frowned. "Yes... but it's very circumstantial, Denise. Mrs. Sinclair could have just had a dizzy spell. And from what I understand, there was no suggestion of poison when she died. Surely if there was real suspicion, there'd have been an investigation."

"But there wasn't any when she actually died," Denise explained, her voice feverish. "That's the problem. It was only when Mrs. Dill started getting sick too that we all got suspicious."

"Who's 'we all'? And when was that? Rosalie Becknell only told Myrtle about the illness symptoms today." Holly stared at Denise. "If you all thought this, why have you been keeping it a secret?"

Before Denise could answer, Holly's phone buzzed. "Hang on, let me just get this."

Jamie's voice erupted in excitement the minute Holly answered. "Myrtle just called! Holly, they have the cause of death! Sally Dill was poisoned! With cyanide! It's now officially a murder investigation!"

15

———

By the time Holly had turned a still-emotional Denise over to Sarah Flynn, who was in charge of the Inn that day, gathered her belongings, and sorted out Truffle, she arrived at the empty Bean café just at closing time.

Angie looked up from behind the counter, where she was stacking clean cups. Her hazel eyes looked worried. "They're all upstairs. I told Jamie I'd close up so she can be at your meeting with you. It's a bit unnerving, isn't it? I mean, poison!"

"Yeah, it is," Holly agreed.

Angie made shooing motions at her. "Well, hurry and get up there. The sooner you all get going, the sooner the case will be solved!"

Holly climbed the stairs, musing on the fact that most of Hibiscus Island seemed to know about, if not support, their detecting. Where was Rob, she wondered, and what was he doing right now?

As she reached the second floor of the Bean café, which housed Jamie's staff room and office, Jamie's voice floated out. Holly paused as she realized exactly where the island's police inspector was.

"You told Holly you'd check with your buddies on Azure to see what was going on. That means you knew what we were doing. And besides, Myrtle and I tried to tell you at the expo, but you walked away from us. So it's no good you getting on your high horse now, Rob, and playing police inspector."

"I am not *playing* inspector." Rob's voice sounded exasperated. "I *am* a police inspector and therefore—" He broke off as Holly walked into the room. "Ah, and here's the final member of the wholly unauthorized Hibiscus Island Detective Club."

Holly blinked, then her lips twitched in amusement. "Good afternoon, Inspector Tucker."

Rob eyed her with suspicion. "Are you laughing at me, Miss Gold?"

"Never," Holly assured him. "I was just thinking about you, though, and lo and behold, here you are."

"Not through any invitation, I assure you. I was passing the Bean on my way to the library when I spotted certain people making a beeline for the place. And knowing that these same people are trouble when they get together..."

Thomas smirked. "He invited himself."

"Come on in, Holls." Jamie shot a satisfied grin her way. "We're discussing the case."

Rob cast his eyes heavenward. "At the risk of repeating myself, I can't discuss murder cases with civilians."

Myrtle tutted. "We're hardly mere civilians, Inspector. Not after our previous cases."

"Yeah. You should think of us as consultants." Jamie eyed the police inspector with some impatience. "What? You're the one who suggested that term in our first case!

Now, enough time wasting! Myrtle told us Sally Dill died from cyanide poisoning. Is that correct?"

"Well, of course it's correct, Jamie," Myrtle replied. "My sources are impeccable."

Rob gave a heavy sigh. "Honestly, I don't know why I bother," he muttered. Sinking down beside Becky on the staff room's turquoise sofa, he moved over to let Holly sit next to him, then narrowed his eyes at the septuagenarian. "I know I've asked this before, but who exactly are these 'sources' of yours, Myrtle?"

"I couldn't possibly tell you that, Inspector."

"No. Sources are sacrosanct," Thomas agreed from his perch on the windowsill. "Got to protect them at all costs. Sorry, Inspector, but it's true." He grinned at the glare Rob sent his way.

"You're as bad as they are. And what I did to deserve this, I'll never know." Rob heaved an enormous sigh, then glanced at Holly before continuing. "But, as some people constantly remind me, Hibiscus Island isn't a normal place."

Ignoring Myrtle's indignant protest, the inspector gazed around the room, catching each eye in turn. "I may be able to share some details. However, I'll need your promise that you won't discuss anything outside this group of people. Excepting François, of course, Becky," he added, turning to his sister. "Although I'd still prefer it if you weren't involved at all at this—"

"Delicate time of her life. Yeah, yeah. We know. Rob, she's pregnant, not made of porcelain." Jamie looked at the inspector in exasperation. "And besides, she's the best researcher we have! You can't keep her on the sidelines."

"I can keep all of you on the sidelines," Rob warned. "And I'll do exactly that if you don't stop pushing, Jamie!"

Jamie had the grace to look abashed at the frowns sent

her way by Myrtle and Thomas. She held up her hands. "Got it. No pushing. Tell us in your own time, Inspector."

Rob's lips twitched as he looked at her wheedling smile. "I'll admit you have been helpful in the past. Very well." He pulled out a small notebook, glancing at the first page. "In brief, tests showed Mrs. Dill had elevated blood lactate and high venous oxygen levels, which are common with cyanide poisoning. The breathlessness, seizure, and subsequent coma suffered by Mrs. Dill are also symptoms of large-dose exposure. And finally, cyanide was detected in blood samples." The inspector leaned back in his seat. "There's no fast test to detect oral cyanide ingestion as yet, which is why it took the lab some time to discover what had happened."

"Oral ingestion?" Myrtle's eyes sharpened. "Are you assuming this happened at the tea on Sunday?"

"It's possible. There is, I've been told by the medical experts, a difference in oral cyanide ingestion and cyanide inhalation. And the onset of symptoms can vary according to dose."

As Rob flipped over pages in the notebook, Holly suppressed a smile. The inspector refused to use a phone or anything digital to take notes on a case.

"Doesn't cyanide poisoning make a person's face turn red? And I thought there was supposed to be a smell of bitter almonds. That's what murder mysteries always say anyway." Jamie looked at Myrtle. "You didn't notice that?"

Thomas spoke up. "I think that happens more often with inhalation, if you were in an enclosed space in a fire, say. I know some products like plastic or vinyl can produce cyanide from incomplete combustion." He glanced at the inspector. "But you think Mrs. Dill ingested cyanide, you said. Could her earlier symptoms have been a result of that as well?"

Myrtle looked at the journalist with approval. "Excellent point, Thomas. Is it possible to systematically poison a person with low doses of cyanide, Inspector?"

"Yes." Rob looked mildly exasperated. "Would you mind if I found my notes before you all start hypothesizing?"

"You should use a phone or tablet," Jamie said. "So much faster."

"So you've said. Multiple times. I have my own methods." Rob paused, a small smile appearing. "Watson."

Jamie grinned in appreciation. "Carry on then, Holmes."

"Ah, here we are. According to the lab folks, oral cyanide is most frequently ingested in the form of cyanide salts—potassium cyanide or sodium cyanide to be precise. I haven't heard exactly what form Mrs. Dill took."

"Took? But... but you don't think she did it deliberately, do you, Rob?" Holly was shocked. "Surely not!"

"Cyanide salts are used to commit suicide. I can't completely rule that out yet."

There was a moment of silence.

"I cannot believe that Sally Hartley Dill would take her own life. And certainly not in such a way." Myrtle's voice was definite. "She was a delightful woman. And full of plans for the future. No. I will not believe this was a deliberate act on her part."

"And besides, what about the others?" Jamie asked. "Daina Trott and Freda Sinclair? They had the same symptoms as Sally Dill."

"There's no evidence to say they were poisoned." Rob spread his hands out. "I contacted my colleagues on Azure and there was nothing at all to indicate foul play. Daina Trott died as a result of her disease. Freda Sinclair passed out while driving, causing her car to crash. She had been diagnosed with the flu and advised to remain in bed." He paused. "There was no autopsy performed on either woman."

Jamie sat up. "No autopsy? Then there could have been something. Couldn't you ask for one?"

Before Rob could respond, Thomas intervened. "The problem with cyanide is that it metabolizes very quickly. It has a really short half-life, so after a couple of days, it can't be easily detected, particularly if the body has already begun to decompose."

"Ugh." Becky's face turned green. "Thomas, would you mind not—"

"Don't be so descriptive, Miller!" Jamie snapped. "Pregnant woman in the house, remember? And how do you know so much about cyanide, anyway?"

"I covered a case several years ago. As a newbie journalist. Young guy committed suicide. It wasn't very pleasant."

"Oh." Jamie's glance at the journalist was apologetic.

"I've heard there're a couple of new detection methods available now—biomarkers in the liver, for instance—but you would still need a good reason to ask for an autopsy, and it doesn't sound like you have one. Right, Inspector?" Thomas directed an enquiring look at Rob, who nodded.

"Correct. As far as the police are concerned, we are dealing with one death. That of Mrs. Dill."

Standing up, Rob closed his notebook, then cast a stern glance around the room. "Now, listen. I know you're all keen to help, and I also know that asking you not to do so is, frankly, a complete waste of time." He paused as Jamie and Thomas grinned. Holly suppressed a smile of her own as Rob glared at them.

"But I want your word, all of you, that you will not—" The inspector held up a hand at the protests that sounded around the room. "Hold the comments, please. I haven't finished. I want your word that you won't put yourselves in dangerous situations. Anything you find out in the course of conversation must be immediately reported to myself or Sergeant Hollis, and you are to confine yourselves to questioning only. You may not take the law into your own hands. Is that clear? You are not, I repeat, *not* police officers and your rights to perform citizens' arrests are limited."

"Well!" Myrtle huffed. "I'm not sure that I appreciate your tone, Inspector."

Rob shrugged. "I'm not concerned with your appreciation, Myrtle. I'm concerned with your safety. You want to be detectives, then you answer to me. Otherwise, I'll have no choice but to place you in protective custody—for your own safety, of course."

Holly choked at the looks of outrage on Jamie and Myrtle's faces. Glancing sideways at Becky, she saw the librarian struggling to contain her own laughter.

"Agreed." Thomas grinned at Rob. "Absolutely fair, Inspector, and no more than what's expected of any investigative reporter. Less, in fact, since we're required by law to identify ourselves when asking questions, to avoid harassing people, and to safeguard privacy. I'm assuming that's expected on Hibiscus Island as well. So yes, you have my word."

"Mine too." Becky raised her hand. "All I'm going to do is research anyway and I doubt I'll find anything you don't."

"Agreed," Holly said.

The inspector nodded, smiling at her before raising an eyebrow at Jamie and Myrtle. "Well?"

"Well, I don't think it's fair," Jamie began. "This is Hibiscus Island! It's different here. Everyone expects us to get involved and help out—and you putting conditions on what we can do is going to get in the way!"

"Is that a no?"

Jamie glared at the impassive inspector. "No, it's not a 'no'! I'll give you my word. But I think you're just... just mean!" She crossed her arms over her chest, transferring her scowl to Thomas as a snort of laughter escaped the journalist. "And you can just zip it, Miller!"

"You have my word as well, Inspector, but I must say I am highly offended you feel the need to ask for it in this insulting fashion."

Myrtle's dignified tone had no effect on Rob. "I think I can live with that, Myrtle. I'd rather you were offended and safe than pleased and in danger."

"Humph!" A flicker of respect crossed Myrtle's face as she gathered her purse and suit jacket. "Well then, if we've discussed everything that needs discussing, I'll go and collect Anne McGinney from the expo and take her home."

"Perhaps you'd let her know that I'll need to talk to her tomorrow." Rob smiled at Myrtle. "It might make her feel more comfortable if I come to your house to ask my questions."

Myrtle huffed again. "Very well, Inspector. We'll expect you at ten o'clock." She sailed out of the room.

"What do you want to ask Mrs. McGinney?" Jamie demanded. "This sharing thing goes two ways, right?"

Rob grinned at her. "Maybe."

"Maybe?! Now look, Rob, that's not fair at all! How come we have to tell you everything, but you don't have to do the same?"

Thomas laughed. "Relax, White. He's just winding you up. Nice speech there, Inspector."

"It wasn't all words," Rob warned. "I really do want to make sure you're all sensible and stay out of danger."

"But you will tell us what's going on?" Jamie prodded. "Right?"

The inspector nodded. "So long as I'm legally able to do so, yes. And the Hibiscus Island Detective Club will have to be content with that."

16

"Would you really lock them up?" Holly asked the inspector as he walked beside her back to her car.

Rob grinned down at her. "Absolutely. It would give me great pleasure to have those two where I could keep an eye on them."

"Just those two? You mean you don't want to keep an eye on the rest of us? Inspector, I'm hurt!" Holly clutched at her chest in mock dismay.

"I'm doing you the courtesy of believing you have more sense than to deliberately put yourself in a dangerous situation." Rob took Holly's hand. "In fact, I'm relying on you, Miller, and Becky to keep them under control."

Holly laughed. "Wishful thinking, I'm afraid. But we'll do our best. Rob, have you spoken to Denise Trott yet?" When the inspector shook his head, she continued, "Well, I think you should. And to Derek Hartley. I know you have no evidence that Freda Sinclair—the Oleander who had the car accident, you know—was murdered, but judging by what Denise told me earlier today, there may be something in it after all."

Rob paused at the door of Holly's car, studying her anxious face. "I'm seeing them both tomorrow. Mr. Hartley was at the quilt expo all day and said he'd prefer not to talk without his attorney present, and Miss Trott was under medical orders."

"Oh, did you meet Derek's dad? Apparently he won't let anyone in the family make statements without him. I picked him up from the airport today," she added when Rob's eyebrows rose.

"Ah. I wondered how you knew that. Yes, I have statements from Mrs. Hartley and Mrs. Worthington. Interesting family dynamic—and no, I can't tell you what they said." Rob grinned at Holly. "I'm scheduled to meet with Mr. Hartley and Miss Trott first thing in the morning, before my visit to Myrtle and her friend, so I'll ask what they know about Mrs. Sinclair, although, as I said, there was nothing suspicious flagged by the Azure police."

He tilted Holly's chin up to give her a light kiss. "I'm going to be tied up with this case, obviously, but, circumstances permitting, shall we try to reschedule our dive for next weekend? I still haven't seen the wreck site and now that you've discovered some treasure out there, I'd like a chance to see it *in situ*, so to speak."

Holly grinned. "I'm free on Sunday. And it's hardly treasure. Just an old glass bottle."

"But possibly an eighteenth-century glass bottle. And sealed, I think you said. Who knows what could be inside it?" Rob smiled. "It's a date, then?"

"For sure. And I'll check and see if Uncle Phil can take us out in his boat."

"Sounds good." Rob gave her another quick kiss before heading back to work.

~

HOLLY WAS SNUGGLED on the sofa with Truffle, a cup of tea by her side and a book in her hand, when Maggie walked into the family room and collapsed beside her with a sigh.

"What a day."

Her mother's woebegone face made Holly drop her book and sit up. "Are you okay, Mama? What's happened now?"

"Apart from murder at the Inn and a hysterical guest? Oh, nothing."

Holly wrapped an arm around her mother. "Aww. Try not to worry about it, Mama." Maggie's incredulous look made her flush. "Well, you know what I mean. Besides, Denise isn't hysterical anymore. I took her to the butterfly garden with me this afternoon, then gave her tea. She was quite calm when I left her with Aunt Sarah." Holly paused. "Unless she had another meltdown. Did she?"

"No, she's fine. And she told me you'd looked after her. Thanks for that, Holly." Maggie patted her daughter's leg. "She's to go see Rob tomorrow morning... Oh, you already knew that too, I see."

"I did. And Derek as well. Do they need a ride down to the station? I can take them if you want."

"No. Mr. Hartley Senior has already organized a taxi to collect them all." Maggie made a slight face. "Not Sybil, of course. She wants her own taxi."

"But I thought Rob already spoke to Sybil and Mrs. Hartley."

"Oh, he did. Sybil needs a taxi to get to the expo." Maggie sighed. "I suggested that the one taxi drop her off, but she won't ride with her son-in-law."

"Yeah, I heard they don't get on very well. I'm surprised

Mrs. Worthington's going to the expo though. I mean, with the death and all."

"I am too," Maggie admitted, "but that's Sybil for you. Stiff upper lip doesn't even begin to describe her. She's also the new vice-president of the club, or will be when the Oleanders have their next meeting, so I suppose she feels she should be present."

"Gosh, they really are a very organized club, aren't they? Do you know Sybil well, Mama? I heard she owns the Daylily Resort! That place is huge."

"Yes, it's lovely. The expo was held there a few years ago. We all wallowed in the height of luxury. And then the following year, we roughed it on Coral Island in church halls." Maggie smiled. "I've known Sybil for a while, although I'm really closer in age to Ellen. They're both excellent, and very talented, quilters."

"What about Jonas Hartley? Do you know him too?"

"We've met a couple of times. I must say, his son is much more personable."

"Handsomer too." Holly grinned. "He's got fabulous eyes, doesn't he? Derek, I mean."

Maggie laughed. "I'll have to look more closely. I can't say I noticed Derek's eyes." She heaved herself up. "Well, I'm turning in early tonight, Holly Berry. I'm manning the Patch-workers stall tomorrow morning, then relieving Sarah for the afternoon. She's covered for me a lot this week. What about you? What are your plans?"

"I'm helping Jamie with the lunches at the expo, and then we're meeting Tansy and Sage Craft. Which reminds me, Sage said she quilted part of your hibiscus block today. She said to tell you it's lovely."

"That was nice of her." Maggie's smile was distracted, as

she mulled over Holly's words. "And why are you and Jamie meeting with the Craft girls?"

"Uh... well..."

Maggie frowned. "Please tell me you're not investigating again, Holly!"

"Rob's okay with it," Holly said quickly. "As long as we don't put ourselves in danger. Which we won't because we're just talking."

"You were 'just talking' last September, too, when you got yourselves in trouble with that pirate thing!" Maggie protested. "Holly, I really don't think—"

"It'll be fine, Mama. Seriously. I mean, how much trouble can we get into at a quilt show?"

AT LUNCH THE FOLLOWING DAY, Jamie and Holly dished out bento boxes to the mob of hungry quilters in record time. As soon as the ice buffet had been emptied, Jamie rubbed her hands together with glee.

"Right. Let's find Tansy. And Holls, no browsing today! We're on a fact-finding expedition. Not a shopping one."

Holly rolled her eyes but followed her friend into the crowded lecture hall. "There she is. Oh, and Sage is with her. That's convenient."

"Mmm. But they look pretty busy. Bother. It doesn't look like we'll be able to have a serious conversation with them right now." Jamie huffed with annoyance. "Now what are we going to do?"

"We could take a quick peek at the Flower Quilt," Holly suggested. "I haven't seen it yet and I wanted to see what Mama's block looks like in it."

"I suppose. I haven't seen it myself yet, come to think

about it." Jamie led the way to the board room, then paused outside to look at the schedule. "Looks like the Tacky Turtles are quilting right now." She sniggered. "I do love that name."

"And it sounds like they're not getting on!" Holly's eyebrows shot up as raised voices sounded inside the room.

The two women sidled inside in time to see Sybil Worthington facing off with another elderly woman.

"And I'm telling you, Caroline, that someone changed the schedule! The Oleanders were originally timetabled to have the quilt bee at this time. Look! It says it right here on the documents we were sent!"

The two Oleanders behind her nodded in agreement.

"And it also says," Caroline responded in a calm tone, "that the schedule is subject to change. Which it clearly has."

The Tacky Turtles around the room nodded with vigor. "That's right."

Jamie's eyes rounded, a grin spreading across her face as she watched the stand-off. "Who knew a quilting schedule was this important?" she whispered to Holly, watching as Sybil Worthington swelled up.

"Well, Caroline, I see I shall have to go and consult the organizer!"

"Do, Sybil. Please do," Caroline replied sweetly. "I'm sure Myrtle knows exactly who should be in here at this time."

"Humph."

Sybil and her coterie exited the board room in a huff while behind them the Tacky Turtles exchanged grins. Catching sight of Jamie and Holly, their leader smiled. "Hello. Have you come to join the bee?"

"We're not Tacky Turtles," Jamie replied with a grin.

Caroline laughed. "Oh, anyone's welcome. Don't pay any

attention to Sybil. She could perfectly well have come in and joined us, but she—"

"Doesn't want to quilt with the competition," another Turtle said in a dry tone.

"At least not the winning competition," another woman added.

"Now, now, ladies. Let's not be petty." Caroline shooed the Turtles back to their places around the quilt frame before turning back to Holly and Jamie. "So, what club do you two belong to? I don't think I've seen you before. Is this your first expo?"

"Oh, we're not quilters," Holly said hastily. "But my mama has a block on the quilt, and I wanted to see it."

"Really? Who's your mom?" Caroline asked.

"Maggie Gold. She made a—"

"Hibiscus. Yes, of course, it's over here. Lovely appliqué, I must say." Caroline eyed Holly with interest as she led the way to the quilt stretched over the large frame. "So, you're Maggie's daughter, are you? Holly, isn't it?" She transferred her gaze to Jamie. "And that means you must be Jamie White, the owner of the legendary Rose Treasure."

Holly blinked, wondering how Caroline knew their names. The answer came almost immediately.

"I hear you two are quite the detectives."

Jamie looked pleased. "Where'd you hear that?"

A woman looked up from where she was quilting along the seam of the bright pink sashing that edged the blocks. "Oh, you're the talk of the expo." Her face sobered. "Particularly after what happened to Sally Dill."

Jamie pulled out a chair next to the quilter. "Did you know Sally?"

"We all knew Sally," Caroline said, sadness in her voice. "She was a lovely woman."

"Yes, very un-Oleander like, in fact." The woman who spoke lowered her needle as everyone frowned at her. "What? I'm only saying what we've all thought."

"Now, now, the Oleanders are perfectly nice, Frances," Caroline said in a soothing voice. "Much more formal than us, but there you are... Different strokes for different folks."

Frances tutted. "Humph. Sybil's daughter's sister-in-law died on Sunday, Caroline. She shouldn't even be at the expo, let alone ordering people around!"

"People deal with grief in different ways. It's not our place to judge." Caroline was firm before changing the subject. "Now, Holly, here's your mom's block. Nice, isn't it?"

Holly nodded, admiring the tiny stitches that various quilters had put into the block. "I love that little butterfly quilted there!"

"Well, thank you. That was my contribution." Caroline smiled. "Would you like to make a few stitches? Look. Your friend is giving it a go."

What? Holly looked across the room, her mouth dropping open as she saw Jamie, thimble on her middle finger, holding a tiny quilting needle. As the quilter beside her demonstrated a rocking motion with her hand, Jamie's eyes met Holly's in a silent plea for help.

Holly started to grin, then stopped when Caroline handed her a thimble of her own before threading a minuscule needle for her.

"Here. Do some stitches on your mom's block. She'll be thrilled."

Despite Holly's protests, she was no match for the determined Turtle and soon found herself pushing the needle through the quilt, wincing at the size of her stitch compared to the others.

"Oh, don't worry about that. That's the charm of the

Flower Quilt. Everyone's stitches are different." Caroline smiled as her own needle flashed in and out of the morning glory block beside Holly's hibiscus, before lowering her voice. "Now, Holly, I hear you and that handsome police inspector are an item. Is that true? Then perhaps you'd like to pass on some information to him."

Holly inadvertently stabbed her finger, then lowered her own voice to a whisper. "What information? Do you know something about Mrs. Dill's death?"

"Not exactly. But I wondered if anyone had told you about Wilhelmina—and her cassava pie."

17

_____

"**A**re you serious? You can't be serious! She said the cassava was poisoned?" Jamie was incredulous.

Holly took a sip of her soda.

After staggering out of the quilt bee following a nerve-wracking quilting experience—the Tacky Turtles had held Holly and Jamie captive for quite some time—the two women had stopped by The Black Cat booth to find out when Tansy and Sage would be free. Learning they'd be taking a break in a few minutes, Holly and Jamie had repaired to the food courtyard to grab some much-needed sugar and catch each other up on their various conversations with the gossipy Turtles.

Now Holly sighed. "No, she didn't say that. Or not in so many words."

"And how does she know anything about this Wilhelmina's cassava pie anyway?" Jamie demanded. "She's a Tacky Turtle and all the victims are Oleanders! They don't even live on the same island, for Pete's sake!"

"She said that at every expo, Wilhelmina goes around to various hosts for dinner, no matter what island she's on.

And she takes her cassava pie with her. All the people she visits prepare a pie of their own. It's some kind of weird tradition because apparently Wilhelmina's cassava pie is amazing. Or so Caroline said. They all try to make one that's better than hers, but so far no one's managed it."

"I have never, in all my life, heard of anything so... so... ludicrous!" Jamie exclaimed. "A cassava pie contest? At an annual quilting expo! How many pies does she bring with her, for goodness' sake? You know what? They all have too much time on their hands." She frowned. "Wilhelmina... the name rings a bell."

"Her name's Wilhelmina Carson. She's been getting your bento lunches every day, remember? Auntie Elma had her for dinner the other night. I remember Gramps telling me he was having cassava pie there."

"Unbelievable." Jamie shook her head.

"Yeah, but here's the thing. According to Caroline, all three of our victims were the recipients of Wilhelmina's cassava pie when they were sick!"

"And she knows that how?" Jamie looked skeptical.

"Because Wilhelmina told all the Oleanders when she delivered them. And then the Oleanders told people and they told people and so on. You know what island gossip is like. She's very proud of her cassava and, according to Caroline, was insistent that Daina and Freda eat it. Claimed it had health properties. But—and here's the kicker, Jamie—she also took her cassava pie to the tea on Sunday!"

Jamie was still gaping when Holly heard their names being called. Glancing across the courtyard, she waved to Tansy and Sage Craft, beckoning them to the table.

"Want a drink?" Holly asked the Juniper islanders, seeing that Jamie was stupefied into silence. "There are sodas and juices in a cooler over there. I have a couple of tickets so my treat. Or would you rather have tea? I think the urns might still have some hot water."

Sage tutted. "You can't make proper tea with hot water from an urn, Holly. And thank you, but I'll stick with my water for now."

"I'll just go grab an orange juice." Tansy waved Holly back into her seat. "I've got my own tickets. I'll be right back."

She strolled off across the courtyard to the small tent manned by the White Horse restaurant, looking very chic in her ankle-length blue dress, patterned with large appliquéd peonies on its irregular hem.

Returning her attention to Sage, Holly realized the older of the Juniper island sisters was wearing a similar dress.

"I love your outfits." Holly admired the layered skirt, whose hem was embroidered with wildflowers and butterflies. "Where'd you find them? They look very... bohemian. In a good way, of course."

Sage laughed. "Thanks. There's a little boutique store on Juniper that brings in all sorts of vintage and one-of-a-kind clothing. You should visit some day. There's lots to see on the island."

"I'd like that," Holly said. "I've only ever been to Coral Island, and the mainland, of course."

"Yes, we do all tend to stay on our own small rocks, don't we? I've been to Azure a couple of times, and Grand Island as you said, but this is my first visit to Hibiscus. It's a bit different from home."

"In what way?"

"We're bigger than you," Sage replied. "More mountainous. Hibiscus has an urban feel to it. Juniper is more wilderness."

"I've heard it's very new age. Is that true?" Jamie asked,

entering the conversation. "Kind of like a tropical Sedona is how someone once described it to me."

Overhearing this as she returned with her orange juice, Tansy snorted in amusement. "No red rocks on Juniper, but yeah, I guess you could say some people have mystical leanings. Holistic living, metaphysical kind of things, tarot readers... there's an eclectic mix on Juniper. It's a fun place to live."

"Is there anyone else who sells teas and stuff like you do? I noticed you were really busy earlier, by the way. Business picking up?"

Tansy sobered. "It has, actually. And it's since Sally Dill died, which is weird."

"Well, she died at a tea party," Holly pointed out. "Which you weren't at."

"No, we had nothing to do with it." Tansy looked thoughtful. "So, you think the Maritime quilters have now decided we're in the clear with regards to the other deaths on Azure because of that?"

"Or they're thronging your stall trying to discover something." Jamie spread out her hands when Holly frowned. "What? That's what they do."

"Have you heard any gossip?" Holly asked Tansy.

"No. But this is our first expo, remember. We're not well-known."

"That doesn't usually stop Hibiscus folk." Jamie's tone was sardonic. "They thrive on supposition, innuendo, and gossip." She glanced at Sage. "You mentioned you've been to Azure a couple of times, and that Daina Trott and Freda Sinclair were customers of yours. And when we met with you earlier, I thought you seemed a little... reluctant to talk about something. Care to share anything now?"

Sage raised an eyebrow. "Reluctant?"

"It was when Myrtle was asking about the products you made," Holly said. "She mentioned teas, and you said both women liked sorrel tea. And then someone asked if they bought any other products from you. I think you mentioned a lotion or something. You did seem to be a bit hesitant to talk about that."

"I feel that customers are entitled to privacy," Sage said in a stiff voice.

"Yeah, well, murder kind of messes that sort of thing up." Jamie raised an eyebrow of her own. "Did you know Daina and Freda were having those symptoms? Is that why you were reluctant to talk to us?"

"Of course she didn't know," Tansy exclaimed. "Why would you say such a thing? Tell her..." Her voice trailed away as she saw the expression on her sister's face. "Sage?"

Sage winced. "I was on Azure in October and December, Tansy. I went to a conference in October at the Daylily Resort, and I had a meeting in December with that little boutique hotel—The Lemontree Inn—to see about potentially supplying them as we do Maggie. I dropped off orders while I was there."

"So, you're saying you were on Azure Island when both women were sick? And you dropped off orders? To Freda and Daina?" Jamie pursed her lips when Sage nodded. "Were they sick when you got there, or did they get sick after you dropped off their products?"

"Hey!" Tansy exclaimed, anger edging her voice. "Don't accuse my sister!"

"I'm not. I just want to know—"

"It's okay." Sage's shoulders drooped slightly. "I should have told you the other night but... Well, honestly, I was scared to."

"Scared? But why?" Holly asked.

"We're a small business, and the few rumors circulating were already making an impact on our bottom line and—"

Tansy, who had been looking at her sister in consternation, now laid a hand over hers. "You didn't want to admit anything to the 'detectives,' right? In case it caused problems."

Sage nodded, looking at Holly. "You do have a bit of a reputation. That article about the Spanish ship kind of went viral among the islands. And..." Sage sighed. "I was a little leery of saying anything that could have incriminated me."

"We're famous, huh?"

A small smile tugged at the corner of Sage's mouth as she took in Jamie's pleased expression. "Yes, even our little island saw the article in *The Island Gazette*." She relaxed suddenly. "I should have been open with you from the start, I guess."

Jamie waved a magnanimous hand. "Oh well, even if you've heard things, you don't really know us properly. And I wasn't actually accusing you of poisoning Daina and Freda..."

"It sounded like it to me." Tansy's voice was skeptical, but a twinkle lurked in her eyes.

Holly restrained the urge to roll her own eyes. It never failed to amaze her how Jamie could say the most outrageous things at times, and yet, somehow, not only get away with it but end up having people like her despite it!

"No, no. What I meant was," Jamie continued, "why would people think there was a connection between you and the victims unless there was a reason?" She paused. "That didn't come out right either. Hmm. Let me see—"

Grinning openly now, Sage cut her off. "How about I just explain?"

"Oh please!" Holly said with exaggerated relief. "Anything to stop her digging a deeper hole!"

A giggle escaped Tansy. "You two have been friends for ages, haven't you?"

"Since preschool," Holly agreed. "And she's been a trial ever since we first met."

"Ha! If it wasn't for me, you'd have cowered in the corner of Mrs. Goodwin's class all year."

Both Juniper islanders chuckled at the mock glare Holly directed at Jamie.

"My sister and I have this same sort of relationship," Tansy said. "Marigold and I are best friends. We're only eleven months apart and born in the same year."

"Really?" Holly asked. "How does that work? Were you in the same class at school?"

Tansy shook her head. "No. I was born in January, so my parents asked if I could start early. The school said yes." She smiled at her sister. "Sage is five years older than us."

"They were a bit of a trial when they were younger too." Sage grinned.

The atmosphere around the table lightened even further.

"So, now that we're all friends," Jamie said, "perhaps we could get back to the interrogation."

All reserve completely gone, Sage laughed. "Ask away, detective. Ask away."

HOLLY EXHALED with relief as the Juniper islanders returned to their booth. "I don't think they had anything to do with it."

"Agreed." Jamie fingered her lip. "Although, knowing

what we do now about cyanide being the poison, I think the information about apple seeds was interesting, don't you?"

"It was apple seed oil Sage mentioned," Holly pointed out. "Used on skin to make it look younger."

"She said sometimes people cook with it." Jamie looked thoughtful. "I wonder if François has ever used it."

Holly ignored the digression. "She also said Sally Dill never bought it. So, if we think all three women were killed in the same way, then apple seed oil is a non-starter for the poison."

"Besides, it's apple seeds that contain cyanide, not so much the oil, right?"

"Umm," Holly hesitated. "To be honest, Sage totally lost me with all her chemistry. I think she said the seeds have something that turns into cyanide when metabolized but you'd have to crush them first, and you'd have to eat several thousand. We can ask Becky to do some more research if you want, but I don't think the apple seed oil Sage gave to Daina and Freda was the poison. And since she showed us a list of every single product from The Black Cat shop... Well, I doubt any of it was poisoned."

Jamie sighed. "Yeah."

"What's the sigh for? I thought you liked Sage and Tansy!"

"I do. And I'm glad we can cross them off the suspect list, but now... Well, what suspects do we have?"

"I think," Holly said, "we should start with the cassava lady."

18

"Mmmm. Wilhelmina Carson, right?" Jamie looked at Holly. "If she's an Oleander, isn't she staying at the Inn? I thought all the Oleanders were there."

"Except for Mrs. McGinney," Holly agreed. "She's staying with Myrtle. But yes, Ms. Carson has the Frangipani Suite. Why do you ask?"

"Well, rather than trying to have a private conversation with her in this madhouse, maybe we could talk to her later. At the Inn."

Holly drank the remainder of her soda. "We could do that. What shall we do now, then? Or do you have to get back to the Bean for the teatime rush? I have some designs to finish for Thomas's gardens—and the butterfly garden to work on—but nothing with a time constraint."

"Angie's handling the tea crowd with some high schoolers—if there is a tea crowd today. Which I doubt, since it looks like everyone's hanging around here as much as they can. She told me I could have the afternoon off."

"Angie told you? And here I thought you were the boss." Holly grinned at the thought.

"She's a good kid. I'm thinking about promoting her."

"Really?" Holly's eyebrows rose.

"Yeah. François and I have talked about maybe having an official catering side to the Bean. We do quite a few events now, and with just the two of us, it eats up a lot of our time. Now that he has a baby on the way, I think we need to consider a different staffing arrangement. Angie's worked for me for the past four years. She's solid. And if she could do more management in the café, I could work on expanding the catering side."

"Wow!" Holly stared at her friend. "How long have you been thinking about this? It's the first I've heard of it."

"Off and on for a year or so. It's the baby that's made me consider it more seriously. François isn't going to want to do lots of evening events. And Becky won't like that either. I'd need to hire someone else, too, though." Jamie eyed Holly. "You wouldn't like a part-time job, would you?"

"No thanks." Holly grimaced. "I feel like I've already got three part-time jobs—helping Gramps with the garden, helping Mama with the Inn, and trying to do my own garden design. But I think the catering idea is great—and you know I'll pitch in if and when I can."

"Yeah, well, it's a future project." Jamie stretched her arms above her head, then tugged her red shirt back into place over the casual jeans she wore. "Why don't we go find our chief researcher and see what she's found out? Myrtle asked her to find everything she could about cyanide poisoning. I'll bet she's in the archives. Come on."

BECKY LOOKED up from the computer as Jamie and Holly entered the blessedly quiet library archives. "Did Myrtle send you? Because if so, you can just tell her I'm doing the best I can and if she keeps harassing me, I'm going to—"

"Whoa, whoa, whoa!" Holly exclaimed, hurrying towards her. "What's the matter? What's Myrtle been doing to get you so upset?"

Becky leaned back in her chair, closing her eyes for a second. She took a deep breath, then sighed. "Nothing really. Just being Myrtle. She asked me to research cyanide, you know."

"We know. That's why we came down." Jamie eyed the librarian with concern. "But if you're too tired to do this, you should stop. We don't want you—"

"I'm not tired!" Becky snapped. "Would you all please stop acting like I'm made of china? I'm pregnant, not incapable!"

Jamie's eyes rounded. "Okay then. Well... uh... hmmm..." She looked at Holly for help.

"When did you last eat?" Holly asked, holding up a hand when Becky spun around. "And don't snarl at me. Or I'll get Rob or François. And I'm sure you don't want them hovering over you." She smiled at her friend. "If you're feeling queasy, what about a soda to sip?"

Becky flushed, then nodded. "A coke would be nice," she said in a small voice before looking at Jamie. "Sorry."

"Oh please! You're growing a human. You're allowed to be snarly. I'll go grab you a drink and some crackers or something. Be right back."

Jamie shot out of the archives, leaving Holly to sit down beside Becky. The sunshine yellow fleecy top the librarian wore was bright and cheerful—a marked contrast to her woebegone expression.

"I'm being nasty, aren't I?"

Holly patted her shoulder. "If this is what you call

'nasty,' you know nothing about it. What've you eaten today? And don't tell me I sound like Myrtle."

There was a tiny laugh from Becky. "I know she means well."

Holly looked sympathetic. "She really does. She cares about you. We all do. Look, Becky, if you don't want to be involved in this, just say so. We'll all back you. This isn't your job—heck, it's not any of our jobs—and you don't have to be part of it."

Becky drew in a deep breath, giving Holly a wobbly smile. "None of you know how to research."

"Of course we do." Holly grinned. "And if we don't, the police do. Rob doesn't really need us, you know."

"Bite your tongue, Holly Gold! How can you call yourself a member of the HIDC and say that?"

Jamie's voice was outraged but her eyes twinkled as she crossed the room with a can of soda and a package of crackers. "Don't listen to this heresy, Becky. Here, have some carbs. Your face looks a little green." She sat down beside her friend. "Seriously, though, if you don't want to do this, just say so. We'll still love you."

"I know you would. If I had sisters, I'd want them to be like you two."

As Becky teared up, Jamie's eyes widened in dismay. "What are you doing? Now look—don't get all emotional on us, Becks! Holly, do something! Make her stop!"

"She's allowed to be teary." Holly rolled her eyes at Jamie while putting an arm around Becky. "Growing a human, remember? Take a sip of this, Becks."

A gurgle of laughter escaped Becky as she took the drink. After a couple of gulps, she wiped her eyes, looking at her friends. "You know, I've been meaning to ask you guys something. When the baby's born—will you be godmothers?"

Jamie and Holly blinked.

"Well, that's a bit of a *non sequitur*, isn't it?" Jamie was taken aback but recovered quickly. "But yes, I'd be honored, although I'm not sure what kind of a role model I'll be for an impressionable youngster."

"You said it, not us," Holly agreed, laughing when Jamie made a face at her. "We'd both love it, Becky."

Jamie looked suddenly struck. "You know, if you could find a third person, we could be like the fairy godmothers in *Sleeping Beauty*! That would be pretty cool. Oh, and then you could call—"

"We're not calling our baby 'Aurora.'" Becky was firm through her laughter. "We don't even know if it's a girl. And besides, Rob and François's brother will be godparents as well."

Holly grinned as Jamie sent a wink her way. Becky looked much happier now.

"So. Do you want to just hand over the research to us?" Jamie peered at the computer. "Is this a good site?"

Becky brushed her hand away from the keyboard. "Don't touch it." She smiled at both women. "Thank you. I'm very lucky to have you as my friends."

"Awww. Don't get mushy, Becks," Jamie begged. "You'll make us cry too."

"Shut up, Jamie." Becky grinned at the look of mock-shock she received. "Move away from the keyboard, and I'll tell you what I've found out."

Holly and Jamie exchanged another smile and pulled their chairs closer.

"So," Becky began, "cyanide is a rapidly acting poison that, as Rob said, can be either in a colorless gas form or a crystal salt. It can also be released from natural substances, like some foods, for instance. I've ignored the gas form, because there seems to be no indication that any of the deaths we're investigating were a result of that. And besides, cyanide gas evaporates and dissipates quite quickly in open spaces, and since Mrs. Dill died outside, I doubt cyanide gas was the cause of death."

Becky had adopted her librarian voice, and apart from sipping occasionally at her coke, seemed to have fully recovered.

"What about apple seeds?" Jamie asked.

Becky blinked. "Apple seeds? Why are you asking that? Were there apple seeds at the tea?"

"I have no idea. I just heard you can get cyanide from apple seeds. Sage Craft told us that today."

"Sage told you?" Becky held up a hand as Jamie started to speak. "Never mind. I don't need to know all the details. Yes, apple seeds contain chemicals that can be metabolized to cyanide when eaten. As do apricot and peach pits. Lima beans, almonds, and cassava also contain cyanide."

"Cassava?!" The word burst from Jamie and Holly at the same time.

Jamie continued, "Are you serious? Cassava is poisonous? But I eat cassava pie every year at Christmas!"

"You also eat apricots, peaches, apples, and almonds." Becky's voice was tart. "Besides, cassava pie's not poisonous."

"You just said cassava had cyanide!" Jamie protested.

Becky sighed. "It does. Raw cassava can contain up to... Hang on, let me just confirm..." She scrolled up the document containing her notes. "Yes, raw cassava can contain up to four hundred milligrams of hydrogen cyanide per kilogram of fresh root weight."

Jamie looked appalled. "But—"

"But you don't eat it raw!" Becky said. "Cassava root is soaked, dried, fermented, boiled, baked, whatever. It's extensively processed before consumption. As long as it's adequately processed, cassava is perfectly safe to eat. Apricot kernels, to be honest, pose a greater threat. Three small raw apricot kernels are considered to be above safe levels. The fruit's fine though."

"But unprocessed cassava can be dangerous?" Holly asked.

"Yes. Why are you fixating on cassava? Do you know something I don't?" Becky sounded exasperated. "What's the big deal about cassava?"

"The big deal," Holly replied, "is that we know cassava pie was given to all three victims at or near the time they died!"

Becky's mouth dropped open. "Really? That is a little... suspicious, I suppose. Did they all actually eat it? And where did it come from?"

"Uh... hmmm... I don't actually know if Mrs. Dill ate any. We should check that," Holly said. "But the pie was prepared by an Oleander—Wilhelmina Carson."

"We're going to try and pin her down later today," Jamie added.

Becky tapped her lip, distracted. "You know, I do think I read something about people being poisoned with cassava, actually."

"But you just said—"

Becky cut Jamie off. "I said if it's properly processed, which most commercial cassava is, then it's quite safe, but..." She tapped away on the computer keys, then sat back. "Yes, here it is. There was an incident in western Uganda in 2017. Suspected cyanide poisoning where ninety-eight people ended up in the hospital and two died." She scrolled down the page. "It says here it was traced to cassava flour made from wild cultivars with a high cyanogenic content."

"But if this cassava pie that we're talking about was made from properly prepared cassava, it couldn't be the cause of death? Right?" Holly asked.

"Not from the naturally occurring cyanide in the cassava." Becky gazed at the two other women, puzzled. "You think this Ms. Carson could have poisoned her pie? Why would she do that? What's her motive?"

Jamie and Holly looked at her, then at each other.

"That's a good point," Holly admitted. "Why would Wilhelmina Carson want to murder three Oleander presidents? Is she in the running for president herself?"

"No. Because Anne McGinney is the current vice-president. Remember she told us that?"

"I do. She went into hysterics, as I recall." Becky's voice was tart.

Holly tapped her lip in thought. "Technically, Mrs. McGinney is now president, and Sybil Worthington is vice-president. Mama told me that," she added. "And there are lots of other motives for murder. Love, revenge, control, money, fear, power. Maybe there's a connection between the victims we don't know about."

"Perhaps Derek would know," Jamie said. "Didn't you say Denise told you he knew Freda Sinclair?"

"As a customer," Holly agreed. "But she did say Derek was suspicious about her mom's death—and Freda's. Yes, we should definitely speak to him again. If he's up to talking to us, that is. After all, his aunt just died."

"He was at the expo yesterday." Becky frowned. "I asked him if there was anyone else who could run his booth, but he said it helped take his mind off things. I hope he's not overdoing it. He looked a little stressed."

Jamie snorted. "Well, judging by what Myrtle told us about that family, I'd be surprised if he wasn't a lot stressed." In an overly nonchalant tone, she added, "We should check up on him—and Denise, of course—after we've spoken to Wilhelmina. Just to make sure they're both okay."

Ignoring the way Becky's eyebrows shot up in surprise, Holly shrugged.

"Sure."

19

As Jamie bounded out of the room, Becky turned to Holly, mouth agape. "What was that? Is she seriously interested in this Derek guy? But... but what about Thomas?"

The librarian's almost-wail made Holly laugh. "I think she just likes Derek's looks, to be honest. And you know your brother thinks we're like high school matchmakers, right?"

"We are not." Becky was indignant. "They're just so well-suited, Thomas and Jamie. If they didn't squabble so much."

"They like it." Holly grinned. "Just wait it out, Becky. Derek's going back to Azure on... When's the award ceremony again? Wednesday? Thursday?"

"Thursday night. The vendors pack up on Wednesday after lunch and we have a day to set up for the awards dinner. Thank goodness. It would have been a horrible rush trying to do the dinner on Wednesday. Most people are leaving on Friday, I believe, although I suppose some might skip the dinner." Becky frowned. "But will they all be allowed to leave? If Rob hasn't solved the case?"

Holly pursed her lips. "Hmmm. I hadn't thought of that. I wonder what he found out today. He said he was going to interview Derek and Denise this morning."

"Maybe they'll tell you when you and Jamie see them." Becky glanced back at her computer. "I'm going to do a little more research to keep Myrtle happy, and then I'm heading home. If you all decide to meet tonight, you could come to me if you like."

"Are you sure?" Holly smiled when her friend nodded. "Okay, I'll let the others know."

Upon leaving the still-crowded quilt expo, Holly paused on the library steps wondering what to do. The butterfly garden needed some more work; there were designs to touch up for Thomas's gardens; there were undoubtedly jobs to be done in both the Inn and in the slat houses. But...

She gazed up at the bright blue sky, with its wisps of clouds. It was a gorgeous day. Truffle would love to go for a walk, Holly mused. And she could use some time away from murder and motives.

Her mind made up, Holly headed for her car, and the Inn. She'd just check that her mother didn't need any help first.

Maggie's voice could be heard coming from the tearoom as Holly pushed open the front door to the Inn.

"Mr. Hartley." Maggie sounded overly patient. "There's nothing I can do. There's only one flight a day to Azure Isle and I'm afraid you've missed it. I'm sorry your meeting with the Inspector ran longer than anticipated, but he is investigating the suspicious death of your sister and I'm sure you want him to do all he can to find out what happened."

"Yes, of course I do!" Jonas Hartley snapped, preceding Maggie out of the room. "But I also have a busy practice and it's imperative I get back to it. If it wasn't that I had to ensure that my son—" He broke off. "Well, I suppose, if there are no charters then I shall just have to wait until tomorrow. Since the suite is not conducive to work, I shall remain here, Mrs. Gold. Perhaps I could have some tea and food?"

"Certainly." Maggie smiled. "I'll bring you a tray."

Holly hastened after her as she went towards the kitchen. "He missed his flight?"

Maggie gritted her teeth as she started preparing a tray with teapot, cup, and plate of pastries. "He did. He insisted on being present for Rob's interview with Derek, which ran later than expected, and then couldn't get to the airport on time. He's been bending my ear about it for the last half hour."

"But his sister died on Sunday!" Holly was flabbergasted.

Maggie set her lips as she poured boiling water into the pot. "It does seem rather coldhearted, I agree."

Holly blinked. That was a strong statement coming from her mother. Maggie usually saw the best in everyone. And for her to criticize a guest... Well, it just wasn't done! Jonas Hartley had really rubbed her mama the wrong way.

"Why are you back so early?" Maggie had a slight frown between her brows. "I thought you were going to be at the expo most of the day."

"No, I just helped Jamie with the lunches, then we got caught by the Tacky Turtles and were forced to do some quilting." Holly grinned as her mother's jaw dropped. "I put some stitches on your block. A Turtle called Caroline told me my sewing would just add to the charm of the quilt."

A snort of amusement escaped Maggie. "Caroline Cunningham?"

Holly shrugged. "Is she a Turtle? Then yeah, it might have been her. She did a butterfly on your block."

"That's her." Maggie smiled. "So, you did some quilting, did you? I'm impressed Holly Berry!"

"Jamie did too." Holly laughed outright at her mother's expression of disbelief. "And then we talked to Tansy and Sage Craft, and then Becky." She sobered. "Becky's a bit emotional right now—and still queasy."

"Mmmm. What is she, just over three months? Things might improve a little now. The first trimester is a roller-coaster, but most people feel better when they hit about thirteen weeks."

"She said her mom and grandma were sick the whole nine months."

"Oh dear. Well, hopefully she won't take after them." Maggie laid some cutlery on the tray and picked it up. "What are your plans for the rest of the day? Working on your butterfly garden? It looks lovely so far. I took a little walk out there earlier with Denise and she showed me what she'd planted. It was nice of you to involve her, Holly."

"Is Denise still here? She hasn't really gone to the expo much at all, has she?"

Maggie sighed. "Rosalie Becknell told me they've been quite worried about Denise since Daina died. They wanted her to come to Hibiscus because they didn't want to leave her alone. Rosalie is her godmother, you know."

"I heard that." Holly looked at her mother. "Where's Denise now? I was going to take Truffle for a walk. Maybe she'd like to join me."

Maggie's face lit up. "I think she'd love that, Holly. She's just taken a book out to the pool if you want to go find her."

DENISE, wrapped in a fluffy pink sweater with a fleecy blanket over her legs, was curled up on a deck chair by the pool. A paperback book lay open beside her, unread as the girl stared vacantly into space.

"Well, you look cozy." Holly was cheerful she approached the younger woman. "I like your sweater. Is it handmade?"

"Aunt Rosalie made it for me. For my eighteenth birthday," Denise answered in a dull tone.

"The color suits you." Holly sat down on a deckchair next to her. "Truffle and I are going for a little walk along the old railway trail. Would you like to come? It's an easy hike. Probably take about forty-five minutes or so. We'll be back in time for tea. What do you say?"

"I suppose." Denise didn't smile but she closed her book and swung her legs down to the ground. "Who's Truffle?"

"Our cavapoo. The little black dog I had when I came to your suite the other day."

A slight look of interest crossed Denise's face. "Oh yes, I remember. The one Derek was playing with. She was cute. She's a cavapoo? That's a cross between a poodle and a..."

"Cavalier spaniel," Holly supplied, standing up. "Come on. I'll introduce you properly, then we can head out. We can access the trail from the far side of the grounds."

TRUFFLE WAS A GREAT ICEBREAKER. Holly watched with amusement as the little dog frolicked and jumped around Denise, making the Azure girl laugh and throw the red ball down the trail again.

"How old is she?" Denise asked, as Truffle raced after it.

"Just over two, nearly two and a half now. My mother got her as a puppy after my dad died. She's a lovely little dog. Very friendly. She's a therapy dog, you know. Well, she's still sort of in training, but she visits the nursing home nearly every week." Holly watched Truffle galloping back with the ball. "Do you have any pets?"

"We used to have a cat. And we were thinking about getting a kitten when my mom got sick. It didn't make sense to get a pet at that time."

"No, probably not," Holly agreed. "Did you have any other family to help you when she was ill?"

"My mom was a single parent and an only child," Denise explained. "And I never knew my dad. Aunt Rosalie is probably the closest I have to a relative. She was my mom's best friend. She's been great. There was a lot to sort out after... after... Well, there was a lot to sort out, and I don't know how I'd have managed if Aunt Rosalie hadn't been there."

"I'm glad she was there for you." Holly picked up the ball that Truffle dropped at her feet. "No more throwing, Truff. We need to turn around now."

"It's a great walk. Did you say it was a railway at one time?"

"Yes. Ages ago. I think the trains stopped running in the 1940s and the trails were designated a National Park in the 1980s. They run right around the edge of the island and one track crosses over from north to south. That's the one we're on. The coastal trail is really pretty."

"So's this." Denise stopped as the path crested a small

hill. "Look, you can see all the way out to that island from here."

"That's Wreck Rock, smallest island in the Maritime Islands."

"The one Jamie's ancestor swam to from the wreck." Denise smiled at Holly's expression. "It was in the newspaper article Mr. Miller wrote. It was big news on Azure when you solved that murder." She paused. "That's why I thought you could help me find out about my mom."

"Did Inspector Tucker ask you about her this morning?" Holly asked.

"Yes. And he told me he'd contacted the police on Azure, and they said there was nothing suspicious. Which is what they kept telling me, too, but I'm sure there was something going on. Mom was getting better! And then suddenly all her symptoms came back in a rush!"

"Couldn't it have been a relapse?" Holly's tone was gentle. "I believe it's quite common for people to seem to improve and then go downhill again. It happened to my dad a couple of times during his treatment."

"I thought that at first," Denise admitted. "But then when Aunt Freda got sick... And now Mrs. Dill too. Well, don't you think it's suspicious?"

Holly was quiet for a moment. "Mrs. Dill was definitely poisoned with cyanide, but so far no one knows how. Unless something's been discovered today that I don't know about yet. If your mom was poisoned—and remember Denise, there's no evidence to say she was—do you have any idea how it could have happened?"

Denise shook her head. "I've thought about it over and over and I have no idea."

"Did..." Holly hesitated, then shrugged internally and

carried on. "Did a Ms. Carson ever visit your mom when she was sick?"

"Wilhelmina Carson? Oh yes. All the time. She kept bringing food for mom. Trying to tempt her appetite, she called it. She drove mom crazy, but she meant well, and neither of us had the heart to tell her to stop."

"What sort of food?"

"Oh, tons of different things. One week it was ginger-bread, then custard, then some weird kind of green smoothie. I can't even remember all the things she brought. Poor mom."

"Did she ever bring her cassava pie?" Holly asked. "Someone mentioned that to me."

Denise groaned. "Oh yes! Multiple times! It's her specialty, you know. Supposedly she makes the best cassava pie in the Maritime Islands!"

"Supposedly?"

"Well, I wouldn't know how good it really is. Neither Mom nor I like—liked—the stuff. Mom would be all polite and say thank you and then as soon as Ms. Carson left, she'd tell me to get rid of it." Denise giggled. "I used to scatter some of it for the birds so Mom could watch them from the window."

Holly stared at her in surprise. "Your mom hated cassava pie? You mean, she never even tried a little bit?"

"Ugh, no!" Denise shuddered. "I don't know how anyone eats it. It's horrible stuff!"

20

Jamie's face fell. "Really? Not even one tiny spoonful?"

Holly shook her head. "And the birds all seem to have survived, too, so I think we can assume there was nothing wrong with the cassava pie."

"Well, that throws that theory out the window, doesn't it? I guess the cassava lady can be crossed off the suspect list." Jamie sounded gloomy as she leaned forward to consider the treats Becky had placed on the coffee table.

Holly had relayed the librarian's invitation to the others and they had all repaired to the tiny cottage after an early supper. Holly loved the sunshine yellow walls, floral sofas, and antique wooden beams and floors in Becky's cozy home.

"Agreed." Myrtle was brisk. "Not that I ever suspected Wilhelmina Carson in the first place. Everyone knows she makes cassava pie. I doubt she'd be so obvious. And what motive could she have? She was good friends with all three women and has no intention of running for president of the Oleanders."

Becky shifted in her armchair, making Hibiscus, her small black cat, mew in protest. She stroked the kitten with a soft finger. "And in any case, I thought you said no one touched the cassava pie at the tea on Sunday, Myrtle."

The septuagenarian nodded. "That's correct. It's not a suitable dish for afternoon tea. I told Wilhelmina that, but she didn't listen."

Holly suppressed a grin at the disapproving expression on Myrtle's face. "Well, I asked Denise as many questions as I could think of—most of which Rob seems to have also asked, by the way—and she couldn't give me a single suggestion for how her mother could have been poisoned!"

Becky pursed her lips. "Or *why* she would have been." She held up a hand as Jamie opened her mouth. "I know what you're going to say. Mrs. McGinney thinks it's because they were quilt club presidents, but that seems highly unlikely to me. I think we should try to find out if there's anything else that links these three women in some way. That could suggest a different motive."

Everyone looked at Myrtle, who frowned. Holly, eyeing her more closely, thought the septuagenarian looked uneasy for some reason.

Myrtle's voice was clipped as she spoke in brief bullet points. "Daina was a single mother, no family, one daughter. She died at the age of fifty-three. Freda was seventy when she died. A widow with two children. Sally was also widowed. No children. Parents deceased. One brother. She was fifty-eight."

"What about jobs?" Becky asked. "What did they all do?"

"Before she got sick, Daina was a teacher; Freda was a homemaker; and Sally ran the family business. I believe they all did yoga at one point, if my memory serves me correctly. You have to remember, I only saw them once a year at the quilt expo. I occasionally visited Azure to see Sally, and we would all have tea if everyone was free. But in general, I relied on emails or social media to keep in touch."

"Did they live near each other?" Jamie was curious. "I've never been to Azure. I know it's bigger than our island, but did Daina, Freda, and Sally move in the same social circles or anything?"

Myrtle snorted. "Azure Isle really only has one social circle—an elite one. It's a very wealthy little island. I know that Freda and Sally both belonged to the same golf club, but I'm not sure if Daina was a member. She wouldn't have been playing during the last couple of years if she was."

"I think we should also consider location and timing," Holly added. "Daina and Freda died on Azure; Sally was poisoned here. There were two months between Daina and Freda's deaths, but only a month between Freda and Sally. Does that mean anything?"

Myrtle pursed her lips. The uneasy expression was back on her face. Holly had opened her mouth to ask why when Becky spoke.

"That's a good point, Holly." The librarian eyed Jamie, who was curled up in a flowered armchair. "Jamie, you said you were going to speak to Derek Hartley. Did he say anything helpful?"

"I only saw him briefly." Jamie frowned. "His mom and grandmother interrupted us. They really don't get on very well in that family. And Mrs. Worthington was quite snippy about Derek's jewelry. I mean, it's not my taste either, but I wouldn't make nasty comments about it."

"What sort of nasty comments?" Holly asked.

Jamie shrugged. "Something about it not paying the bills. It didn't seem to bother Derek, but I thought it was kind of mean."

"Well, from what I understand, Derek chose to study the

arts at college, which annoyed everyone," Myrtle said. "Sybil wanted him to do business, Jonas wanted him to do law and join the family firm, and Ellen wanted him to do medicine. Instead, he opened a jewelry shop."

"Sounds like a pretty strong character to me," Becky noted. "Does he have siblings?"

Myrtle shook her head. "No."

"Well, I only managed to chat with him for a few minutes. He's very upset about his Aunt Sally, of course, but he did say he'd had suspicions about Daina Trott and Freda Sinclair." Jamie nodded at Holly. "Freda, in particular. He said her symptoms were strange."

"Strange in what way?"

"They weren't like regular flu symptoms, he said. They came and went."

"Huh." Holly chewed her lip. "Denise told me Freda Sinclair had an episode in Derek's shop one day. Got dizzy and had to sit down. Is that what he means?"

"Maybe. As I said, we were interrupted."

There was a short silence, causing François, who was ambling through to the kitchen from the den where he was catching up on a soccer game, to pause.

"Why the silence, detectives? Is the case causing problems?"

Jamie scowled at him. "Don't smirk, François."

Her chef and business partner grinned, holding up his hands. "I wouldn't dream of it." He perched on the arm of the chair Becky was sitting in, resting his hand on her shoulder. "Anything I can help with?"

"Sure. Tell us how Sally Dill was poisoned."

François looked surprised. "I heard it was at the tea party on Sunday. I just assumed it was something she ate."

"Well, of course it was something she ate, François," Jamie began.

"No, wait. What *did* she eat?" Holly looked thoughtful. "We've ruled out the cassava pie, but what else was at the tea party?"

"Good point. Because we know it wasn't Maggie who put poisoned food on the table. So, what did Sally Dill eat that no one else did?" Becky looked at François with approval.

"Glad I could help." François's complacent grin faded in sudden concern. "Wait a minute! You're all being careful, right? I hope you're not going to be confronting any murderers like the last time! And you're telling Rob everything, right?"

Jamie rolled her eyes. "Yes, yes, yes. We're under orders from the Inspector. Don't worry! Becky's perfectly safe."

Becky smiled at her husband's dubious expression. "I told you Rob laid down the law. This is more along the lines of a theoretical investigation."

"Keep it that way," François warned before giving the top of Becky's head a kiss and strolling out of the room.

Jamie scowled. "What is it with all these bossy men? 'Keep it that way?' Your husband's getting as bad as your brother, Becks!"

"It's called caring," Becky said with a smile. "I seem to recall Thomas issuing some orders of his own last year."

"Huh. And how did that work for him?" Jamie huffed in remembered annoyance. "Hey, where is Miller anyway? Didn't anyone invite him?"

"I did. He said he was pursuing a lead and couldn't make it." Holly's eyes danced as she waited for the explosion that was sure to come.

"Pursuing a lead?"

"What lead?"

Myrtle and Jamie spoke together. Indignation laced Jamie's voice.

Holly shrugged. "I've no idea. He said he'd catch up with us later when he has time."

"When he has—? The gall of that man!" Jamie's eyes narrowed. "We need to figure out what's going on—and fast!" She rounded on Myrtle. "Exactly who was at that tea party again? And what food was there? Because I think that's what we should focus on."

Again, a reluctant expression crossed Myrtle's face. "Elma Foster, Anne McGinney, Ellen Hartley, Sybil Worthington, Wilhelmina Carson, Rosalie Becknell, and myself. And Sally, of course."

"I think we can rule out Auntie Elma," Holly said, keeping an eye on Myrtle. "She has no motive, and no connection to the deaths on Azure."

"Yeah, and it looks like Wilhelmina's off the hook as well. If no one ate her cassava pie, that is."

"Plus, she doesn't appear to have a motive," Becky agreed with Jamie.

"So... Anne, Ellen, Sybil, and Rosalie..." Jamie pursed her lips before looking at Myrtle. "You know them all better than us. Any grudges?"

Myrtle hesitated. "Sybil and Sally occasionally had words, but that was normal for them. Rosalie was Daina's best friend. She would never have hurt her, and she had a good relationship with Sally, from what I could see. Ellen was Sally's sister-in-law. Anne..."

As Myrtle's voice trailed away, everyone looked at her.

"What about Anne?" Jamie sat up, her eyes narrowed with suspicion. "What have you thought of?"

"Apparently Anne and Sally had a falling-out a few months ago," Myrtle admitted with reluctance.

"What sort of a falling-out?" Holly raised an eyebrow.

"About the structure of the Oleander Quilting Society."

"And?" Jamie prompted with impatience when Myrtle paused. "What happened?"

Myrtle sighed. "I only learned this today. And I was going to tell you but... Well, apparently, Sally put forward a motion to rewrite their constitution. Anne opposed it."

"The Oleanders have an actual constitution? Wow. Is that normal for quilt clubs?" Holly asked in surprise. "Do the Patchworkers have one? I've never heard Mama mention it."

"No. On Hibiscus, we get together very informally because we like quilting. There are lots of little sub-groups that meet, and we only come together as 'Patchworkers' at the annual expo because of the contests—for the Maritime Thimble Award. I believe the other clubs are the same. But the Oleanders have always taken their organization much more seriously."

"It's probably from belonging to all those elite clubs and things." Jamie rolled her eyes. "All those rules and bylaws go to their heads. Snobbish, like you told Mrs. McGinney at dinner the other night."

Myrtle opened her mouth as if to refute the statement, then closed it. "They have a very formal organizational structure, yes."

"Regardless of what we personally think about the internal workings of various clubs," Becky intervened as Jamie looked set to expand on her ideas, "I think what's important is that Anne McGinney had an altercation with Sally Dill over the structure of the Oleanders. When Sally Dill became president in December, did this issue come up again?"

Everyone looked at Myrtle, who winced. "Yes. In fact, it came up when Freda Sinclair was president as well."

"What?" Jamie exclaimed. "Myrtle, this is important! This is a real motive!"

As Myrtle sagged in her seat, Holly looked at the septuagenarian in dismay. Myrtle never wilted in the face of an argument. What was going on?

Before Holly could speak, Becky's gentle voice intervened. "They're your friends. This must be very difficult for you, Myrtle."

Jamie had uncurled from the armchair and was pacing up and down. At Becky's words, however, she stopped to peer at Myrtle. "Oh." After a moment's hesitation, she crossed to the sofa and plopped down beside the older woman. "Sorry. Um... Do you want a cup of tea or something?"

"No, I don't want a cup of tea! And you can stop treating me as if I'm an old woman, Jamie White. I'm perfectly fine!" Myrtle glared at Jamie before smiling across the room at Becky. "But thank you for your concern, my dear."

Holly smothered a smile as Jamie's eyes bulged at this blatant favoritism, noticing that, despite the setdown, Jamie remained sitting next to Myrtle.

Myrtle sighed. "As I said, I only heard about this for the first time today. From Elma. She tracked me down at the expo after speaking to Holly and Thomas. Apparently there was a heated conversation at tea on Sunday before I arrived, and she thought I should know about it."

"That's what she didn't want to tell Thomas and me." Holly nodded in comprehension. "Because Auntie Elma doesn't like to—"

"Wait!" Jamie interrupted. "Did you say Anne and Sally were arguing at the tea?"

"According to Elma, everyone was arguing. She said she felt quite uncomfortable and was about to excuse herself and leave when Sally collapsed." Myrtle cleared her throat.

"What was the argument about?"

"Sally said it didn't matter what Sybil and Anne thought. She was going to raise the issue of the constitution at the next meeting and push to have it altered. According to Elma, she said their club was elitist, snobby, excluded people, and was discriminatory. And that she was going to see to it that it changed, no matter what." Myrtle hesitated.

"And? What else? I know something else happened!" Jamie stared at the older woman.

"And then Anne apparently said she'd see Sally dead before that happened." Myrtle sighed in exasperation as Jamie gave an exclamation. "But it was just a figure of speech. Anne gets overwrought at times. I've heard her say things like that occasionally when she's been carrying on about the Oleanders."

"Yeah, but this time"—and Jamie's voice was dark—"someone actually died!"

21

A stubborn look crossed Myrtle's face. "I refuse to believe that Anne McGinney has anything to do with this. I've known her for years!"

"Plus," Holly began, then paused, trying to gather her thoughts.

Becky leaned forward in a conciliatory manner. "I'm not saying she's responsible, but there are some circumstantial things to consider, Myrtle. Anne and Sally were on opposing sides of what appears to be a controversial topic for the Oleanders. Did the issue actually go to a vote while Daina Trott was president? You didn't say."

Myrtle shook her head. "From what Elma told me, it didn't. Daina was ill and they postponed it. Then she died. When Freda took over, the issue was raised again."

"And then Freda died!" Jamie exclaimed.

"Yes, but—" Holly's attempt to speak was cut off.

"Then Sally became president, declared her intention to change the constitution and died. It's a pattern! This has to be the motive!" Jamie's eyes were bright with excitement.

"The Oleanders have kept this very quiet." Becky

frowned. "I mean, you didn't know about it, Myrtle, and there's been no talk at the expo at all. I wonder why they all let loose in front of Auntie Elma."

"Elma had left the table to chat with Sarah Flynn for a few minutes. When she returned, Sally was speaking her mind. Elma said she tried to change the subject, but no one listened to her. As I said, she was about to excuse herself again when Sally collapsed. I arrived at that moment, but by then, the argument—obviously—was completely forgotten."

"Where's Mrs. McGinney now?" Holly asked.

"Hmm?" Myrtle looked surprised. "Oh, she's having dinner with Sybil and Ellen. I said I'd pick her up afterwards."

"I don't think she should be staying with you," Jamie exclaimed. "It's not safe!"

Myrtle stiffened. "Anne McGinney is not a murderer! And I won't hear another word against her."

Before Jamie could respond, Myrtle's phone rang from inside her bag. With another glare at the younger woman, the septuagenarian picked up her purse and fished around inside. Holding up a hand for silence, she answered the phone. "Hello? Yes... Yes... Sybil, slow down! I can't understand you. What happened?... What?... When?... Good heavens!"

"What's happened?" Jamie hissed.

Myrtle flapped a hand at her. "Has the doctor been called, Sybil?... Yes... Yes... Oh, well, that's a great relief... Yes, of course. I'll be right there."

Hanging up, Myrtle turned to the three younger women, who were now waiting anxiously.

"Well? Don't just sit there! What happened?" Jamie was impatient.

An incongruously smug look crossed Myrtle's face. "What's happened is I've been proven right. Anne McGinney is not a murderer! In fact, there's just been an attempt on her life!"

~

BY THE TIME HOLLY, Myrtle, and Jamie arrived at the Hibiscus Inn, a shaken Anne McGinney was wrapped in a blanket on one of the overstuffed sofas in the lobby, being plied with a cup of tea by a hovering Ellen Hartley while Sybil Worthington huddled with a group of whispering Oleanders just inside the breakfast room. Thomas Miller, notebook in hand, was talking quietly to a worried-looking Derek Hartley at the bottom of the stairway that led to the upper floor of the Inn.

Seeing the two men in intense conversation, Jamie paused in indecision. As Myrtle hurried to her friend's side, and Jamie hovered, Holly detoured to the kitchen, from where she could hear voices. She paused in the doorway.

"She appears to be fine," Doc Eastham was saying to Rob. "A few bruises, but it looks like the bushes broke her fall. I've given her something for the pain, and something to help her sleep if she needs it."

"She fell? From where?" Jamie came up in a rush behind Holly, peering over her shoulder into the kitchen.

Denise Trott sat at the island in the kitchen, a cup of tea in front of her. Maggie, wearing comfortable sweat pants and a grey hoodie, stood beside her, her dark hair disheveled, worried blue eyes watching the inspector and doctor.

Rob's head swung around, then he sighed. "Dare I ask how you heard about this so quickly?"

"Mrs. Worthington called Myrtle," Holly answered, venturing further into the room before looking at her mother. "Are you okay, Mama?"

Doc Eastham produced a reassuring smile for Holly. "Everyone's fine. Just a bit of a shock, that's all."

"A loud scream in the night does that to a person. It definitely startled Wilhelmina and me," Maggie admitted, laying a hand on a pale-faced Denise's shoulder. "Drink that, Denise. I put some extra sugar in."

The young woman shuddered, then sipped at the hot, milky tea.

"I'll just check Mrs. McGinney again and then I'm heading back to the hospital. The stubborn woman's refused to be admitted, and I must say I can't see any reason to force the issue." Doc Eastham grimaced. "I'll swing past Myrtle's house in the morning to do another inspection, but I think she'll be fine. I'd hold off on questioning her anymore until tomorrow, Inspector. She's going to be a bit shaky for a while."

Rob nodded. "I'll do that. Thanks, Doc."

The doctor looked at Denise. "And you, young lady, take those pills I gave you and get some sleep. You'll feel much better for it. Your Aunt Rosalie says she'll stay with you again tonight."

When Denise offered a tremulous nod, he gave her an avuncular pat on the shoulder before swinging out of the room.

"Finish that up, Denise." Maggie spoke briskly. "And then Rosalie and I will get you all settled for the night. Come along."

Denise drained the cup of tea, gave Holly a wobbly smile, then followed Maggie from the kitchen. As soon as they'd disappeared, Jamie rounded on Rob.

"Well?" she demanded. "What happened?"

The inspector pinched the bridge of his nose before directing a plaintive look at Holly. "Do you think I could have a cup of tea as well? Before this one starts badgering me?"

Holly gave him a half-smile. "Don't you have to talk to people?"

"Not now. I've already got statements from everyone who was here. I only have a preliminary statement from Mrs. McGinney, but you heard the doctor about that. I'll visit tomorrow. And yes," he continued as Jamie opened her mouth, "I've already asked Sergeant Hollis to make sure Mrs. McGinney gets home safely, and to have a constable remain outside this evening. Not that I expect there to be any further attempts on her life tonight."

Jamie pounced. "You think there was an attempt on her life? Aha! But do you know that—?" She stopped when Rob turned his back on her.

"The tea?" he begged Holly.

"If you've finished asking questions, let's go through to our part of the Inn," Holly suggested. "There were a lot of Oleanders whispering in doorways when we came in. I think it's better if we go somewhere private."

"What about Miller? Can he come too?" When Rob rolled his eyes but nodded, Jamie disappeared out the door.

Rob glanced sideways at Holly as they walked along the corridor leading to her part of the Inn. "I take it the HIDC had a meeting tonight? I notice Becky's not with you."

"No. François exerted his manly authority and insisted she stay home."

"Good for Francois!"

Rob's look of approval made Holly roll her eyes. "Not," she added in pointed tones, "that it would have stopped her had she wanted to come. But she didn't. She said there'd be enough people here and you wouldn't need another body taking up space."

"Sensible of her." Rob was clearly trying not to smile. Crossing the small interior courtyard that separated the main part of the Inn from Holly and Maggie's family quarters, he held the door open for Holly.

As an excited Truffle cavorted around them, the inspector laughed, crouching down to play with the little dog.

"You don't seem too concerned about this murder attempt," Holly said, glancing over her shoulder as she put the kettle on. "How come?"

Rob gave Truffle a final pat, then stood up. Shrugging out of his dark grey suit jacket, he laid it over the arm of the sofa before loosening his tie and taking a seat at the kitchen island.

"I'm not convinced yet that it was a murder attempt. I don't have enough information."

"So, what? You think she just fell over— Where did she fall anyway?" Holly paused in the making of a pot of tea.

"She toppled over that little stone wall right outside the Lantana room." Thomas's voice was indecently cheerful as he reported this news, Holly thought, watching the journalist and Jamie enter the room.

"The Lantana suite?" she repeated, frowning. "But that's not a long drop at all. It's more like a—"

"Gentle slope full of shrubbery. Yep." Thomas slid onto a stool beside the inspector, directing a grin her way. "Got any coffee, Holls? Tea's insipid stuff."

"Insipid?" Rob looked down his nose at Thomas. "That's my national drink you're maligning, Miller."

"There're two reasons tea was dumped in Boston Harbor, you know. Taxes and taste." Thomas guffawed.

"I won't even dignify that comment with an answer."

"Stop horsing around, you two!" Jamie scolded. "This is serious. If someone actually tried to kill Mrs. McGinney, then she can't be the murderer, can she? And that messes up my theory."

Rob raised an eyebrow. "You think Mrs. McGinney is a murderer? Perhaps you should fill me in."

Thomas smirked. "Yeah, go ahead, White. Tell the inspector why you think the McGinney is a murderess most foul."

As Rob accepted his cup of tea from Holly with a smile, pulling a stool closer to him for her to perch on, Jamie shot an irritated look at the journalist.

"Shut up, Miller. It's a perfectly good theory and you know it. Like I told you, as president, Anne McGinney can refuse to entertain the motion to rewrite the constitution of the Oleanders. Plus, Sally Dill was the one who wanted it rewritten. Remove Sally, become president, and problem solved."

Jamie must have talked Thomas's ear off, Holly thought, for her to have filled him in on everything so fast.

"And I say it's too far-fetched."

"Far-fetched? How's it far-fetched?"

Holly sighed, taking a sip of her tea. Feeling Rob's gaze on her, she glanced sideways to see his eyes dancing with mirth. She elbowed him hard. "You already know about this constitution thing, don't you?"

"I have made some enquiries, you know." Rob's voice was mild. He took a sip from his cup. "And I had an interview with Mrs. Worthington and Mrs. Hartley, you may recall. I heard a good many details about the Oleander Quilting Society."

Holly eyed him with suspicion. "You said you're not sure this was a murder attempt tonight, Rob. How come?"

Jamie's head whipped around. "You're not sure? But she was pushed over a wall!"

"She says she was pushed. No one saw it. And she was a little tipsy." Thomas mimed tilting a drink to his lips. "Besides, no one could be killed rolling down that slope. All those pink-flowered things stopped her fall."

"Dwarf oleanders. There're a few of those in that garden," Holly offered.

Thomas laughed. "Well, that's weirdly appropriate."

"No one saw her fall?" Holly returned to Thomas's earlier comment. "What was she doing out there anyway?"

"Getting some fresh air apparently. Or so Sybil Worthington says. She also said, rather scathingly I thought, that Anne never could handle her wine." Thomas consulted his notes. "Ellen Hartley says they'd had dinner—takeout from The White Horse—and were having an after-dinner aperitif when Anne brought up this constitution topic. According to Mrs. Hartley, she got quite heated when Sybil reminded her she couldn't dismiss the item, since it was already on the agenda."

"Yes, but—"

He held up a hand to stop Jamie from speaking. "My turn now, White. According to Mrs. Hartley, Anne McGinney knew the motion to rewrite the constitution..." Thomas paused, rolling his eyes. "Honestly, I have a hard time believing the things I'm hearing about this. I thought people quilted because it was an enjoyable hobby."

"It's supposed to be," Holly said. "The Oleanders do seem to have rather rigid rules, don't they?"

"I'll say. Anyway, the McGinney knew she couldn't dismiss the item. Ergo, why kill Sally Dill? For that matter, why kill Daina Trott? According to Sybil Worthington, there was a lot of support for Anne's position."

"Huh. Okay, I'll grant you that one," Jamie reluctantly agreed.

"And why kill Freda? All that did was push the vote back even further and it meant Sally would be the next president, which wouldn't help Anne's case at all. Plus," Holly hesitated, then shot an apologetic glance at Jamie, "Anne McGinney is the one who brought all this up in the first place. If she was the murderer, why would she do that?" Holly flinched when her friend turned an accusatory look on her. "I'm just saying—"

"I know what you're saying! I know what Miller's saying too! But who else could it be then?" Jamie exclaimed.

Holly tightened her lips against a smile as Thomas winked at her.

"Well, here's the thing, White"—the journalist's tone was provocative—"if the McGinney is correct in her claim that she was pushed, why would that be? Who wants the— correct me if I'm wrong—new president of the Oleander Quilting Society dead?"

Jamie's head came up, her eyes narrowing in thought.

22

———

Holly paused with her cup of tea midway to her mouth. "Oh wow. You're not suggesting there really is a serial killer on the island, are you?"

"I don't think that's the case at all."

The mildness of Rob's response had both women looking at him with immediate suspicion.

"You know something we don't, don't you? Rob, you said you'd share!" Jamie's accusation morphed into a wail of frustration.

The inspector was unfazed. "You seem to have ferreted out quite a lot on your own."

"We don't know how the cyanide was administered, though." Holly raised an eyebrow at Rob. "Do you? Was it in something at the tea party like we think?"

"Aha! I know that!" Thomas grinned when Jamie transferred her look of frustration to him, holding up his hands in self-defense. "I only just found out! I promise I haven't been hoarding clues, White!"

Rob frowned. "And who provided you with this information?" He sighed when Thomas's grin just widened. "A sacrosanct source. I see. Never mind. I trust I can rely on you not to publish anything that could compromise my case?"

"Of course. *The Island Gazette* is on the side of justice, Inspector. I'm a bit offended you would ask that."

The inspector snorted. "Offended? In a pig's eye, you are! Just keep it out of the paper for now, Miller. I'll tell you when you can publish."

Thomas produced a snappy salute. "Aye, aye, *mon capitaine!*"

"Miller! What. Do. You. Know?" Jamie bit out the words through gritted teeth. "And stop playing games. Sally Dill's death isn't funny."

The journalist sobered immediately. "You're right, Jamie. It's not." He laid a hand over hers. "I'm sorry."

Holly watched her best friend's mouth drop open before she pulled her hand from beneath Thomas's. Clearing her throat, Jamie shot a look of appeal at Holly.

"How was Sally Dill poisoned?" Holly got straight to the point, drawing attention away from her uncharacteristically flustered friend.

"She took it herself."

Holly gaped at Thomas. "What? You're saying it was suicide after all?"

"No. Not unless she was poisoning herself in a very Russian roulette sort of way." Rob set his teacup down on the island counter, his face sober. "This goes no further than here, of course. In Sally Dill's possession we found a box of herbal capsules that had been tampered with. Several capsules contained cyanide salts in varying concentrations."

"Herbal capsules?" Jamie exclaimed. "What kind?"

"Turmeric curcumin. A natural remedy for inflammation. Mrs. Dill used it to help with mild joint pain," Rob said.

"She didn't get those from The Black Cat." Holly was definite.

Rob looked puzzled. "The Black Cat?"

"The shop on Juniper Island run by the Craft family. They supply the Inn with soaps and things. They've had some business problems because of rumors that their products could be poisoned."

The inspector nodded. "Ah. This would be the two sisters you were telling me about earlier. The ones you were meeting with?"

"Yeah, well they're off the hook," Jamie said, twiddling one of the large gold hoops in her ear as she avoided looking at Thomas. "We already checked them out. And they showed us spreadsheets of all their inventory. Holly's right. They don't sell turmeric capsules."

"Good to know." Rob smiled. "And good investigating on your part."

Thomas intervened. "My source told me the capsules were a generic brand but expertly taken apart and re-filled. Most of the tampered-with capsules had very low doses— ones that would only cause very mild symptoms, although cyanide does build up in the body over time."

A frown crossed the inspector's face at the word 'source,' but he agreed. "Yes, that's correct. But some capsules had lethal concentrations of cyanide, including the one Mrs. Dill took on Sunday."

"Anne McGinney and Rosalie Becknell both said Sally had some strange episodes of nausea and weakness." Holly frowned in thought. "And you said it was possible to poison someone with cyanide over a long period of time, right?"

Rob nodded.

"So, if she took a mildly laced capsule every now and then, she could have had those weird symptoms?"

The inspector gave a second nod. "That's our assumption. It would have to be minute amounts in those capsules, I might add. Cyanide is highly toxic."

"Did Sally take these capsules every day?" Jamie asked.

"Apparently not. Mrs. Sybil Worthington informed me that Sally has been taking them for some time, but only as needed. Bearing in mind that her symptoms started very recently, we believe the cyanide was only added in the last month."

Jamie narrowed her eyes at the inspector. "Just how long have you known about these capsules, Rob?"

"We confiscated everything in Mrs. Dill's room on Sunday. Once cyanide was confirmed, the lab checked everything and found the altered capsules. I've also contacted my colleagues on Azure Isle to ask them to search Mrs. Dill's house in case there are more contaminated medications." He shrugged. "I told you I'd share what I was able to. And I'll add that you only told me about your Black Cat information just now."

"Because we haven't seen you!" Jamie retorted.

Rob's look was mild. "Exactly."

"You mentioned Russian roulette, Inspector," Thomas intervened. "What you're saying is that Sally Dill could have died at any time, in any place. In other words—"

Jamie groaned. "You're saying her death is completely unrelated to the tea party on Sunday. It doesn't matter who was there because no one handed her a poisoned parfait. And that means—"

"—the murderer might not even be on Hibiscus Island!" Thomas concluded. "Exactly. Two minds with but a single thought, White."

Jamie flushed and looked at Rob in enquiry. "Well?"

"That's entirely possible," the inspector conceded.

~

"I'M FRUSTRATED!"

"No! Really? I would never have guessed!" Holly rolled her eyes at her friend's dramatic statement.

When a tired-looking Maggie had eventually appeared, the inspector and journalist had immediately said their goodbyes. Jamie had stayed on. With her father and step-mother in Florida, living the "good life" as she called it, and her mother "finding herself" somewhere in the world—last known destination, Arizona—Jamie had adopted the Hibiscus Inn as a second home, and Maggie as her surrogate mother.

The two younger women had fussed over Maggie until, exasperated, she'd ordered them off to bed and disappeared into her own bedroom, taking Truffle with her for company.

Although Jamie frequently slept in one of the Inn's suites, she was also happy to camp out on Holly's sofa when-ever she spent the night. Now she threw herself back against said sofa and repeated her words.

"I'm *very* frustrated!"

Holly, who had been clicking aimlessly through television channels, sighed, clicked the off button on the remote, and turned to give her volatile friend her full attention.

"Okay. Why are you frustrated?" A grin edged Holly's mouth. "Would this have anything to do with a certain newspaper owner calling you 'Jamie' for probably the first time ever and holding your hand? Oh wait! You said 'frus-trated,' not flustered.'"

"He didn't hold my hand! And I wasn't flustered!" Jamie protested.

"Oh, you totally were. You turned those big brown eyes of yours towards me and said, 'Help me.'" Holly laughed and ducked when Jamie picked up a cushion and swung it at her.

"I'm frustrated," Jamie said with dignity, "because first of all, Thomas, Rob, and Myrtle have hoarded clues; and secondly, it could have been anyone who put the cyanide in the capsules!"

Tucking her legs beneath her blue fleecy robe, Holly pushed her red-gold curls off her face and gave the comment some thought. "Not really. It had to be someone who knew Sally took turmeric, had access to the capsules, and time to make the substitutions—oh, and had access to cyanide salts." She frowned. "There's something about those capsules that I think I should know. Something I overheard at some point."

"What?"

"I can't remember. It'll come to me." Holly shrugged. "In the meantime, maybe we need to focus more on means and opportunity instead of motive."

Jamie's eyes narrowed. "You're right. We need to find out if Mrs. McGinney ever visited Sally Dill's house! If so, she could have put the cyanide in the capsules!"

Holly rolled her eyes. "Maybe we shouldn't focus our entire attention on one person. What if the murders have nothing to do with the Oleanders at all?"

"Huh." Jamie gave that some thought.

"I wonder how one gets hold of cyanide salts?" Holly mused.

"What?"

"Well, it's a deadly poison, isn't it? I can't imagine it's sold on shelves, so how did the murderer get hold of it?"

"No idea. We'll have to ask Becky to do some more research."

~

OLEANDERS WERE MILLING around the breakfast room and foyer of the Hibiscus Inn bright and early the next day, buzzing with a mixture of emotions. Excitement about the quilt show judging was tempered with sorrow and speculation about Sally Dill's death. The quilters didn't seem to know exactly what behavior was appropriate.

As Holly pushed a trolley laden with pastries into the room, she spotted Derek Hartley and Denise Trott sitting at a table by the window.

"Good morning. Can I get you a refill of anything?" Holly paused beside them, noticing Denise was just pushing scrambled eggs about her plate in an aimless fashion. "Or something different to eat?"

The younger woman produced a wan smile. "No, this is fine, thanks." She hesitated. "Holly, how's Mrs. McGinney? Have you heard?"

"Myrtle called this morning. She's absolutely fine." Holly gave the Azure islander a reassuring smile. "A couple of bruises, but nothing to worry about."

"Is she still saying she was pushed?"

"Yes. And she was!" Denise glared at Derek.

As Derek sighed, Holly eyed him with interest. "Did you hear it when it happened? I understand she gave quite a loud scream."

"She did. It scared me half to death." Denise shuddered. "I'd just come up to the Inn to get some hot chocolate to take back to my room and there was this almighty screech. She sounded terrified! I just froze at first. I didn't know what to do. And then everyone came running out of the Inn to see what happened, so I went back with them. And then I... Well, I kind of fell apart when I saw what had happened."

"I didn't hear any screams, but I had the television on pretty loud," Derek said. "But I heard the commotion afterwards." He frowned. "Someone hammered on my door, so I came out to see what was going on, and everyone was carrying on in the dark like there was a house on fire. My mother told me what had happened, and I went over the wall after Mrs. McGinney."

"Yeah, he'd just got her up to the top when Maggie, Wilhelmina, and I arrived," Denise offered.

"Someone hammered on your door? Who?"

Derek blinked. "No idea. I assumed it was my grandmother or mother. My room's just round the path from theirs on that level of the garden."

"Yeah, I know. You're in the Poinsettia suite, aren't you?" Holly gazed into space, visualizing the layout of the Inn rooms.

The Hibiscus Inn flowed down a terraced hillside, with rooms and wings being added over time, as the wallets and fancies of previous owners allowed. The result was an intricate labyrinth of interior curving staircases and passages winding down the hillside, connecting the main house and the various levels. Visiting children adored this maze of corridors for the opportunities it afforded hide-and-go-seek games, but adult visitors usually preferred the more straightforward exterior paths that led to the outside entrances of the rooms.

The Poinsettia suite, with four others, sprawled across the second level of the gardens, directly below the main house; three suites were situated in the main Inn building; and the final two reclined on the third terrace level.

Holly mentally reviewed the people in the second level suites. Sybil Worthington and Ellen Hartley shared the Lantana room; Derek occupied the Poinsettia; Denise was in the Nasturtium suite; Wilhelmina had the Frangipani room; and the Bougainvillea suite was occupied by a mousy Oleander who barely spoke—Janet Ross. She'd been having dinner with some quilters from Coral Island, and another couple of Oleanders—the Moncrieffs—and, according to Rob, had driven up in a taxi well after everything had happened.

Holly dismissed the other Oleander guests from consideration. Mr. and Mrs. Cherry, staying in the main house in the Hibiscus suite, and old Mrs. Sullivan in the Rose room had been playing cards in the breakfast room, well supplied with plates of shortbread and cups of tea.

If Mrs. McGinney had indeed been pushed over the wall, it had to have been by someone on the second level— or a complete outsider.

"Derek!" A voice interrupted Holly's musing. "We have to leave now." Mr. Jonas Hartley tapped his watch in a pointed fashion. "The taxi's waiting."

23

Derek got to his feet with a resigned smile. "And duty calls. I'll see you lovely ladies later."

As Holly watched him leave the room to join Jonas Hartley, there was an audible snort from Denise.

"Pitiful," she muttered.

Holly's eyebrows shot up. "What?"

"Well, he is," the younger woman complained.

"Mr. Hartley's pitiful? In what way?"

"Not Mr. Hartley. Derek. He needs to learn to stand up to his dad." Denise was indignant. "Mr. Hartley's always poking around his store, talking about paying bills, and managing finances, as if Derek has no idea how to run a business. And what does Derek do? Just stands there and takes it. He should stick up for himself!"

Intrigued, Holly slid into the chair opposite the young woman. "I heard Derek went against his father's wishes when he chose to go into the jewelry business."

"Well, yeah, okay. He did it one time. But that was because of his Aunt Sally. She thought he had talent and suggested he go for the arts. He makes some cool things."

Denise held up her wrist. "See this? My mom asked him to make me this charm bracelet when I graduated."

Holly admired the delicate chain strung with tiny gold charms. "Very pretty. Sounds like you've known Derek a long time. Has he always been a pitiful specimen?"

Denise blushed at the twinkle in Holly's eyes. "Okay. That was kind of mean, I know. He's not really that wimpy. Yeah, I've known him a while, but he's a good ten years older than me. We're not that close." Denise played with her fork, moving scrambled eggs around her plate. "He's been playing big brother ever since my mom died, though. It's a bit of a pain to be honest. He hovers." She glanced up at Holly.

"Hovers?"

"Yeah. He's always coming around, asking how things are, worrying about me, checking that I'm okay. I'm an adult, you know. I don't need a babysitter."

Holly suppressed a smile. "I'd say that sounds like he cares. Doesn't your Aunt Rosalie come over as well?"

"Yes. And Wilhelmina. And Mrs. Worthington. And Mrs. McGinney. And Pastor Robinson. And a gazillion other people! I'm never alone." Denise sighed. "I sound selfish and self-centered, I know, but I haven't had any real time to myself since Mom died and… I kind of need some space."

"I get that."

"You do?" Denise looked hopeful. "Did you feel like that? When your dad died?"

"I did," Holly replied. "In fact, after my dad died, I left Hibiscus Island altogether. I went back to the mainland for two years. I'd had a job there before Dad got sick, and I went running back to it."

"Really? And Maggie was okay with that? She told me to call her 'Maggie,'" Denise added.

Holly grinned at the quick aside. Despite her assertions of maturity, Denise was still quite young. "She didn't like it, but she said she understood. From where I am now, looking back, I wish I hadn't left. But at the time... I needed to."

Denise was quiet for a moment. She fiddled with her fork before meeting Holly's eyes. "I want to be me. I want to go someplace where people only see me. Not Daina Trott's daughter." Her eyes welled up with tears. "That sounds awful."

"It doesn't. And as I told you before, it will get better. It just takes time." Holly patted her hand in sympathy. "What are your plans for the day? It's the last day of the expo. Are you going?"

"I wanted to. It's the judging today, isn't it?" Denise wiped her eyes. "I'd like to see Aunt Rosalie's quilt in the show. She made it in memory of my mom."

"Oh, then you must see that! How about you come with me today? You can help Jamie and me serve the final lunches, then we'll go to the City Hall art gallery and check out the quilts. I'd like to see Mama's wall-hanging in the show as well. Oh, and the Flower Quilt should be finished by now. We can have a look at that too."

"Are you sure? You don't have to work in your garden or anything?"

"Nope. It can wait. I'll clear the breakfast room, check with Mama just to make sure she doesn't need any help with the rooms, and then we can head out." Holly glanced at her watch. "How about I meet you in the foyer at ten-thirty?"

Denise's smile was wide. "Okay."

∾

JAMIE GREETED the two women with enthusiasm when they walked into the Bean café. "Are you here to help? Oh, good! Come on back into the kitchen. François is just putting the last bento items into the boxes."

The chef looked harried as he zipped along an assembly line of boxes, deftly placing pieces of rolled up ham stuffed with arugula alongside a scoop of red lentil pasta salad. "Close the lids behind me, Jamie," he ordered. "You two can start putting the boxes into the cartons. *Vite, vite, mes amies.* You're going to be late if you don't get moving!"

"Relax, François, we've got plenty of time." But Jamie started snapping boxes shut at full speed.

Holly showed Denise how to pack the cartons and within twenty minutes the three women were in the Bean van, heading towards the library.

"Nice work! If you ever need a job, Denise, look me up." Jamie grinned at the Azure islander, whose eyes widened in surprise.

"Seriously?" she blurted.

"I'm going to need to hire new staff, yeah, but," Jamie added with a smile, "I don't expect you to leave Azure just for me. What'd you do at college, anyway? Got any jobs lined up at home?"

"I studied business. And there's nothing for me at home." Denise lapsed into silence, her brow furrowed.

Catching Jamie's eye, Holly shook her head, mutely telling her friend not to ask any more questions, and changed the subject. "You'll need to put your skates on when lunch starts," she said in a cheerful voice. "Jamie calls this feeding time at the zoo. These quilters definitely like their food."

Denise produced a small smile as they pulled into the parking lot behind the library. Leaping out, Jamie threw open the doors at the back of the van, unloaded the delivery trolley, and started piling cartons on it.

"If you'll take that bag of ice, Denise, you can follow Holly inside. I'll be right behind you."

~

"Phew!" Jamie wiped a dramatic hand across her forehead as the last bento box disappeared from the ice buffet. "And we're done!"

"I thought you were catering dessert for the awards dinner tomorrow night," Holly said in surprise.

"And we're done except for the dessert catering!" Jamie grinned. "But that's easy, Holls. François has everything ready. All we have to do is deliver it and stand back. We're not serving or anything." She looked at Denise in approval. "You were a big help just now. Thanks."

The Azure islander blushed, hesitated, then asked in a rush, "Were you serious about that job offer?"

Jamie blinked. "You want a job at the Bean?"

"I want a job away from Azure." Denise's blunt response made Jamie glance at Holly for help.

"You don't need to make any decisions right now, Denise." Holly was gentle. "You're not leaving till Saturday, I think your Aunt Rosalie said. Why don't you sit down with Jamie on Friday when it's quieter, and see what she has in mind? Then you can think it over."

"I could do that." Jamie nodded when Denise looked her way in appeal. "Afternoon tea? Yes? Cool. Now, weren't you two going to go see the quilt show?"

"Yes, but we can help if—"

"No, no." Jamie cut Holly off with a smile. "I can clean up. Are you going to check out the vendors one last time?

From what I remember there are some good bargains to be had on the final day. No one wants to take things home with them."

"I haven't been in the vendor hall yet," Denise admitted.

Jamie's mouth dropped open in mock-horror. "You haven't been shopping? Good grief, woman. Pull out that wallet. Go purchase something! *Vite, vite*, as François would say." She made shooing motions with her hand.

Denise giggled. "Do we have time?"

"Plenty," Holly assured her, glancing at her watch. "They're not supposed to start packing up the booths for another hour. And the judging's going on right now, so no one's allowed in the art gallery till it finishes. Come on. Let's go find some bargains."

As Jamie had predicted, prices had been lowered and the lecture hall was packed with last minute shoppers thronging the booths.

"Holly!"

Turning at the sound of her name, Holly's eyes widened at the sight of the woman hurrying towards her. "Natasha? When did you get here? *Why* are you here?"

The slim strawberry blonde grinned. "I flew in this morning. Caught a ride on the research center plane. Didn't Jamie tell you I was coming? She told me you found something at the wreck on the weekend."

"It must have slipped her mind," Holly said. "We've had a bit of excitement on the island this week."

"Yeah, I heard." The marine scientist rocked back on her heels, shoving her hands into the pockets of her khaki cargo pants. Her blue polo shirt sported the crest of the Ocean

Science Research Center. Seeing Denise eyeing it, Natasha stuck out her hand.

"Hi. I'm Natasha. Natasha Skinner. I work at the research center on Turtle Island. I'm helping with the *La Rosa de España* wreck project."

"Denise Trott. From Azure Isle."

Natasha's eyes lit up. "Really? Now that's an interesting island. I haven't made it there yet, but I hear you have a crater lake in the middle of the island. Right?"

Denise nodded. "Yeah. Mist Lake. It's inside our highest mountain. It's a fresh water nature reserve so lots of birds go there."

"One day I'll get there." Natasha grinned before turning to Holly. "Where's Jamie? Think she's free to chat? If not, I'm going to do a bit of shopping. I found this booth with the most amazing cookies!"

Holly laughed. "She's just packing up her lunch table in the courtyard, through there."

"I'll check in with her first, then. Where's the courtyard?" Natasha smiled her thanks as Holly pointed. "Nice to meet you, Denise. I'll look you up when I make it to Mist Lake. See you."

Denise laughed as the tall woman loped away. "She seems nice. What's her accent? She's not from the islands, is she?"

"No. England somewhere, she said. Devon? Or was it Cornwall?" Holly frowned. "I'm sorry. I can't quite remember. Somewhere down south, anyway. Natasha's a marine scientist, but don't ask me what she does because she lost me totally when she tried to explain it. She's helping to coordinate the wreck... uh... operations, I guess you'd say. I think mainly because she has a lot of contacts—marine archaeologists and people like that."

"Have you been to the wreck yet?" Denise asked as she and Holly threaded their way through the booths.

"Yes, a couple of times," Holly replied, pleased to see Denise looking cheerful. "There's not a lot to see but the main excavation doesn't start till the spring. We're all hoping there's stuff buried beneath the sand." Holly paused at a booth. "Look, Denise. These are the cookies we all think are fantastic!"

Denise had just finished purchasing a bag of cookies iced to look like a Bear Claw quilt block when the two women heard their names being called. At the sight of Jamie and Natasha heading towards them, Denise uttered a heart-felt sigh.

"What's that for?" Holly asked with amusement.

"Well, just look at them! They could be cover models." Denise sighed again with envy.

"It is pretty disgusting, I agree." Holly's comment made Denise giggle.

"Wait up!" Jamie called.

Holly smiled as the two women reached them. "Are you joining us? We're just about to head to the art gallery to see the results of the judging."

"We'll go there later but I wanted you to hear what Natasha just told me." Jamie lowered her voice. "You know we were wondering where you could get cyanide salts?"

"Yes, but we've asked Becky to research that for us."

"Well, Natasha says— You tell them, Nat." Jamie waved a hand for her friend to proceed.

"It's used as a pesticide," the marine scientist said.

"A pesticide? In today's world? Are you sure?" Holly asked in surprise. "I'd have thought there were better things to use than cyanide now."

Natasha nodded. "Yeah, I saw it in New Zealand when I

was on a job there. They use it for possum control. They're a pest because they're the primary wildlife carriers for bovine TB."

"They use cyanide to kill possums?" Holly repeated, incredulous.

"Well, they did a few years ago. I assume they still do, but you could check. It was in these green pellets or paste that were put in bait stations. It was only handled by licensed personnel, of course."

Holly stared at her. "I've never heard of such a thing. How do you know this?"

"Oh, I had a couple of days leave off the science ship, so I went touring."

"You went and watched possums being killed?" Denise stared at her in slightly horrified wonder.

Natasha laughed. "No, of course not. But the guy in charge of the tour told us all about them. Said they're an environmental threat. Anyway, I just remembered it when Jamie was telling me about what was going on here. So yeah, cyanide is used as a pesticide."

"Not here." Holly was definite.

"We don't have possums on Azure Isle either," Denise said. "And besides, my mom was environmentally friendly. We never used pesticides."

Natasha's eyes widened. "Oh, my goodness! Oh, honey, I am so sorry! I didn't know it was your mom—" She stopped talking and took Denise's hands in hers. "I am *so* sorry. Really."

Denise looked into the kind blue eyes now gazing at her in remorse. "It's okay. And... Well, we're not really sure if my mom was... She had cancer, you see, so it might have just been that." She glanced at Holly, who wrapped an arm around her shoulders.

"It might have been," she agreed. "We're hoping Inspector Tucker can find out one way or the other."

Natasha gave Denise's hands another compassionate squeeze. "Cancer sucks too." She stared into the young woman's face for a moment, then smiled warmly. "But I can see you're a strong person. You're going to get through this, I know. And you'll be happy again."

Denise blinked. "Th...thanks." She flushed before producing a shy smile. "Thanks. I think I will too."

Jamie, who had been gazing at Natasha in surprise, now turned her attention to Denise with a smile of her own. "We know you will! And you can be sure we'll find out what happened, Denise. One way or the other."

24

_____

A voice interrupted the women's conversation. "Well, here's a bevy of beauties. Hello ladies." Holding a cup of coffee in one hand, Derek Hartley's eyes gleamed with appreciation as he sauntered towards them before he turned a concerned look on Denise. "Should you be here, Denise? Shouldn't you be resting? You've been through a lot, you know."

"I'm fine, Derek." Denise rolled her eyes slightly.

Jamie jumped in. "I was just going to come and see you, Derek. This is my friend, Natasha. She's—"

"—in charge of the shipwreck project. Yes, I remember you told me." Derek held out his hand. "Pleasure to meet you, Natasha. I had an amazing dive out at the site on Sunday. Has Jamie told you about her find? What do you think? Is it long-lost treasure? She's very excited about it." He sent a twinkling look Jamie's way.

Natasha's answering smile was cool as she shook the jeweler's hand. "It could be an artifact from the wreck, yes. I'll know more when I see it. And we're all very excited about *La Rosa*. It's a historic find of some significance to the island."

"Yes, I read the article in *The Island Gazette* last year. It has a fascinating history." Derek turned to Jamie. "Speaking of historical treasures, I meant to ask if you still wanted me to have a look at the Rose Treasure? You said it was a bit tarnished, remember?"

Holly stifled a grin at Jamie's blank look. Her friend had clearly forgotten all about her original ploy to question the jeweler.

Jamie's face cleared. "Oh yeah. Do you actually have time though?"

"I'm not leaving until Friday morning. Come back to the booth with me for a minute and we'll work out a time."

"Okay. But just for a second. We want to go see the results of the quilt show." Jamie glanced at Natasha. "You coming, Nat? You could have a look at Derek's jewelry— don't you have a friend in England who quilts? —and then we'll catch up to these two later."

"Be right there." Curiosity radiating from her, Natasha turned to Holly as the other two walked away. "So, who's the wolf?"

"The what?" Holly laughed.

"Wolf. He has wolf eyes."

Denise giggled. "You know, you're right. Wolves do have amber eyes, don't they? Derek's are gorgeous. And his eyelashes! It's not fair he has such long ones." A vendor packing up caught her eye. "Oh! Look at that. Can you wait a second, Holly? I just want to see that."

As Denise hustled over to the nearest booth, Holly grinned at Natasha. "Wolf eyes, huh?"

"I'm not really a fan of wolves." Natasha shrugged at Holly's look of surprise. "They're predators, aren't they?"

～

DENISE GLANCED sideways at Holly as they walked up Windward Street towards the City Hall art gallery. "Do you think she's psychic or something? Natasha, I mean."

"Psychic? Why on earth would you think that?" Holly laughed. "You wouldn't say that if you'd heard her on the topic of marine thermoclines or whatever it is she does. She's a scientist through and through."

Denise shrugged. "She was kind of intense."

"She didn't mean to upset you." Worried, Holly paused. "Nat's very kind, really. Are you okay?"

"Yes, I'm fine," Denise assured her. "The thing is... I wasn't upset." Her voice was half surprised, half thoughtful. "I've been thinking a lot about what you said when we were on the railway trail. That people have relapses, then improve, then relapse again. It happened to my mom, just like you said it happened to your dad, and I didn't think anything of it at the time. So I'm not really sure why I suddenly became convinced there was something... oh, I don't know... unnatural, I guess, about her death. I've been trying to pinpoint when it happened, and I can't, but I think it was around the time Mrs. Sinclair had her accident."

Holly gazed at her in surprise. "Are you saying you don't think there was anything suspicious about your mom's death now?"

Denise's face flushed. "I don't know. But talking to you... Well, it's been really helpful, Holly. You understand how I feel and... and... it's just helped me think about it differently, I guess."

Holly felt her own face redden. "Oh. Well, I'm glad." Her thoughts whirled as both women walked on in silence.

If Denise was having second thoughts about her mother

being murdered, what did that mean in terms of the investigation? The police and doctors on Azure Isle had said there was nothing suspicious about Daina Trott's death; they'd also said there was nothing suspicious about Freda Sinclair's car accident. What if they were correct? What if both women had died from tragic but completely natural causes?

Holly frowned. They really needed to find out more about Mrs. McGinney's accident. If she really had been pushed, that suggested she might be right about Daina and Freda's deaths. If, however, she'd just fallen, then perhaps there was nothing to her suspicions. Holly wondered if Myrtle had cross-examined her friend about her accident yet. She'd have to check.

Her thoughts veered towards the pesticide Natasha had talked about. Imagine cyanide being used to kill possums! Holly found it hard to believe such a lethal substance was put in bait stations. She'd have to remember to ask Becky to see if that was still the case. And see if their expert researcher had found out anything else about how cyanide could be obtained.

Holly was still pondering when they arrived at the City Hall and Arts Center.

Bridgeport's seat of administration had been built in the 1960s and was a beautiful example of island architecture. Massive cedar doors opened out from the main wing of the building, with cedar also being used prominently inside on the stairs that led to the second floor.

Two wings jutted out from the central foyer. A small theater occupied one of them, with the Dramatic Society putting on a few productions a year, whereas the other side housed municipal offices. On the second floor, the Arts Center housed two art galleries, one at either end. In the larger of these, the Maritime Quilting Expo quilt competition was being held.

A buzz of voices filled the building, drifting down from the second-floor balcony, where quilters clustered in groups discussing the results.

Holly ushered Denise up the stairs. Spotting Myrtle chatting with one of the docents at the door of the gallery, she paused.

"Go and get a guide to the show, Denise, and I'll join you in two seconds. I just want a quick word with Myrtle, okay?"

"I'll see if I can find Aunt Rosalie. She said she'd be here today."

Holly nodded, then hovered, waiting to catch Myrtle's eye. Finally noticing her, the septuagenarian said a few more words to the docent, then bustled over to Holly, who wasted no time.

"How's Mrs. McGinney?"

"Shaken, bruised, inclined to be teary, but coping remarkably well, all things considered."

"Bruised?" Holly repeated. "What kind of bruises? From rolling down the hill?"

Myrtle nodded. "Yes. And also a rather large bruise in the small of her back. She was definitely pushed, Holly. There's no doubt about it."

"Has she told you what happened?"

"According to Anne, she had a bit of a row with Sybil Worthington." Myrtle sniffed. "Not unusual. Sybil has quite a high opinion of herself and doesn't hesitate to share it."

Holly kept a straight face. "What was the row about? Did Mrs. McGinney say?"

"Oh, about this silly constitution thing. I've told Anne she should give it up, but she just won't listen. I believe Sybil said that since Sally died, many of the Oleanders feel they should carry out her wishes with regards to changing the constitution. Anne was upset and went outside to clear her head."

"Who was in the suite? Did anyone follow her out?"

Myrtle looked at her in approval. "Exactly what I asked. Ellen and Sybil were the only ones in the room and they both say they stayed inside. Anne went out alone."

"Hmm." Holly pondered for a moment. "So, someone else at the Inn last night pushed her. But why there? It's a very gentle slope. Even if she hadn't been caught in the oleanders, she'd have stopped eventually. There's no steep drop off there at all. It certainly couldn't have killed her."

Myrtle nodded. "And there's another thing we should consider. Why did the murderer change their *modus operandi*? If they poisoned three presidents, why would they resort to pushing the fourth?"

HOLLY WAS STILL PONDERING Myrtle's final comment as she approached the door of the main gallery where Denise was waiting for her.

"I've got a map." The younger woman waved a brochure at Holly. "Look. They have all the entries listed and where to find them."

Smiling at Denise's eager expression, Holly pushed Anne McGinney's fall from her mind. "Come on then. Let's go find your Aunt Rosalie's quilt first. Which category did she enter?"

"Traditional pieced." Denise consulted the brochure. "It's at the far end of the gallery on the left, near the traditional appliqué quilts."

As they walked through the gallery, both women

stopped at intervals to "ooh" and "ahh" over the brightly colored intricate patchwork creations that hung on the walls. Holly was admiring a small sampler quilt, trying to remember the names of the blocks Becky had told her, when she heard an exclamation.

"Oh, there's Aunt Rosalie!" Denise waved to catch the attention of a small and chubby blonde-haired woman in a pink-and-white floral dress, who was closely examining a wall-hanging near the entrance. "Aunt Rosalie!"

The woman turned, her face lighting up at the sight of her goddaughter. "Well now. Look at you, out and about finally." She gave Denise a hug before smiling at Holly. "Holly, right? I've seen you around at the Inn but haven't had a chance to talk to you all week. Denise says you put her to work in the garden." Her dark brown eyes twinkled. "A butterfly garden, wasn't it?"

Holly grinned. "She was a big help."

"We've come to see your quilt," Denise said. "Did it win anything?"

"Honorable mention," Rosalie Becknell replied. "I'm very pleased. There was a lot of competition this year—and there are some very talented quilters on the islands. Your mom did well, Holly. Second place in the small pictorial quilt category."

Holly beamed. "Really? That's awesome. I'll go check it out in a bit. Denise tells me your quilt is a memory piece."

"Yes. It's called *A Rainbow for Daina*." Rosalie smiled. "Denise helped me sew parts of it."

"Not much," Denise said. "You did most of it. And you did all the quilting. Oh, there it is!" She trotted ahead of the other two.

Following more slowly, Rosalie turned her face toward Holly. "Thank you for taking some time with Denise this week. She said you helped her put things in perspective. You've probably noticed she's quite a young twenty-two-year-old."

"Oh, well, she's been through a rough time lately."

"Yes, it's been difficult for her. She and Daina were very close," Rosalie said. "Her mother doted on her—so Denise was rather spoiled, I'm afraid. She's had to grow up quite quickly in a short time."

Holly nodded. "I don't imagine all the talk about murder has helped either."

"Oh honestly, I don't know how that all started!" Rosalie rolled her eyes in irritation. "No matter what Anne McGinney's been running around telling everyone, Daina was not murdered! Nobody thought anything of the sort until after Freda Sinclair had her accident. I'm not even sure how it started, but it was definitely after Christmas that rumors began flying. I've told Denise over and over that there's no connection whatsoever, but what with both Anne and Derek constantly worrying her about it, the poor child's been overwhelmed."

Holly stopped in her tracks. "But I thought you were the one who said you were worried about Sally Dill?"

"Sally, yes. Her bouts of illness were concerning. There was no rhyme or reason to them, and she had no health concerns. But Daina had terminal cancer. Her death, sad as it was, was expected."

As other people walked around them, Holly drew Rosalie to the side of the room, lowering her voice a little. "And Freda Sinclair?"

"Freda had the flu." Rosalie tutted in annoyance. "I know what people are saying and I've told Anne McGinney repeatedly that it's completely unfounded. I saw Freda the day before her accident. She looked absolutely dreadful, said she'd just been to the doctor and her flu test had come back positive. She told me she'd been ordered back to bed. And instead of doing what she was told, she went out again the following day to collect a Christmas gift of all things!" Sadness laced the Azure islander's voice. "Such a dreadful waste. She was a lovely woman. Her family were just devastated when they got that phone call."

"Her flu test was positive?" Holly repeated. "Did she have any other symptoms? Like the ones Sally Dill had?"

"She had regular flu symptoms." Rosalie was firm. "I've told your inspector this, Holly. Sally's illness was strange. It came out of nowhere, just after Freda died. She would feel queasy, weak, dizzy, then get better for a while. Then it would happen again. I did notice that each episode seemed worse—and that the effects seemed to last longer."

"How many 'episodes' did she have?" Holly wondered how long someone could ingest minute doses of cyanide and continue to survive.

Rosalie frowned. "Not many. Perhaps three? I live—lived —next door to Sally, you know, so I saw her most days. Let me think... Freda died just before Christmas, on the twentieth of December—her poor family!—and Sally didn't start feeling ill until, oh, the end of the month for sure. Perhaps even the first week of January. I remember because she said she thought she might have a touch of flu but then everything went away, or so she thought."

"So it was only going on for a couple of weeks?" Holly said in surprise.

"Oh yes. It's a recent occurrence. But, as I told Myrtle, it was odd." Rosalie's eyes suddenly welled up. "And now she's gone."

"Myrtle told us Sally lived alone."

"Yes, that's right. Her husband died more than ten years

ago now and she was never interested in another relationship. Besides, she was a workaholic." Rosalie gave a wan smile. "I was always telling her she needed to slow down, take more time for herself, but other than our once-a-month quilting meetings, all she was interested in was that business of hers."

"What did she do?" Holly asked. "Was she a lawyer too?"

"Like Jonas?" Rosalie snorted. "Certainly not. Oh, Jonas is successful—he certainly represents enough people on Azure—but he and Sally barely spoke to each other. Although I must say, I did notice him visiting her a couple of times around Christmas. Perhaps he was attempting a reconciliation of sorts."

"I noticed he and Mrs. Worthington didn't get on very well either."

Rosalie laughed. "Oh, the feud between Sybil and Jonas is legendary. The problem with Jonas and Sally came from the fact that Sally owns—owned—a chain of small hotels on Azure. They're more like very exclusive inns, but she was investigating the possibility of investing in some smaller, more eco-friendly family-style resorts near Mist Lake.

"The Hartleys own a big chunk of land there. Well, Sally did. Her parents left it all to her after Jonas married Ellen Worthington. Said they couldn't risk the Worthingtons getting their hands on it."

"Are you guys coming or not?" Denise stood a few feet away. "I found the Flower Quilt, Holly. Didn't you say you wanted to see it?"

Still trying to digest Rosalie's final flood of information, Holly blinked at the younger woman. "What? The Flower Quilt?"

"Oh yes, you must see that. It's quite gorgeous! And you must buy a raffle ticket! The draw is tomorrow night. We're donating all the proceeds to an environmental charity this year. Something to do with conserving the ocean around the islands. Reducing plastics, pollution, saving turtles, all that kind of thing. A very worthy cause."

Still talking, Rosalie swept Holly and Denise away to purchase Flower Quilt raffle tickets.

25

H olly was gazing with pride at the red rosette on her mother's wall-hanging when Jamie bounced up.

"Hey, look at that! Maggie won a prize! Awesome!" Jamie's beam rivaled Holly's. "Wait. Isn't that Becky's garden?"

"It is. Mama says she's giving it to Becky as a gift."

"Nice. She should hang it above that floral sofa of hers. It'll look great there." Jamie stood back, tilting her head to the side as she considered the wall-hanging. "Do you think Maggie would make me something like this? But maybe with my garden gate and a bit of the old wall in the front?"

"You can ask her." Holly grinned before glancing around. "Where's Natasha? And have you got your raffle tickets for the quilt yet?"

"Natasha's still at the library. She bumped into Mr. Graham and got talking about diving stuff. She's staying at my house tonight." Jamie frowned, then pulled out her phone. "Which reminds me. I asked Miller to send me the photos he took when we were out at *La Rosa* on Sunday, and he hasn't done it yet. I need them to give to Nat."

"What's she going to do with them?"

Busily texting, Jamie didn't look up. "She knows some guy who's a marine archaeologist. She's already contacted him about coming out in the spring, but she said she'd send him the photos to see what he thinks."

"But aren't you going to get the actual bottle?" Holly asked.

"That's what Nat and Mr. Graham were talking about. They might go out there tomorrow, take more photos, then retrieve it."

"I don't know why we didn't just bring it back," Holly commented. "I mean, it was only partly buried. I get that an excavation has to be done carefully, but this was just one bottle."

Jamie finished her text. "Yeah, I know, and it would probably have been fine, really, but I'm not taking any chances. I want qualified people removing any artifacts. That way we have proper evidence, witnesses—all that kind of thing."

Putting her phone away, she looked at Holly. "What were you saying about raffle tickets? Why would I want tickets for a quilt?"

"Maybe because you actually quilted part of it? Come see it anyway." As Holly led the way to the Flower Quilt, she filled Jamie in on her talk with Rosalie Becknell.

Jamie frowned. "She said Anne McGinney had been 'worrying' Denise about her mom's death?"

"Yeah. It sounds like she and Derek were probably the ones who started all the rumors."

Jamie fingered her lip in thought. "And Rosalie sounded plausible? You believe her when she says they were just rumors? I mean, Mrs. McGinney seemed pretty certain they'd been murdered when she was first telling us about all this. And if she really was pushed off the wall—"

"Myrtle says she was," Holly interrupted. "She said Mrs. McGinney has a huge bruise on her back from being shoved."

"Oh, well then, that definitely lends credence to her belief, right?"

Holly's eyebrows shot up. "When did you become a talking dictionary? Credence?"

"It's all this association with librarians and journalists. Their vocabulary has inspired me to collect words." Jamie grinned, then sobered again. "But you say Rosalie thinks the first two women died of natural causes. What does it mean if she's right?"

"It means that only Sally Dill has been murdered." Holly paused. "But if Mrs. McGinney really was pushed, then who did it and why? Myrtle raised a good point. Why would the murderer change his or her method? Why push someone when the other three were poisoned?"

"Huh." Jamie thought for a moment. "Well, we know Sally Dill died from a poisoned capsule of turmeric, but we haven't been able to discover how Daina Trott or Freda Sinclair could have been given cyanide. And it's unlikely we will, since no one in authority on Azure Isle even believes they were murdered."

"No," Holly mused. "I wonder if they took the same capsules as Sally. Perhaps Rob could find out."

"Maybe. But what we have to do now is find out who could have pushed Anne McGinney. Who was at the Inn last night, and who had the opportunity?"

Holly frowned suddenly. "Wait a minute..."

"What? What have you thought of?"

"Derek said someone hammered on his door. Who was it?" Holly paused. "Where was Jonas Hartley last night?"

Jamie's mouth dropped open. "Jonas Hartley? You think Derek's father has something to do with this? Why?"

"I'll tell you later. Look, here's the quilt."

They'd reached the Flower Quilt, hanging in all its tropical splendor in a corner of the gallery, with Auntie Elma doing a brisk business in raffle ticket sales at a table beside it.

Holly admired the appliquéd collaborative project again. "It looks great, doesn't it? I'd love to win it! How many tickets are you going to get, Jamie? I got five."

Auntie Elma turned from her previous customers to raise an eyebrow at Jamie, who quickly plastered a bright smile on her face. "I'm sure you've told me many times that you have absolutely no desire to own a quilt, Jamie White. What's changed your mind?"

"Well, it just so happens, Auntie Elma, that I actually put some stitches in this work of art. Right there!" Jamie pointed at a block with a cluster of frangipani flowers appliquéd on it.

"Did you indeed?" Elma Foster peered at the block in question. "Well, I can see which ones are yours by the size, but they're very neatly stitched, I must say. Quite nice work, Jamie."

A pleased expression spread across Jamie's face as she pulled out her wallet. "I'll buy five tickets too, Auntie Elma. Maybe I'll be lucky."

"I hope so." The older woman smiled at them, handed Jamie her raffle tickets, then turned her attention to another couple.

Shoving the raffle tickets in her pocket, Jamie grabbed Holly's arm, towing her towards the exit as she hissed, "What do you mean, you want to know where Jonas Hartley was? Why? Wasn't he with his wife inside the room?"

Holly shrugged. "Myrtle says Sybil Worthington and Ellen Hartley were together in the room when Anne went outside. And Jonas wasn't in the Inn lobby like everyone else was when we got there last night. So, where was he?"

"You think he might have pushed Mrs. McGinney? For what reason?"

"I don't know," Holly admitted. "I'm just curious about where he was."

"But why?" Jamie's eyes narrowed. "Do you know something about him that I don't?"

"Rosalie Becknell told me his parents left the whole family business to Sally when he married Ellen Worthington. The Hartleys own a chain of small hotels and a chunk of land Sally was considering developing."

"They disinherited their son?" Jamie blinked. "What is it with these two families? Ellen doesn't get the Daylily Resort because of Jonas and now Jonas doesn't get the Hartley hotels because of Ellen. Talk about the Montagues and Capulets."

Holly choked. "I can't quite see Ellen and Jonas as Romeo and Juliet!"

"No, I guess not." Jamie snorted, then her expression darkened. "So, what's your point?"

"Well," Holly said, "I'm just wondering what happens to all that land and property now that Sally's dead."

Jamie was still talking as the two women reached the Bridgeport Library. "But even if Jonas does inherit everything, I don't see what he had to gain from killing Daina and Freda."

Holly frowned. "I know. Unless Rosalie Becknell is right

after all, and Daina and Freda weren't killed. Then that means the only murder we're talking about is Sally's. And Sally had a lot of property. If Jonas inherits—and he's her only sibling, she has no husband and no children—then the motive for killing her could be simple greed."

"Yes, but what about Mrs. McGinney?" Jamie argued. "Myrtle said she was pushed. If the first two women weren't killed, and Sally was the only target, why would Jonas push Mrs. McGinney? It doesn't make sense."

Holly sighed. "I know."

"And besides, how'd he do it?"

"What?"

"How did Jonas poison Sally? You said Rosalie told you they barely spoke to each other. So how did Jonas manage to get cyanide into those turmeric capsules? I doubt she just handed them to him. And where'd he get the cyanide in the first place?"

"I don't know," Holly retorted. "It's a theory, that's all. Just like your theory about Anne McGinney when you thought she was the murderess. Where would she have gotten cyanide?"

"Heck if I know. Where does anyone get cyanide? If they're not possum control, that is."

Annoyance warred with amusement as Holly stared at her friend. "You could try the patience of a saint, you know that?"

"It's been said before," Jamie admitted with a smirk. "Tell you what, Holls, let's go find Becky and see if she has any more information for us. I tried to find out some stuff about cyanide last night when I got home but I must be useless at search terms. I found lots of information about what happens when you take it, but precious little about how to buy it!"

"Your search history must be fascinating." Holly couldn't suppress a grin at the thought. "I hope no one looks at your computer. They'll think you're contemplating murder yourself."

"Tell me about it," Jamie said with a snicker as she pushed open the library door. "Wow, it's a lot quieter in here, isn't it? Hey, Stephanie!" She hailed the children's librarian from across the nearly empty foyer. "Have you seen Becky around? Is she in her office?"

Stephanie nodded. "I saw her go that way about twenty minutes or so ago."

Waving in thanks, both women made their way to the head librarian's tiny office on the ground floor. The door was ajar, and Becky's voice could be heard talking to someone. Holly poked her head into the room.

"Oh, hi, Mr. Graham. Are you guys having a meeting? We can come back later."

"No, no." The president of the Hibiscus Island Historical Society beckoned Holly in. "Please come in. I'm just about finished. Oh, Jamie, I'm glad you're here. Did you see Natasha yet? She said she'll be able to go out to the wreck tomorrow."

Mr. Graham took his glasses off, placing them in the pocket of the brightly colored Hawaiian shirt he wore over khaki trousers. His grey hair was standing on end—he had a habit of running his hands through it when researching—but his blue eyes were smiling. "I saw the photos of that bottle, Jamie, and it looks very promising. Very promising indeed. We'll retrieve it tomorrow and Natasha tells me her friend, that marine archaeologist chap, will take a look at it. Apparently he'll be on Turtle Island in two weeks, and may be able to take a side trip here."

Jamie beamed. "Oh, that's awesome! Maybe he'll be able

to give us a time estimate for his excavation as well. Gosh, I hope there's something below all that sand! Gold maybe, or jewels."

"Well, don't get your hopes up too high," Mr. Graham warned. "And just remember—anything we find is of historical significance. A simple carpenter's chisel, for instance, lowly as it is, can tell us a lot, you know." He glanced at his watch. "I must go. When you see Natasha, let her know we'll be leaving from Castlebay Harbor at ten in the morning."

As the historian trotted out of the office, Becky leaned back in her chair with a sigh. "You don't know how nice it will be to have our library just be a library again. Although I must say, it's all gone very smoothly. The booths have all been dismantled and everything packed up in record time. We have a breathing space now before we set up the hall for the awards dinner tomorrow night. I'll say this for Myrtle: she's a superb organizer."

"Bossy, you mean," Jamie commented, collapsing into one of the little armchairs in front of the desk. "But yeah, she's done a great job. We were just up at the quilt show, by the way. Maggie got second place for the quilt she made of your garden."

Becky's face lit up. "Really? Oh, that's wonderful. She must be so pleased."

"I don't know if she's seen it yet," Holly said, "but she'll be thrilled."

"Anyway," Jamie interrupted, "we're here to see if you've had time to do any more research on this poison. Did you find out anything else?"

Becky rolled her eyes. "No, I haven't had time to research. Despite Myrtle's amazing organization with the expo, this is still a library, and believe it or not, some patrons expect service. And then there's the awards dinner tomorrow, remember. It's a big job setting that up. It'll take all day."

"What are you doing about the carpet in the lecture hall?" Holly asked curiously. "Wasn't that a bone of contention with your library board?"

"Yes, but everyone agreed that a temporary tiled dance floor laid over said carpet would do the trick. They'll be here bright and early in the morning." Becky looked at her friends. "I can do some more research at home tonight, if you want."

"You don't have to," Holly began.

Jamie overrode her. "That would be great because Holly and I are useless at it! How about we meet for tea or coffee tomorrow at the Bean and you can fill us in? Or lunch? What would work better for you, Becks? Holly's free any time, right, Holls?"

"I'm flexible," Holly corrected. "Gramps decided today he wants to completely redo one of the beds on the fourth level, so tomorrow I'll be up to my knees in mud, digging up spider lilies the size of triffids!"

Laughing at Holly's reference to John Wyndham's science fiction classic, Becky stood up. "Well, I need to get back out there, but I'll be at the Bean at... Shall we say two-thirty tomorrow? I think I'll be needing a cup of tea by then. I'll have my research in hand."

26

Gramps frowned at the nearly empty bed, then at Holly. "A break? Again?"

"We've been at this since eight this morning with only one short coffee break, Gramps. That's six hours already and I'm starving! And I said I'd meet Jamie and Becky at two-thirty. Which will now be my lunch break, I'd like to point out." Holly looked at the remaining spider lilies with dislike. "We should never have let these things get so big. They're a nightmare to remove."

"They're low-maintenance," Gramps said, "but yes, they have spread a little too much, I agree. Well then, go get your lunch." He glanced at his watch. "Three o'clock back here?"

Holly gazed at him in exasperation, mixed with admiration for his stamina. "I'm going to the Bean. And there's a dinner to go to tonight, remember? Why don't we call it quits for the day, Gramps?"

Her grandfather's white eyebrows beetled. "We can finish this if we work till five."

"Fine." Holly sighed. "I'll be back at three-thirty. And

wait for me to get back, you hear. You need to eat something too."

Gramps rolled his eyes. "You sound like your mother." His lips twitched as he gazed at his granddaughter. "You'd better clean up a bit before you go into town. There's mud on your face."

Holly ignored his comment and the chortle that followed her as she marched away.

THE LUNCH CROWD had departed by the time Holly collapsed into a chair in the Bean café with a groan. "Every muscle in my body aches! And I'm on the clock, by the way. Gramps is determined to clear this garden today. The man has energy to burn! I don't know how he does it."

"What's a word for that, Becks?" Jamie asked as she put a plate of toasty grilled cheese in front of Holly. "I know you know one."

The librarian looked surprised. "A word? For 'energy to burn'? Um... Indefatigable, maybe? Why?"

"Just curious." Jamie grinned.

"What's so funny?" Becky looked at her warily.

Holly rolled her eyes. "She's trying to improve her vocabulary. Just ignore her, Becks. Did you find time to do any research?"

"Yeah, what else have you found out about cyanide?" Jamie asked, sliding into her own seat with a cup of coffee.

Becky eyed her with suspicion, then surrendered. "Well, I found out it's considered a rising chemical threat in terms of terrorism and is supposedly readily available. Also, over eighty percent of acute cyanide cases are from oral inges-tion, as opposed to gas inhalation, which surprised me. I thought there'd be more cases of inhalation since cyanide is used in several industries. And I also learned that when cyanide is ingested, symptoms don't always appear immediately. There can be a delay."

"A delay? How long a delay?" Holly asked in surprise. "I always thought death was instantaneous."

Becky shook her head. "Low dose exposure causes the symptoms that Sally Dill had—headache, dizziness, nausea, vomiting. High doses lead to respiratory failure, apnea, heart arrhythmia, seizure, and coma. But from what I understand, the time to onset of symptoms is flexible. Symptoms can occur anywhere from minutes to hours after ingestion. Up to four hours after, in fact, if taken on a full stomach."

"So, you're saying that Sally Dill might not have taken the cyanide at the tea?" Holly pondered. "You know, we haven't even asked anyone if she took a capsule there. If she didn't, then she had to have taken it in her room before the tea."

"Which would actually make more sense," Becky agreed. "People don't normally pop a joint pain medicine at a tea party. I would think she'd take it in the mornings. Or possibly at lunch—which would have delayed her symptoms."

Joint pain. Holly frowned in thought.

"I don't think that's the important point," Jamie interrupted. "Regardless of when she took the capsule, someone still had to tamper with it, and that had to have been done on Azure Isle. How could someone get hold of these cyanide salts that Rob mentioned? Where do you find them?"

"Cyanide is mainly used in silver and gold mining, it seems. They mix the ore with cyanide, which dissolves the metals, and allows them to be separated from other materials." Becky consulted some printouts of paper on the table. "Then there's industrial organic chemistry use—which was too complicated for me to plow through for very long, and cyanide fishing—"

"Cyanide *fishing*?" Holly gaped at her. "What on earth's that?"

"It's totally bizarre is what it is. Ornamental fish for fish tanks are often captured in the wild, and cyanide is used to stun them, if you can believe it. Fishermen make a diluted solution of cyanide by crushing pills into a water bottle. It's a banned practice because it can harm the fish and damage the reefs, but it's hard to enforce. So poachers keep doing it."

"Wow." Holly stared at her friend. "I had no idea."

"Me either." Becky continued. "Cyanide is used as a pesticide in some places, and as a rodenticide, and also to cull animals like coyotes and—"

"Possums." Jamie nodded. "Natasha told us about the possums. But what I want to know is where can an ordinary person get this cyanide? Is it available online? Can I just call up somewhere and say, 'Can I have some cyanide please?' Where does a murderer get it?"

"Well, if you'd let me finish," Becky began, only to be interrupted by a crash from the kitchen, followed by a flood of impassioned French. "Oh dear! That's François. What's happened?"

Becky started to get up, but Jamie beat her to it. "I'll go. Be right back."

Glancing at her watch, Holly gave an exclamation of her own. "Oh gosh, look at the time. I've got to go too. Gramps is going to be spitting mad if I'm late!"

"Holly, wait!" Becky put a restraining hand on her arm. "There's one more thing about cyanide and I'm not sure how Jamie will take it."

"What?" Holly stared at her in surprise.

"It's sometimes used by jewelers to clean jewelry."

Another burst of French from the kitchen had both women turning their heads.

"All right, François! Chill out. We'll handle it." Jamie emerged from the kitchen looking harried. After a quick word with Angie, she went over to the door and flipped the sign to CLOSED.

Holly's eyebrows rose as she watched her friend stop at the two remaining tables with customers, who looked curious, then smiled in understanding, flapping their hands at Jamie as if to say, 'Don't worry about us.'

Signaling her friend over to the table, Holly asked, "What's the problem?"

"The problem," Jamie snapped, "is that François has been far too fancy with desserts for the awards dinner and is now in a tizzy that things won't be ready in time."

Becky winced. "I did try to tell him just to do cookies."

"So did I!" Jamie sighed. "I've closed the café so I can get things packed in the van. Angie will help as soon as these last customers go, but I'm not rushing them out. Sorry, guys, but I'll have to leave you to it."

"I wish I could help," Becky began, "but I have to get back to the library myself."

Holly glanced at her watch again. "I'll stay. I'll just call Gramps and let him know. The spider lilies can wait till tomorrow."

A relieved expression crossed Jamie's face. "Seriously? That would be great, Holls. Thank you!"

As Becky said an apologetic goodbye and left to return to the library and her own undoubted chaos, Holly made a quick phone call to her grandfather, who was surprisingly amenable to the change in plan. He was probably tired himself, Holly thought with a grin, putting her phone back in her pocket.

Pushing through the door into the kitchen, she could see François waving his arms in a frenzy as he pointed this way and that, issuing orders to Jamie even as he carefully cut a slab of—Holly's eyes widened. Was that *tablet*?

Catching sight of Holly's face, the chef beckoned her in. "*Entrez! Vous pouvez nous aidez!*"

"Uh..." Holly blinked.

"He said 'you can help us,'" Jamie said in a sour tone, glancing up from packing beautifully iced cupcakes into a large box. "I told you. He's in a French tizzy."

"I am not in a tizzy!" François roared. "*Tout ce que j'ai demandé...*" He paused, then took a deep breath. "All I asked for was some help! Is it too much to expect? *Mon Dieu!*"

"Oh, let it go, François!" Jamie snapped. "I told you not to be too fancy. It's your own fault if you're stressed."

As François's eyebrows lowered even further, Holly intervened. "Is that tablet, François?" She pointed to the pale caramel-colored candy spread out on wax paper on the counter. "Real tablet?"

Distracted, the chef glanced down. "*Oui.* Why?"

"I didn't know you knew how to make it! I love tablet! It's a Scottish recipe, you know. Gramps makes it for Christmas every year."

"Mr. Mack is the one who gave me the recipe." François was calming down. He cut a tiny piece of the fudge-like candy and gave it to Holly. "What do you think?"

As it melted in her mouth, Holly gave a moan of pure pleasure. "Oh wow, it's fantastic! Just like Gramps makes it."

François beamed. "*Bien.* We're going to put them in little bags as favors. Here, you can do it. Wash your hands first. I'll go start packing the crème brûlées." He shot Jamie a glare as he hustled toward the large walk-in fridge at the far end of the kitchen. "We may just get everything done on time, after all."

"If he didn't insist on doing so much, it wouldn't be a problem," Jamie muttered, rolling her eyes as she closed the lid on the cupcake box before moving to trays of caramel shortbread slices. Heaving an enormous sigh, she started transferring them onto what looked like a glass plate.

"Isn't glass a little risky?" Holly asked.

Jamie grinned. "It's eco-friendly plastic. Pretty cool, huh? And it has a cover too. Easy presentation."

"Are these bags eco-friendly too?" Holly asked, glancing at the pile of little cellophane bags waiting for candy.

"Yep." Jamie moved like lightning as she popped the last square on a dish, snapped on the clear lid, and moved to the next tray. "Oh hi, Angie. Are they all gone? Good. What's next? I'll be finished with these in a jiffy."

Angie looked around the kitchen. "Well, the fruit salad stays in the bowls and people can serve themselves, but there are chocolate cups, mini cheesecakes, and pecan tartlets still to go."

"See what I mean?" Jamie groaned. "All he had to do was an assortment of cookies. It would have been so much easier."

"Not as pretty though. And I like the idea of bite-sized desserts," Holly said, slicing her candy into strips, then squares.

"*Merci!*" Francois had returned, and now directed a somewhat sheepish look at his business partner. "Leave the rest to me, Angie, and Holly. You can start loading the van. The crème brûlées are in the coolers. Be careful with them."

"Ah, you're feeling better. Good." Jamie gave him a reassuring pat on the shoulder. "Everything looks great, François."

"Better than cookies, that's for sure." A grin crossed the chef's face. "Let's hustle, people. As soon as we've delivered and set up, we're free for the night!" He looked over at Holly. "Two pieces to a bag, Holly. And no sampling."

Holly laughed and picked up the tongs to start filling her order.

SHOOTING into the Inn just after five o'clock, Holly was surprised to find her mother sitting at the table in the kitchen, poking through colorful brochures.

"Hey, Ms. Prizewinner, what are you doing? I thought you'd be getting beautified for your big night." She grinned. "You know, I was thinking we should do something of our own later this week to celebrate. How about dinner? Just the two of us!" Holly did a little dance shimmy as she sang the last few words.

Maggie laughed. "You sound like your father when you sing."

Holly grinned. "Off-key, huh? I'll take it as a compliment anyway. So, where do you want to go to celebrate? Later, I mean."

"We could go to Wahoo. I haven't been there in some time."

"It's a deal." Holly inspected a plate of leftovers from afternoon tea. "Any of these gluten-free?"

Maggie shook her head. "No, and are you sure you want to eat now? There'll be tons of food at the awards dinner, you know." At Holly's pleading look, she smiled. "Well, if you're starving, there's some biscotti in the cupboard. I'm trying out a new supplier. Tell me what you think. I quite liked them."

Holly found the biscotti, turned on the kettle, and got cups down while she waited for it to boil. "So, what are you looking at over there?"

"Brochures from vendors at the quilt show," Maggie replied. "I like to support local businesses and some of these ship throughout the islands."

Holly poured the tea and brought the cups to the table before returning for the plate of biscotti. Crunching into one, she shuffled through the pile of paper, her eyebrows rising in pleasure at the almondy taste. "These are good, Mama. Oh, here's the Cookie Encounter lady. I can vouch for these. Her gluten-free cookies were awesome."

"She said she could make us custom designed cookies for the Inn. I'm just trying to think what we should have. Any ideas?"

"Hibiscus." Holly spoke around a mouthful of biscotti. "Or wait, I know! Let's get different flowers to match the suites."

Maggie pursed her lips in thought. "That's not a bad idea. She wraps them individually. We could use them as welcome gifts for guests. And perhaps have a basket of cookies on the front desk? Iced with our logo?"

"It's a great idea. Let's do it." Holly grinned at her mother, who smiled back and laid a hand over hers.

"Have I told you how glad I am to have you back, Holly Berry?"

"I'm glad to be back," Holly assured her.

The sound of a throat being cleared interrupted the two women.

"Mrs. Gold, could I trouble you for a cup of coffee?"

Holly looked around in surprise as Maggie stood up.

"Certainly, Mr. Hartley. Would you like to have it in the tearoom?"

The slim dark-haired lawyer sighed. "Yes, that will be fine. It's been a long day. I need something before this dinner tonight."

"I'll bring it straight through."

As Jonas trailed away, Holly jumped up to follow her mother across the kitchen. "I thought he was supposed to be leaving. What happened? Why's he still here? He said he had to get back to Azure."

Maggie replaced the filter in the coffee pot and found the ground coffee beans. "Apparently, Rob asked him to remain on the island."

"Rob asked him—?" Holly gawked. "But why?"

"Inspector Tucker hasn't taken me into his confidence." Maggie's tone discouraged her daughter from asking questions.

"Wow. Wait till Jamie hears this!" Holly ignored the warning in her mother's voice as she pulled out her phone. Catching sight of the clock on it, she squawked. "Is that the time already? Mama! We're going to be late. Pour that coffee fast and let's get ready!"

27

A little later, Holly whistled as her mother came into the living room. "Wow, Mama! You look amazing. I love that jacket."

"Yes, well, it's tradition to wear something quilted to the awards ceremony of the Maritime Quilting Expo." Maggie smiled as she fingered the jewel-toned crazy quilted long satin jacket she wore over slim black trousers and a black camisole top. "And it hides my tummy, which is great."

"What tummy?" Holly scoffed. "You don't have a tummy! Seriously, you look fantastic!"

Maggie blushed. "Well, thank you. You look lovely as well. Green is definitely your color." She admired the forest green long-sleeved flared dress Holly wore, then laughed when her daughter spun in a circle. "Are you driving, or am I?"

"Neither." Holly looked smug. "Rob's picking us both up. We're going in style."

"Rob is? I didn't think he'd be able to take time off from his case."

Holly shrugged. "Well, he was planning to come before

this happened, and he says he can, so I took him at his word. Besides..."

As her voice trailed away, Maggie sighed. "I hope you're not planning to cross-examine the man about murder when you're on a date, Holly."

"Oh listen, I think that's him now." Holly avoided looking at her mother. "You ready, Mama? Let's go get your prize!"

Rob's eyes widened in appreciation as he held the door of his car open. "Well, you two look stunning! I feel a little under-dressed. Maybe I should have pulled out my dinner jacket."

Holly eyed the inspector's crisp white shirt and tie, black suit, and dress shoes. "You look okay to me."

"Holly!" Maggie scolded, then smiled at Rob. "You look very smart, Rob."

As the inspector helped her mother into the front seat, Holly caught his eye and grinned, receiving a quick return wink before she slid into the back of the car.

"You ready to receive your award, Maggie? Second place, I understand. You must be pleased." Rob smiled at Holly's mother.

"Did you go to the quilt show?" Holly asked, surprised.

"I didn't, no, but Becky told me all about it. She's thrilled her little garden was the subject of a prize-winning quilt. She's already got a place of honor reserved for it in the living room."

Maggie blushed with pleasure. "I'll have to make her something for the nursery as well. Do you know what theme she's planning, Rob?"

The inspector blinked. "Theme? What do you mean, 'theme'?"

"A theme for the baby room," Holly explained. "You

know, like sloths or elephants or something. Becky said she's doing green and yellow, Mama, and she's turning her sampler quilt into a baby quilt. You'll have to do her a wall hanging with those colors."

"Sloths or elephants," Rob repeated. "Are you serious? Does François know this?"

Holly laughed and leaned back in the car. "Well, if he doesn't yet, he soon will."

∾

JAMIE WAVED to them from her table as Rob, Holly, and Maggie entered the lecture hall of the library. "Over here. We saved you guys seats."

Maggie demurred. "I'm going to sit with the Patch-workers. All the clubs sit together at the final dinner. It's—"

"—tradition," Holly finished with a grin. "Okay. We'll cheer from over there when you get your award!"

"Not too loudly," Maggie cautioned, a look of alarm on her face at the thought.

Holly's grin widened. "No promises, Mama." She watched her mother greet some fellow quilters, then turned back to Rob. "Well, come on then."

"You really do look lovely tonight." Rob's admiring look turned into a smile at Holly's sudden blush. Taking her hand and tucking it into his elbow, he escorted her across the room towards the table Jamie had reserved, nodding to people along the way.

"Evening, Inspector."

"Nice to see you, Inspector."

"Got yourself a right fine date there, Inspector. You take good care of her, you hear?"

Holly's face reddened even more. "Uncle Stanley!" she hissed.

Beside him, Gramps chortled as Rob just grinned. "I intend to, Mr. Foster. Mr. Mack, how are you, sir?"

Gramps laughed again. "Just fine, son. Just fine. You go and enjoy yourselves tonight."

Jamie's grin was almost splitting her face when Holly finally arrived at the table and sank into a seat. "Quite the royal progress there, Holls. Nice dress!"

"Thanks. Yours too! Both of you." Holly smiled at Jamie and Becky. "Where's Natasha? I thought she was coming too."

"Her marine archaeologist guy called, and she said she wanted to show him the bottle she and Mr. Graham retrieved today, so she stayed at the cottage." Jamie's off-the-shoulder short black cocktail dress clung to her body, her hair was loose, big gold earrings dangled from her ears, and her eyes sparkled.

Across from her, in a pretty pink sheath dress, Becky sipped at a drink while François warily inspected his wine glass, swirling it around with a suspicious look on his face.

"What's wrong with the wine, François?" Rob grinned at his brother-in-law.

"Nothing, nothing." François took a hasty sip.

"He's a wine snob." Jamie rolled her eyes. "Miller's already at the bar, Rob."

"I'll go get something for us, then. What do you want, Holly?" Rob asked.

"A soda, I think. Thanks."

Jamie winked at Holly as Rob smiled before heading to the drinks table on the far side of the room. "Look how cute you two are. This is your first public date, isn't it?"

"I don't think this counts as a date," Holly said, gesturing around the crowded lecture hall full of quilters wearing an eye-dazzling array of patchwork-inspired clothing.

"Sure it does. Fancy dress, dinner, guy in suit and tie. It's a date."

"Oh yeah?" Holly looked in a meaningful way at Jamie. "So, fancy dress, dinner, guy in suit and tie..." She glanced over at Thomas as he approached with two drinks in his hands, then back at her friend. "And he's bringing you a drink. Guess you're on a date too then."

Becky giggled as Jamie spluttered.

"What? We are not!"

Thomas whistled as he drew closer. "Nice dress, Holls! Don't we all look grown-up tonight? Here's your wine, White." He pulled out the chair next to Jamie, then looked surprised when she glared at him. "What? You said white wine, didn't you?"

"I could have gotten my own wine, you know."

Thomas blinked. "Yeah, but I was going there anyway. You asked for wine; I brought wine. What's the problem? You can get the next round."

"I will." Jamie frowned, twiddling her earring between her fingers. Catching Holly's amused eye on her, she straightened up, ignoring Thomas's puzzled look.

Remembering her news, Holly leaned across the table towards Jamie. "Hey, guess what I found out today. Jonas Hartley's still here."

Her friend looked puzzled. "Yeah, I saw him. The whole family's down there by the platform. So?"

"Sooo, he was supposed to go back to Azure the day before yesterday, but Rob told him to stay here." A smug look crossed Holly's face as Jamie's mouth dropped open.

"Rob told Hartley he couldn't leave?"

Thomas leaned forward, frowning. "Why? Is he a person

of interest? Or is this something to do with him representing his family?"

"I don't know. I was going to ask Rob tonight." Holly shrugged.

"Holly thinks Jonas was the one who pushed Anne McGinney," Jamie said.

Thomas's eyebrows shot up. "Jonas Hartley? Why?"

As Holly explained about the Hartley land, the journalist's eyes narrowed. "Huh. I wonder what Sally's will says." He glanced at his watch. "I have a contact on Azure. I'll give him a quick call. See if he knows anything."

"You have a contact on Azure Isle? Who?" Jamie demanded. "You only moved here four months ago!"

Thomas's grin was smug. "I have contacts everywhere."

As Jamie continued to cross-examine the journalist, Becky leaned forward to whisper to Holly. "Did you tell Jamie about the jewelry cleaner? What did she say?"

"I didn't get a chance. We were working flat out getting the desserts ready." Holly frowned. "Is it common in the business? I've never heard of cyanide being used for cleaning jewelry."

"It doesn't appear to be common here, no," Becky admitted. "Some countries still use it though. I thought Derek might know."

"You think he uses it?" Holly asked, her eyes widening at the thought. If so, that could be how Jonas Hartley had acquired the poison. "Does Rob know what you found out?"

"I haven't told him." Becky shook her head.

"Good grief! Just *look* at Myrtle!" Thomas's awed exclamation drew everyone's attention.

As Myrtle swept onto the platform at the front of the hall, a murmur of appreciation swept around the room. Quilters stood up to snap photos on their phones.

The journalist's mouth dropped open. "I've got to get closer! I need photos! What an outfit!" He leapt up from the table, narrowly missing upsetting the drinks in Rob's hands as the inspector returned to the table.

"Where's he going?" Rob placed Holly's soda in front of her.

There was no way Holly could talk to Rob about his case right now. Instead, she nodded towards the front of the hall. "To get photos of that."

Myrtle was still crossing the stage, as stately as a queen in her floor-length quilted creation. Floor-length work of art, Holly amended. You couldn't really call what Myrtle was wearing a dress. It was definitely a piece of art.

Made up of what looked like thousands of hexagons in gold, silver, emerald, ruby, sapphire, and jade satin, the dress shimmered under the chandelier lights of the hall, a moving tapestry of treasure that flowed out in a train across the stage. Long billowing sleeves in the same exquisite pattern covered her arms, while the bodice of the dress was composed only of gold hexagons. And on Myrtle's snowy white head, a gold tiara completed the fantastical outfit.

The applause began as Myrtle reached the microphone. She paused, her face composed as the cheers increased, reverberating around the lecture hall. Quilters from every club rose to their feet in acclamation.

"Did she actually make that?" Holly asked Becky, who shrugged, clapping as hard as she could.

"I have no idea, but it's stunning! Do you have any idea how much work went into that?"

Jamie was laughing as she applauded. "You've got to hand it to her. Myrtle has style! She'll be the talk of every club in the Maritime Islands after this!"

"Is there an award for best outfit?" Rob asked.

Becky looked struck. "There is! You know, the Patch-workers might just win the Maritime Thimble this year! Auntie Elma won the pieced traditional quilt category; Miss Greenley came second in traditional appliqué; Maggie came second in small pictorial…"

"How do you know all this?" Holly asked, watching Becky muttering to herself and counting on her fingers.

"Oh, I saw the results earlier. But it's not complete until the apparel contest is judged tonight." Becky looked up, her face shining. "You know, they really might win!"

"Well, if it depends on a dress, I can't imagine Myrtle not winning." Rob gestured around the room of cheering quilters. "Looks pretty unanimous to me."

Caroline Cunningham strode on stage. Her patchwork skirt paired with a black velvet top was pretty, but it paled in comparison to Myrtle's outfit. Holding up her hands, she signaled the room to be quiet.

"Well, ladies and gentlemen, I think we can forego the fashion show tonight. I don't think any of us can match Myrtle's work of art, can we?" As the room erupted in applause, she smiled at the Hibiscus islander. "Congratulations, Myrtle!"

Myrtle stepped up to the microphone. "I thank you all, but I cannot take credit for this magnificent piece of art." She swallowed hard, then said, "It belongs to one who is no longer with us, and I am honored to wear it in memory of Sally Hartley Dill."

The room went silent as Myrtle's voice shook slightly. Caroline Cunningham raised her hand to her mouth, then lowered it, stepping closer to Myrtle to take her hand. The septuagenarian cast her a grateful look as she cleared her throat. "I call upon the Maritime Quilters to stand as we remember Sally with a moment of silence."

There was a rustling of skirts and a slight clinking of glasses as everyone in the room stood. The Oleanders took each other's hands in silence.

Holly glanced around her own table. Becky leaned against her husband, and Jamie looked solemn. Feeling a hand take hers, Holly looked up at Rob. His warm fingers gently squeezing hers, they watched Myrtle standing with her head slightly bowed at the front of the room.

When the moment ended. Myrtle cleared her throat again, nodding to her fellow quilters. "Thank you." As everyone took their seats, she continued, "I knew Sally well and I am sure she would have appreciated—but likely been quite embarrassed by—our gesture of respect. I also know she would have wanted the Expo to continue, which is why we, the organizers, decided not to cancel. I know that some of you wondered about that and yes, it was a difficult decision to make—but I think it was the right one. Sally was a wonderful woman and a gifted artist. The piece of art that I wear tonight took her four years to make."

Applause broke out again. Myrtle waited for it to die down. "Sally's life ended too soon, but her killer will soon be brought to justice."

Heads turned to look at Rob, whose face remained impassive, his eyes watchful, then swiveled back to the stage as Myrtle continued.

"Sally would not have wanted this dinner or the awards ceremony to be a time of grief. So, although we mourn her, we will also honor her memory by celebrating her passion." A half smile appeared on Myrtle's face. "We all have quilt sayings that we use. Things like 'quilting forever, housework never'—"

"When life gives you scraps, make a quilt," someone called out.

"So much fabric, so little time," another woman said.

There were a few laughs.

"Sally's favorite was: 'Quilts are like friends, a great source of comfort.'" Myrtle looked around the room. "Tonight, let's reverse that. 'Friends are like quilts, a great source of comfort.' As friends, let's comfort each other, and celebrate Sally Hartley Dill and what she meant to us. Thank you."

As Myrtle left the platform, the room once again rose to its feet applauding.

Becky wiped her eyes, then blew her nose on the handkerchief François handed her. She gave a shaky smile. "That was lovely."

Before anyone could answer, Thomas arrived back at the table, grinning. "I'm telling you, Myrtle is incredible! That dress, the speech, the moment of silence, the call to action! Fantastic! What a story."

"Thomas! How can you?"

The journalist blinked at Becky's protest.

"What? It was a great tribute! Sally Dill was clearly very well respected and loved. I can't not report that! Everyone will expect to see Myrtle's speech on the front page tomorrow."

"He's right." Jamie nodded. "In fact, people will be mortally offended if he doesn't write it. Make it good, Miller." Ignoring Thomas's blink of surprise, she turned her attention to Rob. "Myrtle put you on the spot there, Inspector. Got anything to report?"

Rob shook his head. "Not here. And not now. Maybe later," he conceded as Jamie opened her mouth.

"I agree. Let's have no murder talk tonight," François interrupted, his voice firm. "*Parce que le plus beau cadeau de la vie est l'amitié*. The best present in life is friendship. I think we should celebrate that tonight. As Myrtle said."

There was a moment of astonished quiet then Thomas raised his glass in approval. "Cheers to that, mate." He turned to Jamie. "To friendship, Jamie?"

Jamie blinked. "Uh... Sure. To friendship."

As their glasses clinked, and Thomas turned to toast Becky, Holly's lips twitched in amusement at her best friend's bemused expression. Rob's breath brushed against her cheek as he leaned towards her.

"Stop smirking. She'll notice." He held up his glass. "Here's to our friendship, Holly. And maybe to more than just friendship?"

Blushing furiously at the warm look in his eyes, Holly touched her glass to his.

28

***

olly was smiling as she left Tansy and Sage Craft's table. She'd stopped for a moment on the way back from getting herself a dessert and had stayed a little longer than anticipated. The Juniper Island quilters were an eclectic bunch and definitely fun. After listening to stories about their island home, Holly was determined to visit it someday.

Rob grinned at her as she returned to their table. "Ready to cheer for Maggie? Someone just told me they're getting ready for the presentations."

"Well, it's about time. Where's everyone else?" Holly looked around at the empty table.

"Becky and François are talking to Stanley and Elma; Miller's getting fodder for his paper; and Jamie's over there at the Oleander table." Rob pulled Holly's chair closer to his, angling it so that she could lean against him. "You okay for drinks?"

"Yeah, I'm fine. What do you mean, Thomas is getting fodder?"

"He said he had to make a phone call."

"Oh. About the will, I guess." Holly paused, her earlier conversation with Becky coming back to her.

"The will?"

Holly swiveled to face the inspector. "Yeah. Sally's will." Before Rob could speak, she continued, "I've got to tell you something, Rob, but first, did you really tell Jonas Hartley he couldn't leave?"

"Where'd you hear that?"

Holly stared at him. "You did. Is it because of Anne McGinney? Do you think Jonas is the one who pushed her?"

"I thought we'd agreed we weren't talking about this tonight."

"The thing is, I don't remember seeing him that night, and Derek said someone banged on his door right around the time Mrs. McGinney fell."

"Derek Hartley told you someone banged on his door? Did he say who?" Rob's expression changed from vague irritation to alertness.

"No. He didn't know."

Rob eyed her for a moment. "But you think it was Jonas Hartley? Why?"

"Well," Holly hesitated, then forged on. "Sally Dill had no children, and her only sibling was Jonas. I wondered if he inherited the Hartley property now that she's gone, and I thought that might be why you told Mr. Hartley he couldn't leave. Do you know if he does? Inherit, that is?"

"I've asked Mrs. Dill's attorney for a copy of her will."

Holly barely listened. "Do you know anything about jewelry cleaner?"

"Jewelry cleaner?" Rob stiffened. "How do you know about *that*?"

Holly's jaw dropped. "Well, I was just about to tell you, but it sounds like you already know. Wow! Is that really how it was done?" When Rob just stared at her without speaking, Holly hurried on. "Becky reminded me about it just now. She said sometimes cyanide is used for cleaning jewelry. And Denise told me Jonas Hartley was often in Derek's shop. Plus, Rosalie Becknell told me he'd been visiting his sister lately and thought they might have been reconciling. It fits, don't you see? If he inherits, that is."

Rob pinched the bridge of his nose. "I thought you told me you weren't that interested in solving cases?"

"I'm not, but—"

"And I thought you also all assured me you wouldn't run around putting yourselves in danger. And that you would tell me anything and everything you found out." Rob raised an eyebrow as Holly flushed. "Well?"

"Well, we haven't been in any danger—and I've just told you everything we know. More or less."

"More or less?"

"Yes. Unless you really want the details of every single conversation we've had with people. Because I can share everything I now know about cassava if you're interested!"

"Cassava? Why on earth were you talking to people about cassava?" Rob's mouth quirked in sudden amusement before he sobered just as quickly. "Holly... Murder's not a game."

"And none of us think it is!" Holly snapped, annoyed now.

"No, I know you're trying to help. But I also know that someone killed Sally Hartley Dill. Killed her with cold, calculated deliberation. And that person won't hesitate to kill again if he—or she—feels threatened in any way." Rob took her hands in his. "So, please—will you stop asking questions?"

Suspicion filled Holly as she stared at his pleading

expression. "You already know who did it, don't you? Am I right? Is it Jonas?"

"I can't answer that right now, Holly. I'm sorry. I'm waiting for a call from Azure."

Holly followed the inspector's gaze towards the table of Oleanders.

Jonas Hartley texted on his phone, ignoring the conversation around him; Sybil Worthington was delivering a lecture to Anne McGinney, who looked annoyed at what she was hearing; Ellen Hartley and Wilhelmina Carson were in fits of laughter at something on Wilhelmina's phone; Derek Hartley grinned up at Jamie, who had just stood up to leave, saying something that made her laugh; Denise Trott looked bored as she played with a bowl of fruit salad; and Rosalie Becknell was coming back to the table with a plate of dessert.

Holly stared at them, her gaze dwelling longest on Jonas. He—they all—looked like normal people. It was hard to believe one was a cold and deliberate killer. Goosebumps covered her arms under the long sleeves of her dress, and she shivered suddenly.

"Cold?" Rob asked, rubbing his hands over her arms. "There's tea and coffee over there. Shall I get you a cup?"

Holly's irritation vanished as she looked at his slightly anxious expression. "I'm fine." She paused. "And I'll stop pestering you. You're right, we did say we'd give murder a miss tonight."

The inspector's eyes warmed. "You all mean well, I know. But thanks, Holly." He pulled her back against him, nodding towards the stage. "I think they're getting ready to hand out the awards now."

~

WHEN MAGGIE CROSSED the stage to receive her red rosette, Holly and Jamie jumped to their feet, cheering loudly. Maggie's blush rivaled the color of the rosette as she sent a quelling stare their way. The two younger women laughed, clapping even harder as Maggie shook Myrtle's hand, then Caroline Cunningham's, before leaving the stage.

"And now, first place in the small pictorial category goes to Mrs. Sybil Worthington of the Oleander Quilting Society. Sybil, please come and collect your award," Myrtle announced.

Sybil Worthington's slight limp as she went up to receive her trophy made Holly's eyes widen in sudden remembrance.

"Joint pain!" she whispered in Jamie's ear, making her friend start in surprise.

"What?"

"Sybil Worthington. She has joint pain! Just like Sally Dill had. I remember the day she arrived at the Inn, Wilhelmina Carson told her she should take her joint pills!"

Under the cover of the applause that followed the next awardee's progress across the platform, Jamie asked, "So what? Oh, wait, I get it! You think she uses the same turmeric capsules as Sally did. Oh! Do you think the others took them too? Daina and Freda, I mean? That could be the way the murderer poisoned them all!"

Holly cast a quick glance at a smiling, clapping Rob. "Only if they *were* actually murdered."

ROB DROVE into the main driveway of the Hibiscus Inn just after ten o'clock, pulling up behind a veritable convoy of taxis filled with happy Oleanders.

Watching the quilters pile out of their vehicles, Maggie smiled. "They all look like they've had a good evening, don't they?"

"Well, they won the Maritime Thimble award. They should be happy," Holly pointed out.

The Oleanders had beaten the Patchworkers by just one point—a point Myrtle had given them when she'd worn Sally Dill's dress to the awards ceremony.

The septuagenarian hadn't been upset at losing though. Honoring her friend had been more important than a trophy, Holly thought, remembering Myrtle's expression when the Oleanders surged on stage to take their bows.

Echoing her thoughts, Maggie agreed. "They deserved it. Sally's fashion entry was stunning. I'm glad Myrtle wore it." She looked at Rob with a smile as he opened the front door for her. "Thanks for the ride, Rob. Would you like to come in for a cup of tea?"

"I won't, thanks, Maggie. I've got to check in at the office before I go home tonight."

Maggie sobered. "Do you—" She stopped, then forced another smile. "Never mind. I know you can't tell me anything."

"It'll all be okay, Maggie." Rob's voice was kind.

"I know." Maggie gave a resolute smile. "I'd better go see if I can help Sarah with the tea and coffee requests that will undoubtedly be coming from our jubilant quilters."

"I'll be right behind you, Mama." Holly turned to Rob as Maggie nodded, then went inside. "Rob, I know you said you didn't want to talk about it, but I just have one question."

Rob raised an enquiring eyebrow.

"Did you know Sybil Worthington takes pills for joint pain?"

The inspector eyed Holly with a curious expression. "And you know that how?"

"Oh, Wilhelmina Carson said it the day they first arrived. And she was limping a bit tonight, so it reminded me." Holly shivered as a gust of wind blew across the driveway.

"Here, get back in the car. You're cold." Rob held the door open. "And I'd rather not have this conversation out in the open where everyone can hear, anyway."

Once in the car, Rob turned on the engine and started the heater. He made a wry face. "It's ridiculous to be using a heater on a tropical island, but you all have such thin blood here. Feel better?"

Holly nodded, a small grin appearing. "We don't have thin blood. It's chilly tonight."

"Chilly!" Rob snorted. "You don't know the meaning of the word." He sobered quickly, angling his body to face Holly. "Now, to answer your question: yes, I did know that Sybil Worthington took the same turmeric capsules as Sally Dill. And no, hers have not been tampered with. And before you ask, Freda Sinclair also used these capsules, but Daina Trott and Anne McGinney did not."

Holly's mouth dropped open, making Rob sigh. "I do know how to do my job, Holly."

Finding her voice, Holly retorted, "I know you do. I never said you didn't!" At Rob's raised eyebrow, she had the grace to flush, remembering some of the things she'd said to the inspector in the past. "Oh, come on. You can't hold initial impressions against me after all this time! Besides, you really were obnoxious the first time we met."

Relaxing, Rob grinned. "We didn't get off to the best of starts, I must admit. But you were very snooty, you know."

"I was snooty?" Holly gasped. "And what about you? You

kept calling me 'Miss Gold' all the time, and you said some really offensive things about the island!"

Rob leaned back in his seat, his grin widening as he took Holly's hand. "Yeah, but Myrtle put me in my place, as I recall. As did you."

"I did no such thing."

"Mmm. I seem to remember a lecture about how things are done on the island, about going with the flow, getting to know the people. Walking the beat, I think your dad called it." Rob sobered. "I've thought about that a lot, and I think people are more accepting of me now, but—"

"Of course people accept you!" Holly exclaimed, interrupting him. She squeezed his hand. "And you're doing a great job, Inspector Tucker."

"Yeah?" Rob leaned over to kiss her. After a moment, he drew back. "Tell me something. Why the sudden focus on Jonas Hartley? I thought Jamie favored Anne McGinney."

Holly eyed him with suspicion. "You actually want to discuss this?"

"Well, let's just say I'm curious."

"Huh. Well, Jamie's been forced to let go of Mrs. McGinney because Myrtle said she has a huge bruise on her back. Which means she *was* pushed over the wall. And that means she can't be the murderer."

"Agreed."

"So, when Mrs. McGinney was being pushed, Ellen Hartley and Sybil Worthington were together in their suite; Denise was just entering the Inn; Derek was watching television; and Wilhelmina Carson was with Mama in the kitchen." Holly paused, looking at Rob.

"Carry on." The inspector's tone was genial.

"So that means only Jonas Hartley is unaccounted for.

Which means he had to have pushed Mrs. McGinney. Unless you happen to know something I don't?"

"Well..." Rob looked apologetic. "Sorry. I'm afraid Jonas couldn't have done it. He was in the Oleander suite."

"In the Oleander suite?" Holly gaped at him. "But that's in the main house. It was Sally Dill's room. What was he doing there? And how do you know?"

"He came downstairs when all the hubbub started. I talked to him briefly when I arrived, then he returned to the room. Said he had work to do."

"Work to do? His sister was murdered, then someone gets pushed over a wall, and he had work to do? Seriously?"

"Plus," Rob added, "he was seen by another Oleander, a Mr. Cherry, moments before Anne McGinney screamed."

Holly stared at him in irritation. "Well, I wish we'd known that earlier! All right, so, it *wasn't* Jonas. But that means..." She thought for a moment, running everything she knew through her head, before looking at Rob. "You *do* think the person who pushed Mrs. McGinney also killed Sally Dill, right?"

The inspector nodded.

"And do you think that person also killed Daina Trott and Freda Sinclair?"

"No. I believe the deaths of both Mrs. Trott and Mrs. Sinclair, although tragic, were completely natural." Rob's face was sober.

Holly hesitated, not really wanting to ask the next question. "And... Becky is right? Jewelry cleaner *was* used?"

Rob's silence gave her the answer.

"Oh." Holly's heart sank. "Well, that only leaves one person who—"

Rob's phone buzzed. With an apologetic glance at her, he answered it.

"Yes, Sergeant?... Oh, it did?" Rob glanced at his watch. "No, just read it to me, will you? Uh-huh... Mmm... I see... And the other item? Did they find anything? I see... Yes, come along to the Hibiscus Inn now, will you? I'm already here. I'll wait for you." Hanging up, he sighed. "Our colleagues on Azure just called. We have our proof."

29

Holly watched the initial surprise on Jamie's face when she opened the door of the Bean café morph into instant suspicion. She looked at the group on the doorstep, then groaned. "The case is solved, isn't it? I knew it! I knew Rob was holding out on us! That rat! I really thought— Well, come in, then."

Becky shot a nervous glance at Holly, but Myrtle swept into the café without a second thought. Natasha looked up from the table, where she was studying a pile of photographs.

"Hi! You're here early! Did Jamie tell you about the bottle? It's so cool, isn't it? My friend thinks it might actually be possible to..." Her voice trailed away. "Oh. You haven't come about the bottle, have you?"

Myrtle sat down at the table. "I'm afraid not. Inspector Tucker arrested the murderer of Sally Hartley Dill last night."

"I tried to call you," Holly said, looking at Jamie, "but you didn't answer. And I considered driving out, but it was already so late. I phoned Becky first thing this morning and we thought we'd just come here before opening time."

"Yeah, well, I went straight to bed last night when I got home. Nothing could have woken me." Jamie made a face as she pushed another table up against Natasha's, then pulled up some more chairs. "Anyone want a coffee? Tea?" She gazed at her business partner. "Or François could rustle up breakfast!"

François rolled his eyes with a good-natured mock sigh. "I'll make pancakes, I think. Go ahead and start without me. Becky can catch me up later." He patted his wife's shoulder. "See? I told you it would be fine."

"What would be fine?" Jamie stared after the chef as he pushed open the doors to the kitchen and disappeared inside. "What's the problem? Come on, share all the gory details!"

"Well," Becky began gently.

"Inspector Tucker arrested Derek Hartley." Myrtle's tone was uncompromising.

"What?" Jamie's mouth dropped open. "Derek? Derek the jeweler? But what about Jonas? We suspected Jonas! What happened? What did I miss?"

Becky stared at her in bewilderment.

"I *told* you he was a predator!" Natasha sat up.

A hammering on the front door made them all turn their heads in surprise. Thomas Miller peered in over the CLOSED sign.

Jamie huffed with irritation, then jumped up, striding to the doors. "Stop banging on my glass, Miller!"

Becky gaped after her. "But... but I thought she'd be upset! Didn't she like the man?"

Natasha shrugged. "I don't think so. Or not really. She

259

liked Derek's looks, I think, but it seems to me she's more interested in this Miller chap."

Holly bit her bottom lip, trying not to laugh as Jamie unlocked the door to let Thomas in, her expression sour.

"Well, come in, then! The gang's all here. I suppose you're bursting at the seams with information as well."

Thomas grinned at her. "And good morning to you too, White. The inspector said he'd be here shortly, and he'd like a large coffee, eggs, and bacon." The journalist sniffed the air. "Hey, is that pancakes I smell? François, mate! Are you making pancakes?"

"*Mais oui.*" Francois grinned at Thomas from the kitchen pass-through. "You want eggs and bacon too?"

"And a coffee! I'm dying for a coffee." Thomas clutched his throat dramatically.

"Oh, for Pete's sake!" Jamie stalked behind the café counter to pull out mugs. "Who else wants something?"

Holly raised her hand. "I'd love a cup of tea if you're making it." As her friend rolled her eyes with vigor, Holly grinned, then pulled up a chair for herself, gesturing to Becky to sit beside her. "You said Rob's coming, Thomas? How'd you know that?"

"Oh, I was down at the station this morning getting approval for my piece in the paper. As per our inspector's instructions." Thomas glanced at his watch. "The online version is scheduled to release shortly. We held back the paper edition when we got the news last night so it will be delayed a bit this morning." He shrugged. "Most people don't pick up their hard copies till around ten anyway, so it shouldn't matter."

Holly sighed, drawing the journalist's attention to her. His face softened in sympathy.

"I hear it was a bit rough last night."

Holly nodded. "Yeah. People were... upset."

There was a snort from Myrtle. "No need for euphemisms, Holly. It was a very ugly scene! I hope Maggie hasn't taken any of it personally."

"She was better this morning," Holly said, "but yeah, it was hard on her."

"You were there too, Myrtle?" Thomas asked. "I didn't know that."

"Anne and I drove Wilhelmina back to the Inn. We were late leaving the dinner so we walked in just as Inspector Tucker made his arrest."

Jamie brought over a tray and plunked it down on the table. "Two coffees—I got you another one too, Nat—one herbal tea for Becky, and two regular teas." She put her hands on her hips. "And could you all stop talking about things while I'm not here!" She glared at the journalist. "I suppose you were in on all the action last night as well."

Thomas shook his head. "No, unfortunately. We only found out after they were on their way back to the station. I caught up with them there." He made a face. "Mrs. Hartley was still hysterical."

"And Derek?" Jamie hooked a chair with her foot, pulling it towards the table before sitting down. "How was he?"

"Normal."

"Normal?" Becky repeated. "What do you mean?"

"I mean, he was his usual obnoxious self!" Thomas snapped. "Zero remorse that I could see. Just sat there smiling in that supercilious way he has! I knew the guy was crooked the minute I saw him."

"Oh, you did not!" Jamie exclaimed.

"Well, you certainly didn't," Thomas retorted. "He took you in completely."

Becky's head was turning back and forth between the two. Holly caught Natasha's amused look, then leaned back, enjoying the show.

"He did not! It was obvious he was a player. I'll admit, I didn't think he was a murderer, but I certainly wasn't blinded by his charm." Jamie's voice was heated.

"Could've fooled me," Thomas muttered.

Jamie threw him a look of disdain. "You didn't suspect him either, Miller, and you know it. Seems to me the only one who did was our inspector. As usual. Where is he, anyway?"

Natasha grinned, nodding towards the plate glass windows. "There's a hunk coming towards us now. Is that him? I've gotta say, you have some handsome men on this island, Jamie." She shot an admiring look at Thomas. "Present company included, of course."

"Pfft." Jamie shot one more scowl at Thomas before going to open the door for the inspector.

Natasha's eyes twinkled, then widened in appreciation as François emerged from the kitchen laden down with a tray of plates. "Yep," she sighed. "Very handsome men. It's such a shame they're all taken."

"Not all of us." Thomas sent a mock leer Natasha's way. "This handsome man is free and single still."

The marine scientist shook her head with pity. "Tsk. And here I thought journalists prided themselves on reporting facts."

Holly, who had just taken a sip of tea, choked, then spluttered as Thomas gaped at the strawberry blonde. A flush appeared on his face before his eyes narrowed.

"Don't hold back, do you?"

Natasha grinned. "Nope. And can I just say... I'm enjoying the dance."

"Is that so?" Thomas leaned back in his seat, studying her. "Got any suggestions for improvement?"

Myrtle's voice was tart as she interrupted. "May I remind you that, fascinating as this conversation is, we are not here to discuss the 'dancing' habits of various species. Instead—" She broke off as Rob approached. "Ah, Inspector Tucker. I'm glad you could join us. We were about to start."

Natasha raised an eyebrow, another grin sliding over her face. "Start?"

"Yeah, it's tradition." Jamie collapsed into the chair beside her. "We dissect each case after it's over and Myrtle tells us what we all missed."

"I most certainly do not!" Myrtle frowned at an impenitent Jamie. "I merely put all the facts into their correct order."

"Well, just be brief this time, okay? Because I have to open the café in half an hour."

Rob held up his hand. "How about I do the dissertation this time? In the interest of brevity, Myrtle."

"Very well, Inspector." Myrtle directed a quelling frown at Jamie, before adding, "I understand Mr. Hartley Junior confessed. Is that correct?"

"How did you know—?" Rob stopped, took a deep breath, then smiled. "Never mind. Your source told you. You are correct, Myrtle. Derek Hartley confessed in full, despite his father's attempts to get him to stop speaking."

"Why'd he do it?"

"It was the will, wasn't it?"

"Did he kill Daina and Freda too?"

The spate of questions made Natasha laugh. Rob held up his hands for silence.

"No one speak until I've finished! Understood?" He

glared around the table until he received nods. "Right then. In brief bullet point form:

"Derek Hartley did not kill Daina Trott or Freda Sinclair. Their deaths were completely natural. He did, however—"

"Spread rumors and get Denise and Anne McGinney to *think* they were murdered!" Holly exclaimed. She flushed as Rob leveled a steely look at her. "Oh. Sorry."

"He spread rumors, yes. Apparently our Mr. Hartley is a fan of Agatha Christie and took one of her plots for inspiration."

"He told you that? No way."

"Humph. That would be from the film festival they had on Azure, I'm sure."

"Hang on, let me take some notes!"

"Used an Agatha Christie plot? Are you serious? Who does that?"

"Which book?"

All eyes swung to Becky at Natasha's final question. The librarian blinked, then frowned. "Which book? Well, how on earth would I know?"

Everyone's head turned back to Rob, who shrugged. "Something about an alphabet killer? I don't read murder mysteries. It's too much like work."

Becky's frown cleared. "Alphabet? Oh, I know, then. It has to be *The ABC Murders*. The murderer kills two people to hide the reason for his third murder."

"So, Derek started rumors about Daina and Freda's death so that Sally's death would be seen as part of a series. I get it." Holly nodded.

"And the fact that they were all presidents of the quilt club just made it more plausible," Jamie interjected.

Holly shook her head in disgust. "He must have got the idea when Freda Sinclair collapsed in his shop. When she was looking at Christmas gifts. Denise told us Derek said he was worried Freda had the same symptoms as her mother and that they were odd. Poor Denise. What a rotten thing to do to a young woman!"

"But why *did* he want to kill his aunt?" Natasha asked, curious.

Thomas looked up from his phone, upon which he was frantically typing notes. "Oh, I know that. My contact on Azure told me Hartley was the sole beneficiary in Sally Dill's will. He would inherit the entire estate upon her death."

"A greedy and unscrupulous young man." Myrtle frowned in disapproval before looking at Rob. "I presume you found evidence of cyanide-based jewelry cleaner in his shop, Inspector?"

Rob sighed in resignation. "We did." He picked up his coffee cup and gestured towards her with it. "Why don't you just take it from here, Myrtle?"

"Very well." Myrtle cleared her throat, ignoring Jamie's eyeroll. "As a jeweler, Derek had access to cyanide salts. Not quite usual in this part of the world but I understand it's a common practice in other areas. I'd be interested to know, Inspector, whether he obtained these salts recently or if he's always used them."

Rob opened his mouth, then closed it as Myrtle carried on.

"Personally, I incline to the theory that the idea came to him following the prolonged illness of Daina Trott. And then, as Holly said, the collapse of Freda Sinclair, another Oleander Quilting Society president, in his shop, further inspired our murderer's insidious plan."

Thomas choked, taking a hasty sip of coffee to hide the mirth in his eyes.

"Derek was Sally's only nephew," Myrtle continued. "He

frequently visited her, so was aware she took turmeric capsules for joint pain. It would have been an easy task to confiscate a packet of capsules, take them to his shop, and add minute amounts of cyanide to some of them. He could also have obtained the capsules from his grandmother, Sybil Worthington, since she also used the remedy. Regardless, he could plant the tampered capsules at his leisure in Sally's house, knowing she would eventually take them." She looked at Rob. "I imagine he planned to remove said capsules from her house after her death."

Rob nodded. "Yes. From his point of view, it was unfortunate Mrs. Dill took the capsules so sporadically, and that she took one of the fatal ones while on Hibiscus Island."

Natasha raised a hand. "I still don't see why he had to *kill* his aunt, though. If he was going to inherit anyway, what was the rush?"

"Debt, I gather." Rob took a sip of coffee. "His shop wasn't doing that well and he'd taken out a couple of rather large loans."

"Denise did say Mr. Hartley Senior was always in Derek's shop talking about paying bills," Holly said.

"Why didn't he just ask his parents, or grandmother, for help?" Becky asked.

"Oh, he'd never have done that!" Myrtle scoffed. "After all the fuss that was made when he went against every single one of their wishes? The only one who ever supported his plan to open that shop was Sally. She always encouraged his artistic leanings." Before anyone could say anything, Myrtle added, "But Sally was a hardheaded businesswoman. She wouldn't have bailed him out of debt either. No, the only way Derek Hartley would get money from Sally was after she was dead."

There was a moment of silence before Holly spoke. "And

then he pushed Mrs. McGinney over the wall to make it seem like it really was quilt club presidents who were being targeted."

"It would fit the book he was copying," Becky agreed. "In Agatha Christie's plot, the murderer killed a random fourth person to make it look like the serial murders were continuing."

"He should have poisoned her." Jamie sounded critical. "The push was out of character. Myrtle called it when she said he'd changed his *modus operandi*."

"Yes, well, unfortunately for Mr. Hartley"—Rob's voice was wry—"Anne McGinney didn't take the turmeric capsules, didn't have cancer, and didn't have the flu."

"No, so he was forced to resort to a rather amateur attempt to throw us off the scent." Myrtle sniffed. "It wasn't even a steep hill."

"Yeah, I could think of a dozen better places to push someone," Jamie agreed.

"For heaven's sake, Jamie!" Becky protested as Thomas's shoulders started to shake with laughter.

Rob cast his eyes heavenward as the table erupted in chatter.

30

Rob and Holly cut through Waterfront Park as she accompanied the inspector partway back to the station.

"You must be glad it's over," Holly remarked, looking sideways at him.

"Yes. We have to sort out a few things with the authorities on Azure Isle. I imagine Hartley will be tried over there. His attorney is angling for that, anyway. He'll stay in custody here until an escort arrives."

"What will his family do?"

"Sybil Worthington was booking a flight when I left the station this morning. It got a bit heated between her and Jonas Hartley, but he finally agreed that Mrs. Hartley would be better off if she was away from the island." Rob sighed, reaching over to take Holly's hand. "I haven't had a chance to ask, but how is Maggie? I'm sorry it all had to happen at the Inn."

"Oh well, she was upset, of course. So were all the Oleanders. After you all left, everyone stayed in the foyer talking. They all really liked Sally Dill, but they were sorry for Mrs. Hartley and Mrs. Worthington as well. I don't think people really knew how to behave. Mama was feeling better this morning. And most of the Oleanders are leaving today anyway. Denise and Rosalie Becknell will be the only ones there tonight. And Rosalie was very supportive to Mama."

"Good." Rob was silent for a while as they crossed the grass, passing beneath a tall, leafless poinciana tree. "So, what are your plans for the rest of the day?"

Holly grinned. "Nat's going to tell us what her marine archaeologist guy had to say about that bottle. And then, sadly, I promised Gramps I'd help him take out the last of the spider lily triffids in the garden."

"And what about the evening?" Rob stopped, pulling Holly closer to him.

Her eyes laughed up at him. "Depends on what you have in mind, Inspector."

HOLLY WAS GLOWING when she returned to the Bean, a fact Jamie immediately commented on.

"Had a nice romantic walk, Holls?"

"I did, thanks." Holly grinned at her best friend as she joined her and Natasha at the table.

Natasha gave an envious sigh. "Such a handsome man, that inspector."

"Yes, so you've said. Repeatedly." Jamie nudged the marine scientist. "Stop drooling over Holly's boyfriend and focus on these photos. What did—what's his name again? —say?"

"His name is Peter Mackenzie. Also a handsome man but a complete pain in the neck. Virtually impossible to pin down, but he knows his stuff." Natasha leaned back in her chair with a grin. "I showed Mackenzie the bottle over a video call—and sent him photos—and he thinks it's a perfume bottle."

"A perfume bottle?" Holly exclaimed. "Really? How weird."

"Possibly late seventeenth century, but he'd have to see it in person to confirm." Natasha flipped through the photos. "But the thing that most interests him is the fact that it's sealed still."

"What, you think it still has perfume inside it?" Holly peered at the photo. "I can't tell from this."

"Oh, it does. Well," Natasha clarified, "it has liquid inside it. Mr. Graham and I, obviously, haven't opened it."

Jamie leaned back in her chair, staring at her friend. "So, what are you leading up to here?"

"Well!" Natasha's face brightened. "There's this old perfumery on Turtle Island near the Ocean Science Research Center—"

"Plumeria Perfumery," Holly said. "That's where Tansy and Sage Craft get their essential oils and things. They use some old method of making perfume. Tansy said they're having a bunch of perfumiers come in May for a workshop or something."

"That's right!" Natasha beamed at Holly. "It's going to be a big deal on the island. Anyway, Peter Mackenzie said he knows one of the guys who's going to be there. He's an expert in seventeenth- and eighteenth-century perfumes. Apparently he's analyzed and reproduced old perfumes before. Wouldn't that be cool? A *La Rosa de España* fragrance!"

Jamie pursed her lips. "Well, it's not as exciting as gold or emeralds, but yeah, it's pretty cool, I guess. When's this guy going to be on Turtle?"

"Sometime in May. You can come stay with me. Have a holiday. Bring your handsome men with you! I'll bet Thomas could write a good story about an old perfume." Natasha grinned as Holly and Jamie exchanged speculative glances. "It's not as good as a murder story, of course, but... Well, I'm afraid nothing like that ever happens on Turtle Island."

ALSO BY LUCY NORMAN

Buried in Bougainvillea

Remains Among the Roses

Obituary for an Oleander

And coming in summer 2023:

Frangipani can be Fatal

Also available by subscription to my newsletter:

Haunted by Hibiscus

The Poinsettia Puzzle

Visit lucynorman.net

ACKNOWLEDGMENTS

As always, a huge thank you to my family and friends for their support and encouragement; to Lida, my wonderful editor, who fixes all those pesky commas; and to Donna, the talented artist who brings Hibiscus Island to life in her wonderful cover art.

Thank you also to Sarah, for the absolutely gorgeous map of Hibiscus Island at the front of this book!!

ABOUT THE AUTHOR

Lucy Norman is the author of the Hibiscus Island Mystery series - lighthearted cozy mystery books inspired by the small Atlantic island home where she was born and still resides.

Lucy has a degree in horticulture, loves to read (mystery is her genre of choice but she also likes science fiction and fantasy), occasionally quilts, and collects old children's school stories. She shares her home with an adorable cavapoo, enjoys walking on the island's railway trails, and her favorite place in the world is Scotland, in particular the Cairngorms.

To find out about new releases, please visit lucynorman.net